CW01432424

The Perfect Christmas Engagement

HISTORICAL REGENCY ROMANCE NOVEL

Dorothy Sheldon

Table Of Contents

Chapter One

London in winter was an odd place indeed.

For starters, most of the *ton* had retired to the country for the unfashionable months. The Season was over, and without the lure of friends and social occasions to keep people in town, they quickly abandoned the smelly, dirty London streets for the fresh, clean countryside.

Augusta envied them. London was an unpleasant place at the best of times. The streets were clogged with dirt, and bad smells floated through the air, impossible to escape even in the safety of a carriage. Smog hung over the streets, blocking out all but the clearest and brightest skies.

Now the long, cold trudge towards the dead of winter had begun, London had become grey. Grey skies, grey streets, grey rain. The last ball had been danced, the last piece of gossip had been shared, and the last supper eaten. The colour and music had faded out of the world, leaving Augusta behind, alone.

Not quite alone, of course. That was rather unfair to the rest of them.

The Duke and Duchess of Radford, Patrick and Dorothy, had stayed behind, of course. Timothy and his wife were still in town, too, although Augusta didn't see them very often.

Patrick's work had kept him in town when the Season ended, so he'd been forced to remain. Dorothy, of course, did not want to leave her husband, and so naturally, Augusta had stayed too. Their pleasant little country-seat, far away from the clamour and dirt of London, stayed shut up in the country for the time being.

Augusta had no reason to complain, however. She knew she was lucky. She was reminded of her good luck every time her carriage drove past beggars in the street, cold and wet and begging for coins. It made Augusta's heart twist. She always insisted on giving them whatever money she had available, even though

Ambrose told her not to.

"They'll just spend it on gin," he chided almost every time. And almost every time, Augusta smiled and said that she doubted it.

It was more than a little embarrassing, actually. He always made the accusation loudly, usually well in earshot of whichever poor person was currently receiving Augusta's charity.

There wasn't much to dislike about Ambrose, but Augusta hated it whenever he did that. In fact, he always pressed his lips together and sighed heavily when she insisted on giving away her money.

As always, Augusta's thoughts wandered when she thought about Ambrose. He was a good man, but not exactly an exciting one.

Well, what was wrong with that? *Exciting* men tended to make bad husbands, or so her mother kept telling her.

"Don't fidget so much, miss," Betsey chided gently. "You want your hair to be just so for your engagement party tonight, don't you?"

Augusta smiled weakly. "You always do a marvellous job, Betsey. No need to fuss."

Betsey clicked her tongue. "As if I'd let you go out looking less than perfect on tonight of all nights, miss! We're nearly done, just hold still."

It felt as though Augusta had been sitting in her dressing-table chair for hours. Her back ached, her neck twinged, and she was so *bored*. Betsey wouldn't even allow her to read a book while her hair was being done because she tended to crane her neck downwards, she said. Augusta smiled at that, wondering whether other ladies would let their maids set such standards.

Not that Augusta minded, of course. Betsey was a skilled maid, and she'd waited on Augusta since she had come out of the schoolroom. At the age of twenty-one, Augusta was now a far cry from that schoolgirl, and she could pride herself on having her fair share of feminine beauty.

The fashion was for dark beauties at the moment—glossy black or deep-brown hair, flashing onyx eyes, and dark brows. That made the fair beauties look pixie-like and ethereal in comparison.

Augusta fell somewhere in between. She had medium-brown hair, not dark enough to be a "dark" beauty, but not light enough to be pale and interesting. Her eyes were pale-brown, a colour most often compared to honey, and the whole picture was finished off by a spray of freckles on her nose. Plenty of the Season's beauties—the Season's Diamond included—were visibly horrified at even the notion of freckles, but Augusta had gotten used to hers. If she wanted them to fade, she'd use a parasol.

All in all, Augusta was happy enough with her looks not to think much about them. She was no competition to the Diamond and the other highly praised Belles, and that was quite all right. Why would she want to collect conquest after conquest as they did anyway?

This Season's Diamond, a young lady by the name of Miss Rebecca White, was a dark beauty, and a fine one at that. She *was* beautiful and had a decent dowry to her name too. Men threw themselves at her feet, and she received dozens of offers of marriage.

That was all very nice, but Augusta couldn't imagine why anyone—man or woman—would need so many hearts offered on a plate. When it came to conquests of love, you only needed one— the right one.

She couldn't help but feel a *little* smug that Miss White had ended the Season still unmarried. By that time, Augusta had met Ambrose Finch, the Earl of Firnsdale, and their relationship was already progressing rapidly towards engagement. He was a good man, and Augusta saw no reason why she couldn't be as happy with him as with anyone. Even if he wasn't . . .

No.

She would not allow herself to think that way. It had been five years, and Augusta told herself that she ought to grow up and move forward with her life. *He* wasn't coming back. Even if he was, what good would it do her to wait? What would have changed by the time he returned?

"All done, miss!" Betsey said, standing back with a sigh of satisfaction. "You're ready."

Augusta eyed her reflection complacently. Her hair was long, almost waist-length, which made Betsey's daily job of dressing her hair much harder. Augusta knew she ought to get it cut—most ladies favoured hair that ended at their mid-back—but she'd always liked her long, warm, silky curtain of hair. At the moment, it was piled neatly on top of her head in elaborate braids and curls, with one thick, long ringlet draping down her neck. Her dress was watered silk, a pretty lavender colour with expensive lace at the cuffs and neckline, and she'd chosen opals for her jewels.

"You've done a marvellous job, as always, Betsey. Thank you."

Betsey beamed. "Enjoy your party, miss. Oh, and congratulations!"

Augusta smiled weakly. She'd been getting a lot of congratulations recently. Her writing desk was overflowing with notes and letters from friends in the country, congratulating her on her engagement, and scolding her for not getting engaged during the Season so they could attend her party.

As it was, Augusta's engagement party would be a sorry affair. It was small, of course, and few of her friends would be in attendance. There were always a few members of the *ton* who stayed in London all year round—strange creatures that they were—and they would be there, of course, along with Patrick and Ambrose's various business acquaintances. All of Augusta's friends in the country had made their apologies, and she couldn't really blame them. Who wanted to make an uncomfortable carriage journey of several laborious hours simply to attend an engagement party?

It wasn't as if it was the wedding. Besides, in a day or two's time, the family would finally, *finally* pack up to leave London behind and head to the countryside. Augusta was relieved. Christmastide was fast approaching, and she didn't want to spend it in London. It wouldn't feel the same. Even the snow would feel dirty.

It would probably *look* dirty, too. People still threw their rubbish and waste out of their windows, not caring who it landed upon in the streets. The richer areas of London, where the *ton* preferred to live, were kept a little cleaner by the street sweepers. But Augusta knew that the dirt and tide of human misery lay just beyond the hastily swept streets. Christmas was a time for giving, but there were just so *many* people who needed help. It was overwhelming at times.

Ambrose would tell me not to worry so much. He'd tell me

7

they are poor for a reason. He never tells me what reason, though. I wonder if he even knows.

She paused in front of the full-length hallway mirror on her way to the ballroom, checking over her appearance one last time.

The truth was that Ambrose's offer had come at the perfect time. This was her third Season, and it was getting a little embarrassing now. Augusta had received plenty of offers, but none that were deemed suitable.

No one she could see herself marrying, at least.

And, of course, none of them were *you-know-who*.

Augusta didn't even let herself think his name anymore. He wasn't coming back, so why waste time thinking about him? She'd already wasted her first Season and at least half of her second living in hope that *he* would return and sweep her off her feet.

She was relieved to be a more realistic, practical sort of person these days.

The door to the ballroom opened, and Dorothy popped her head out.

"I thought I heard footsteps. There you are, Darling! We were just about to send out a search party. You look lovely, by the way."

Augusta smiled. "Thank you, Mama. Is everyone here?"

"More or less."

Dorothy was one of those unfortunate women who had gone grey early on in their youth. Augusta couldn't remember a time when her mother *didn't* have iron-grey hair. She was still a handsome woman, with the oval face and high cheekbones she'd bequeathed to her son and daughter, and the ice-blue eyes Timothy had inherited, and which Augusta had always envied.

"I suppose I'd better go in," Augusta said, drawing in a breath. Now the moment had arrived, she felt nervous. This was it—her official outing to the world, the announcement that Lady Augusta and Lord Firnsdale were engaged, and planning their nuptial trip down the church aisle.

Was it normal to feel nervous? Surely, it was.

Dorothy smiled at her daughter and held out her hand.

"Come on, we'll go in together."

**

It was a modest party. Pleasant, warm, and well-catered, with polite if unimpressive guests. Augusta mingled, as was expected of her, answering polite, frequently asked questions. She wondered, not for the first time, if she could write up some sort of card to hand to people when they asked the same questions over and over again.

Are you excited to be getting married?
Yes, I am. I think I'll make a good wife.
I daresay you can't wait to have children.
I am fond of children, yes. "Can't wait" may be an overstatement, however. (She'd have to edit that last part out. Ladies weren't permitted to look on motherhood with anything but doting, thrilled excitement.)
Will you miss your parents when you leave?
Yes, terribly. I am fond of my parents.
Are you quite rushed off your feet with wedding preparations?
Not particularly, Mama is handling most of the preparations. We haven't even started on most of them.
Married by Christmas! How exciting!
Not quite. We'll be married after Christmas, about a week after Epiphany. I'll have one last Christmas with my family.

Augusta didn't let her boredom show on her face. She answered query after query smoothly and calmly, every bit the mature and contented betrothed lady.

Still, it was a relief when the music started up. There were just a few couples planning to dance, and Augusta found herself missing the Season, when ballrooms would be crammed with couples, every lady's dance card full of gentlemen's names. Augusta wasn't the finest dancer around, she knew, but she was good enough, and she enjoyed it.

There was really only one man she could dance with that night, though, and Augusta craned her neck to look out for him.

Ah, there he was. Augusta watched Ambrose push through the sparse crowds to greet her, wishing her heart would skip at the sight of him. But no, the beat of her stalwart heart continued as evenly as ever, entirely unmoved by the sight of her betrothed.

Oh, well. One couldn't have everything.

Ambrose was around thirty years old, with a widowed mother who did not seem to like Augusta very much. He had straw-coloured hair and matching whiskers, and pale-blue eyes that seemed to have had the colour leeched out of them. He was of average height, with a genial, pleasant face. He wasn't considered a very handsome man, but neither was he plain either.

"Good evening, my dear betrothed." Ambrose made a flamboyant bow, and Augusta laughed, just as she was expected to. "You look lovely."

"Thank you. And you look very dashing, Ambrose. That's a pretty cravat pin."

Ambrose fingered a ruby pin, a drop of blood-red nestled in the folds of his cravat.

"Thank you. A present to myself. Silly, I suppose."

"Not at all. Are you going to dance, Ambrose?"

"I shall if you want to dance."

Augusta raised an eyebrow. "It is our engagement party, after all."

Ambrose laughed self-consciously. "That is an excellent point. The first dance is to be a waltz, I hear. Shall we stand up for that? I'm not sure I can manage more than a set or two, though. I'm rather tired today."

Augusta nodded. "One dance will do."

They moved to the dance floor together, and Augusta noticed with a twinge of embarrassment that everyone had been waiting for her and Ambrose to start the dancing. They took their positions, and the music began in earnest.

Ambrose wasn't a natural dancer. He was stiff-backed and uncomfortable, and Augusta was sure he'd refuse to dance altogether once they were safely married. She told herself that she didn't mind—a husband and wife didn't have to agree on everything, did they? Dancing was a pastime—a popular one, true, but still just a pastime.

"I imagine you're reluctant to leave London," Ambrose commented a minute or two into the dance.

"Quite the opposite, in fact. I don't mind London, but once the glamour of the Season is gone, it's a very drab, dull place."

10

"Really? How differently we think. I enjoy London much more once all the garish *ton* have packed up and gone, leaving London to the true city-lovers. I shall stay in London all the time once we are married, I think. You can stay in the country if you like, of course, but naturally, I'd much rather you stayed with me."

Augusta swallowed. "I'm sure I'll get used to London."

"Oh, you will! You'll love it all year round, I'm sure. Although, when the Season ends, the card-tables are never quite so good. Not that it matters, of course. Oh, and I have something else to tell you. Bad news, I'm afraid."

Augusta raised an eyebrow. "Bad news?"

"Yes. I know I was supposed to come with you to the country, but something has come up. Business, you know. Dull stuff. I'll have to stay in London, I'm afraid."

Augusta didn't feel disappointed in the slightest. She wished she *could* feel disappointed.

"That's all right, Ambrose. I understand."

"I'm glad. You are very sensible, Augusta. I knew you wouldn't throw a tantrum or sulk. You're never ruffled—that's one of the things I like about you."

Augusta forced a smile. Yes, that was right. Sensible, unruffled old Augusta, who always maintains a degree of civility. You could disappoint her as much as you liked, and she'd never bat an eyelid.

Or perhaps it was that someone had disappointed her so badly once before, she'd never been able to get over it.

Chapter Two

The coach jolted over a particularly nasty pothole, shaking the whole structure and jerking Silas awake. He sat up, blinking groggy eyes and wincing at the pain in his neck and back. Sleeping in the coach had been a terrible idea. Truly horrendous. Part of Silas thought his sea voyage home from the Americas had been less uncomfortable than this trip from the dock to his parents' house.

He missed his home. Not his parents' home, where he was heading, but the little apartment he'd set up for himself while he studied. It was small and serviceable, but it certainly felt like home.

And, of course, there was the lovely English weather. He hadn't missed that at all.

It was snowing, or something close to snowing. A soft, slushy sort of cold rain was falling and being churned up into filthy mud beneath the horses' hooves and the coach wheels. It was icy cold even inside the carriage, no matter how tightly Silas pulled his shawl against him.

He was riding alone and had been for the past few stops. It was colder that way, but at least he didn't have to deal with talkative passengers, most of whom smelled a little ripe. One old lady had smelled so unpleasant he would have sworn she was carrying manure in her basket. It had been a thorough relief when she had left, although the unpleasant scent had lingered for quite some time.

The Mitchell family had never been the wealthiest, and Silas knew it was high time to return home and help the failing family business. His father hadn't asked him to do so, of course, but Silas could read between the lines. He would never have had the opportunity to educate himself in the Americas if it hadn't been for a bequest in his grandfather's will, so now was the time to make use of his good luck.

He leaned forward with a sigh, his breath crystallising and hanging in the air in front of him. Through the misty window, he could see Rasbury House in the distance, almost hidden by trees and hills. He'd known the Radford family very well once upon a time and hoped his parents had kept up the acquaintance.

Although, if Augusta had told them about the kiss he'd stolen from her on Christmas Eve five years ago, perhaps he wouldn't be well received.

Silas sat back abruptly, not wanting to see Rasbury House anymore. He thought of Augusta every day, and often berated himself for being so selfish, so stupid as to kiss her like that. She had been sixteen, and he had been eighteen. She hadn't even been out yet, and he'd had no idea his grandfather was about to die suddenly and leave him a priceless opportunity. He'd been planning an apology letter to Augusta when news of his grandfather's sudden illness had arrived, and the whole family had rushed to be by the old man's side. Then, the will had been read, and Silas was packed off to the Americas without ever returning to Rasbury Village, without ever seeing Augusta again.

Silas closed his eyes, seeing Augusta's shocked face after he'd kissed her, one hand lifting to her lips, eyes wide as a startled rabbit's. They'd had no time to say anything because the rest of the guests had come trudging out onto the terrace at that moment, keen to look up at the stars and toast the Christmas festivities.

Silas had retreated red-faced, and he hadn't spoken to Augusta since. Was she still angry at him? Perhaps she'd completely forgotten the kiss. Either way, Silas wasn't sure if he wanted to see her again or not. He hadn't heard much about her since he'd left England and was too afraid to ask his brother and sister for information. Augusta would certainly be out, and possibly even married, by now.

The coach lurched to a halt.

"Rasbury Village," the coachman announced, sounding bored.

Silas peered out of the window. The coachman had stopped on the edge of town, leaving Silas with an estimated mile-long walk to his home, through a fast-growing blanket of snow.

"Couldn't you take me a bit closer?"

"No," the coachman responded bluntly.

13

Silas sighed. This was it, then. He climbed stiffly out of the carriage, wincing as he straightened his cramped limbs, and the coachman tossed his case down to him, letting it thump into the snow. Silas shot the man a glare which the surly fellow didn't seem to notice. He simply cracked the reins, and the coach rolled forward, scattering a spray of snow over Silas.

He hauled the case up onto his shoulder and started the final stretch of his homeward journey on foot.

***

The imaginatively named Mitchell Cottage was glowing with light and warmth. Silas, who was thoroughly chilled from his trek, was already dreaming of the delightful moment when he'd step over the threshold.

He didn't have to wait long.

Helen Mitchell, his mother, saw him coming, and she threw open the door with such force that it dislodged some snow from the roof.

"Silas, there you are! Come in, come in! Supper is almost ready. Charles, look, Silas is home! Eliza, Colin, come and greet your brother!"

Silas stepped inside, setting down his heavy case with a sigh of relief. Five years had etched themselves harshly on his mother. There was more grey in her brown hair than before, and more wrinkles around her eyes and forehead. There was a line between her eyebrows that hadn't been there when he went away.

Colin peeped out of the parlour door, eyeing his older brother.

Silas sucked in a breath. "Goodness, Colin, you've grown up."

"Well, yes, Silas." Colin retorted. "That's what people do. I'm eighteen now, you know."

Eighteen! That didn't sit right with Silas. After all, Colin had been only thirteen when Silas had left, a gawky young man with ears too big for him and a habit of saying exactly what he thought. Colin was just as tall as Silas now, with the same blue-green eyes and poker-straight black hair. Somehow, he still looked young, and the idea of sending Colin overseas to the Americas, alone, made Silas feel sick.

How had his parents let him go?

"Silas, you're home!" Eliza came next, racing out from the parlour in a flurry of brown curls and green satin, flinging her arms around Silas in a choking hug. "I missed you so much."

Eliza is nineteen, Silas reminded himself. Not the schoolgirl I remember.

He wasn't going to know how to treat his siblings. It would certainly feel strange.

Last, but certainly not least, Silas' father appeared in the doorway. Charles Mitchell had changed the least of all, only filling out a little around his middle, and growing a few silver streaks in his dark hair.

"Silas, my boy!" Charles boomed. "Home at last. And just in time, too—Mrs Brigham is just setting out supper. Let's eat, and Silas can fill us all in on his adventures."

Adventures. Silas thought about it. Day after day, week after week, he'd spent closeted in libraries and poring over old books. He wondered if his family would consider that an adventure.

***

"Who was feeding you over in the Americas?" Helen demanded. "You look as thin as a rake."

"No, he doesn't. He looks fat as anything," Colin commented. "Ouch! Mother, Eliza kicked me."

"Liar!"

"Hush, Children. Well, Silas?"

Silas pushed some more apple pie onto his fork. "Nobody, Mother. I fed myself. I had my own apartment, and I either made my own food or I paid for meals at a lodging house. I didn't have much time to eat, really."

Helen tutted. "You should always make time to eat. Well, Mrs Brigham is still with us, as you can see, so be sure to ask her for some of her old recipes. Remember how much you used to love her jam roly-poly?"

Silas grinned. "I don't think I could ever forget."

"We should have had jam roly-poly tonight. Shouldn't we, Charles?"

"You never make my favourite puddings especially!" Colin

complained.

"That is because you are a thorn in my side, Colin, and your sweet tooth will result in rotting teeth and a growing waistline if you are not careful. What other things would you like to eat, Silas?"

"I don't mind." Silas laughed. "I'm just glad to be home."

"Was the journey terrifying?" Eliza asked eagerly. "Were there storms? Were you nearly wrecked? Were there pirates?"

"There were storms, yes, but we didn't come close to being wrecked. But the storms were unpleasant enough. There wasn't a whiff of pirates, I'm afraid."

"Oh." Eliza sighed. "That's very disappointing."

"What about all of you? Come on, it's been five years. What have I missed? How are the orchards?"

Silas had asked light-heartedly, almost as a joke, but an odd sort of stillness came over the room. Even Colin didn't seem to have a witty quip to make.

Then Eliza muttered something he couldn't make out, and the lively conversation resumed. The silence had rattled Silas, however. Something was wrong, he knew it. He glanced from face to face, finally settling on his father's. Charles' expression was grim and set as he ploughed his way through his food determinedly. He'd never been one for chat at the dinner table, but surely his eldest son returning after a five-year absence warranted some talk, didn't it? Something was on his mind, and Silas was beginning to feel worried.

The meal ended, and the family got up to move through to the drawing room.

"Stay a minute, Silas," Charles said pleasantly. "The rest of you go on, we'll join you in a moment. I want to have a word with my boy."

Silas sat down again, and the rest of them filed out. The door closed, and silence descended.

"I'm glad to have you back, Son," Charles said finally. "You've been missed here, very much. By all of us. Even Colin, although he pretends otherwise."

Silas smiled weakly. "It feels strange to be back, but I'm so happy to see all of you. What's wrong, Father?"

Charles chuckled dryly. "Nothing gets past you, does it?"

"It's got something to do with the orchards, hasn't it?" Silas leaned forward, resting his elbows on the table. The Mitchell orchards had supported the family for years—generations, even. Silas had never thought much about them, except that one day he'd have to come home and tend them, to carry on the family business and continue earning a living. The Mitchells employed a lot of local workers and earned enough money and had enough status to merit invites from the ton. Most of them, anyway. The Radford family, for instance, had always seen fit to be friendly with the Mitchells.

And now something was wrong. Very wrong, judging by the new worry lines etched on his father's face.

Charles sighed. "I didn't intend to burden you with bad news so soon after your return. You've barely shaken the travel dust from your feet, for crying out loud."

"Father, just tell me, please. I've been away long enough."

"Very well. The truth is that our orchards are not doing well. I am concerned. We've . . . we've rather backed ourselves into a financial corner."

Silas swallowed hard. "What does that mean?"

"Nothing good, as I'm sure you can imagine." Charles leaned forward and picked up the decanter of port. He poured himself a generous measure, and after a moment's hesitation, poured Silas one too.

That was a compliment which Silas treasured despite the worried tone of his father's voice. Charles would never have offered eighteen-year-old Silas good port. Eighteen-year-old Silas would have swigged it instead of sipping it and wouldn't have appreciated the aged alcohol in any case.

Silas took a sip.

Yes, he still didn't like port. But that wasn't the point. He kept his expression straight and appreciative, and carefully replaced the glass on the table.

"What are we going to do about it, Father?"

"Truthfully, I don't know." Charles raked a hand through his hair, a nervous gesture that Silas copied whenever he was anxious. "We can discuss it in detail tomorrow. I'm rather tired now, if you don't mind, and I'd like to enjoy your company for one evening at least before we go plunging into business matters. It's almost

Christmastide, after all."

"Yes, people keep reminding me of that. Father, why didn't you tell me all this before? You and Mother wrote letter after letter, and so did Eliza and Colin, but nobody breathed a word of any of this. Why didn't you say?"

"What exactly would you have done about it, Silas?"

"I would have come home immediately. I would have booked passage on the earliest ship sailing to England and returned to help you as best as I could."

Charles chuckled. "And that is exactly why I didn't tell you. I told the others not to tell you, too. You're a clever boy, Silas. Your grandfather wanted you to study, and an opportunity like that wouldn't have come again. I had no intention of letting you cut short your studies. And since I wasn't going to allow you to come back, what would be the use of telling you? So you could worry about it, all the way over in the Americas? No, I think not." Charles tipped back his head, drinking his port in one gulp, the way he'd always forbidden his children to do with their beverages.

"Well, I'm here now," Silas said as firmly as he could. "I have my education behind me, and I'm here to help. We'll get out of this corner, Father, I promise."

"That's my boy. You're giving me confidence already. Now drink your port, don't let it go to waste."

Silas eyed the unappetizing ruby liquid and sighed.

Chapter Three

Five Days Later, Rasbury Village

"What do you think, Augusta? White or green? I really can't decide," Dorothy mused, holding up two rolls of ribbons.

Augusta blinked, suddenly aware that she'd spent the last fifteen minutes letting her mind wander and not paying attention at all. She cleared her throat, hoping she'd looked wisely lost in thought and not like a slack-jawed idiot.

"Um . . . the green, I think. White will get dirty easily. People reuse these baskets, you know."

Dorothy gave her daughter a pointed look. "Yes, Augusta, I do know. I've been making up the poor baskets since well before you were born."

Augusta flushed. "Sorry, Mama. I didn't mean to be rude."

Dorothy tutted, patting Augusta's shoulder. "You weren't rude, my dear. I'm not a fool, you know. This is about Ambrose, isn't it?"

Augusta stiffened. "What do you mean?"

Surely, Dorothy couldn't know. Augusta had assured her parents that she felt strongly for Ambrose, and it wasn't necessarily a lie, even though she'd known her parents meant love, or something close to it, and Augusta's feelings toward Ambrose were . . . was tepid the right word?

Then Dorothy sighed, lifting a new roll of ribbon—purple this time—and inspecting it closely.

"It's a pity he can't be here with us, sure enough. Still, lots of businessmen end up being extra busy around Christmas. He'll be here for the day itself, I'm sure. I remember how I used to feel when your father wasn't around during the holidays. There's nothing quite so miserable as being without your other half at Christmas."

Oh, of course! She thinks I'm missing Ambrose.

She didn't bother to correct her mother.

"Well, I'm sure concentrating on the poor baskets will help to cheer me up," Augusta said lightly, and Dorothy chuckled.

Every year, the Radford family made up dozens upon dozens of baskets for the poor around Christmastide. The baskets themselves were sturdy and good quality, suitable for use after the holiday, and pleasantly decorated. They filled the baskets with food and goodies, a mixture of treats like pastries, sweetmeats, sugared fruits, and more practical groceries, like bread, flour, salted meats, and so on. The baskets would be delivered to the church on Boxing Day, whereupon the vicar would distribute the baskets to whomever he and his wife thought needed them most. In the months running up to Christmastide, he would make a rough calculation of which families were likely to need a Christmas basket from the Radfords and would ask the Duchess to make up the required amount. Then Dorothy and Augusta would make them up.

Augusta enjoyed the work. It kept them all busy, and she liked putting in extra treats and presents for the families to enjoy. Sometimes it was just a few pairs of mittens, or expensive sweetmeats, or tiny pieces of marzipan shaped like fruit, or something similar. She liked their tenants and enjoyed giving out some little extra surprises.

"Let's have white, green, and purple," Dorothy decided. "We can alternate colours."

"That sounds like an excellent idea, Mama."

They gathered up their rolls of ribbon and swathes of fabric they would use to decorate the handles of the baskets and headed to the counter to pay for their purchases.

"Your Grace! Lady Augusta! I thought it was you!"

They paused at the familiar voice, turning to smile at the lady who had hailed them.

It was Mrs Helen Mitchell, an old family friend. Augusta had many happy memories of Mrs Mitchell's warm, cosy little house, and her rambunctious children.

The oldest of whom had stolen a kiss from Augusta, five whole years ago, and she'd never quite been able to forget it.

She should have been able to forget it quite easily since it had clearly meant nothing to him. Perhaps he'd had too much champagne and it had made him bold that evening. He'd left for the Americas only a week or two later, so she was quite certain the kiss had meant nothing at all.

Strangely enough, the idea was more upsetting than anything else. Because the sad truth was, the kiss had meant something to Augusta.

But that was her fault, not his. And, of course, she had no right to take it out on his poor mother. Mrs Mitchell was a lovely woman, and very kind.

So, Augusta pasted a polite smile on her face and turned to greet her.

"Helen, how lovely to see you!" Dorothy smiled. "And please, it's just us—Dorothy will do quite nicely. I hate all this Your Grace nonsense."

Mrs Mitchell chuckled. "Well, it's good to see you. We've missed having your family around the Village at Christmastide. So much has changed!"

"Certainly. How is Eliza? And Colin?"

"Colin is tall and gawky now; you'd hardly recognise him. He's got quite the sharp tongue, too—sometimes I don't know whether to laugh at him or scold him!"

Dorothy laughed at that. "That reminds me of Timothy when he was young. And what about Eliza?"

"Oh, she's so beautiful now. She's here with me now, in fact. Eliza, darling, come over here!"

Augusta craned her neck to spot Eliza. All in all, they hadn't gone back to Rasbury House for at least three years. Her grandfather had been ill, and they'd spent every Christmas since with him in the wilds of Scotland. Augusta had enjoyed her visits, although it hadn't been pleasant to watch her grandfather fade away with every successive visit, and now he was dead. At least it hadn't been in London.

Eliza must have been around sixteen when Augusta saw her last.

The same age you were when Silas Mitchell kissed you.

She came skipping over, the epitome of grace and beauty. She really was a beautiful young woman. She had chestnut brown curls and large, expressive eyes. Augusta didn't believe she was out yet, but when she made her debut, no doubt she would be a huge success.

"Your Grace, what a surprise! And Lady Augusta, it's good to

21

see you again," Eliza greeted them, entirely free of any sort of affectation or shyness. She dropped a neat curtsey, and Augusta bobbed one in return.

"Hello, Eliza. You look very grown up."

Eliza beamed. "Thank you! I'm coming out next Season, all being well. I'm quite thrilled. Can you give me some tips on how to move in Society?"

"Eliza, don't be so forward," Mrs Mitchell said sternly.

"Not at all, she's quite wise to ask," Augusta assured her. "There are lots of unspoken rules in Society, and you ought to know them before you start out. People expect you to know them. Many a debutante has ruined her social career by saying the wrong thing or dressing in the wrong way."

Eliza's smile faded a little, and Augusta felt a little guilty. Still, the fact was that she knew the truth. Society during the Season wasn't enjoyable, not for ladies. It was a vicious place, and an unforgiving one. Finding yourself alone in a quiet room with a gentleman could destroy a lady's reputation forever—not that the gentleman would suffer very much besides a few gossipy comments and a few glares from the more protective mamas—and there was nothing to be done about it.

The ton had a long memory, and mistakes weren't forgiven. Not easily, at least.

"What should I know about?" Eliza asked, looking a little concerned now.

"No waltzing at Almack's for debutantes, no dancing if you refuse a gentleman's invitation to dance . . ."

"But what if I don't like him?"

Augusta smiled pityingly at her. "That doesn't matter. Country manners are very different from Town manners. If you refuse to dance with a gentleman, for any reason at all, you mustn't dance again for the rest of the night."

"What else?"

"Don't force your attentions on a gentleman, even if you're already friends. You ought to wait for the gentleman to approach you. Catch his eye if you must, but don't be too bold. Be careful with your opinions—people remember what you say, and it can be twisted. Read the gossip columns, even though they're absolute nonsense and quite malicious. Pray you don't get mentioned; it's safer that way. Don't spill your tea, don't slurp your soup . . . that sort of thing."

Eliza pulled a face. "That sounds tiresome."

Augusta had to laugh. "I agree, but there it is. If you want to catch yourself a decent husband, you need to play by the rules. It's just a game, but there are serious punishments if you don't follow the rules."

She glanced at Mrs Mitchell's anxious face and her mother's impassive one and wondered if she'd said too much. Probably. But it was worth it if Eliza went into Society a little more prepared than Augusta had been. She had enjoyed her first Season but hadn't approached it with any real seriousness. Debutantes were usually terrified, and for good reason.

It was a game, but one ladies had to take very, very seriously.

Augusta cleared her throat, taking a little step back to indicate that she'd finished terrifying Eliza about the London Season.

"Well, I'm sure Eliza is quite equal to handling herself in Society," Dorothy said quietly, and Augusta nodded.

"I know, Mama. But it's not a nice place for a debutante."

"Charles and I will be there, of course," Mrs Mitchell added. "Eliza won't be alone. Can we expect to see you there too, Lady Augusta?"

"Perhaps."

"Well, I'll have one friend in London then, at least," Eliza said with a short laugh. Augusta smiled weakly. The truth was that a pretty girl like Eliza would have more enemies than friends. Plainer ladies and their aggressive mamas would resent Eliza's pretty face and easy manners, and they were the sort of people who could start unpleasant rumours or cause trouble. Eliza was a good-natured, kind girl, raised in the country by a delightful family, and she only saw the good in the world. She would find the unpleasant undercurrent of London Society something of a shock.

"Oh, Helen, I almost forgot to say. I hear that congratulations are in order. You must be thrilled to have him back after so long," Dorothy said, clearly eager to change the subject.

Mrs Mitchell's face brightened. "Ah, I wondered if you had heard! Yes, we are delighted. Silas has been gone for far too long.

Five years, can you believe it?"

Augusta sucked in a short breath involuntarily. She glanced subtly around, assuring herself that nobody had noticed her reaction. They hadn't, thankfully.

Silas Mitchell was home? Why had nobody told her?

Well, why would they? It wasn't as if you told anyone about the kiss. No doubt he wasn't foolish enough to tell anyone, either.

Augusta forced herself to regain her composure. So, Silas was home. That didn't mean anything, did it? It wasn't as though she was going to see him. Perhaps he was just in England in general, not necessarily home.

"It's so odd to see his old room occupied again," Mrs Mitchell continued blithely, oblivious to Augusta's discomfort. "I know it was a wonderful opportunity for him—for any young man—but it was a wrench, having him so far away." She glanced down, fiddling with the lace on her sleeve cuff. "Mothers worry, you know. Well, I don't have to tell you, Dorothy. But I hated having him so far away. If something went wrong—well, he was all on his own, wasn't he? By the time a letter even arrived, weeks or even months could have gone past. Then it would take more months for our reply to arrive. I'm sure he wasn't afraid at all—young people are so bold, aren't they? But that's all in the past now." She drew in a deep breath. "He's home. I keep reminding myself of it and smiling like a fool. He's home."

"I can't imagine letting Timothy or Augusta go to the Americas for so long," Dorothy admitted. "I daresay I would have let them go, if it came to it . . ." she trailed off, giving herself a little shake, then drawing herself up again. "I am grateful Timothy only wanted to go to Eton. Now, we really must get going—we have the poor baskets to make up for this year. But we really must have you all over for a dinner one day. A nice, informal occasion, where we can all laugh and talk and catch up."

"Oh, that sounds wonderful! I'm sure we'd all love that. Silas especially—he'll be thrilled to see how you've all changed since he left."

Augusta's heart sank. A quiet, informal dinner with wretched Silas Mitchell. She couldn't think of anything she'd find more uncomfortable.

Dorothy didn't seem to pick up on her daughter's

discomfort.

"Excellent! Well, let's set a date at once—you know what this season is like, we'll all be busy every day until Christmastide, won't we? How about tomorrow evening?"

Please say no. Please have an engagement. I don't want to see Silas Mitchell!

"That sounds wonderful!"

"Then it's arranged. We must dash, but we'll see you then! Goodbye, Helen, goodbye, Eliza!"

Augusta forced herself to bid her goodbyes, but her head was reeling.

She didn't want to see Silas. It had taken her years to get over her feelings, her disappointment. She'd missed countless opportunities because of Silas and his thoughtless kiss. Now, she had a fiancé and a decent future ahead of her.

Augusta was determined not to allow those feelings to be stirred up again.

Silas Mitchell, good luck to you.

Chapter Four

Silas made himself as comfortable as he could in the stiff, straight-backed chair, giving Elton a few minutes to collect his papers.

Elton Hargreaves was Silas' cousin, his mother's nephew, and was currently employed as Charles' man of business. He was thirty years old, married to a nice woman, had no children, and had a weak, rabbity sort of face. As far as Silas could tell, Elton was a staid, sensible man, a little dull, but hard-working and honest. More importantly, Elton had no interest in sugar-coating any hard facts, and Silas very much wanted to hear the raw truth about their business. Something was wrong, that much was clear. But how badly wrong was the question.

After his conversation with his father on his first night home, Charles had avoided any in-depth questions about their financial affairs. The exhaustion of travelling had crept up on Silas, and he found he had hardly any energy to pursue his own lines of inquiry.

Five days after his arrival home, however, Silas had finally recovered, and took himself into town to visit Elton's office. It was time to get to the bottom of the matter.

To the untrained eye, Elton's office was a shocking mess. Papers were piled everywhere, in hazardous, lopsided piles. There was a small square of free space on Elton's desk, and the rest of the surface was taken up with papers, folders, and other paraphernalia.

Silas knew from experience, however, that Elton could find any single document in an instant. He knew where everything was, and nothing was ever misplaced or forgotten. He had a remarkable memory to boot, and a knack for accounts.

"I'm glad to see you safely home, Cousin," Elton said brusquely, finally settling himself down. "The trip from the Americas back to England is a long and dangerous one."

"Yes, I know. I miss my studies and the Americas, but I don't think I'll be making the trip again anytime soon."

Elton nodded. "Very wise. Now, what can I help you with?"

Straight to business, then. Silas leaned forward in his seat, back already aching.

"Father has told me that our finances are not in good health. I'd like a little more clarity on that."

Elton pursed his lips. "Uncle Charles is right. We're not quite on the verge of bankruptcy, fortuitously, but I'd be lying if I said things weren't getting worryingly close."

Silas sucked in a breath. "That bad?"

"That bad," Elton confirmed. "The issue is that Uncle Charles has made some bad investments. He'd helped too many tenants who cannot afford to repay him as stipulated. While that is the mark of a good, kind man and an excellent landlord, we simply can't afford to support tenants who weren't prepared for what has happened."

"And what has happened? Remember, I've been gone for five years, Elton, and Father and the others saw fit to hide all of this from me in their letters."

"The rains," Elton said simply. "We've had too much hard, heavy rain for the past few years, interposed with hot summers. That means when the rain comes again, it comes suddenly and heavily, and washes away too much of the topsoil, which is now too dry to absorb the sudden rain. Crops have suffered, and our orchards are no exception."

Silas ran a hand through his hair, feeling pomade stick to his palm. "Are our orchards ruined?"

"Not quite, but if the rain continues, we might find ourselves in a bad situation. What's worse, a lot of our tenants are unable to pay their rent. Uncle Charles gives them far more credit than he should. It's kind, and I hate to tell him to turn out innocent families, but the fact remains that we need that rent. There's no more money, Silas. Our luck needs to change, and soon."

"What would you recommend? There must be something we can do."

Elton shrugged. "Uncle Charles has made a few investments, but they've all gone bad. I'm a man of business, and I prefer solid profit-and-loss accounts to investments. I'm not qualified to give the best advice, but I think Uncle Charles was given very bad advice. And, of course, Cousin Eliza is coming out next Season, which will be another great expense, taking the whole family to London. We have a lot of payments coming up, and not enough money to cover them all. Uncle Charles is keen that Eliza and Colin shouldn't know how bad things here. I believe he also wants Aunt Helen to be kept in the dark, but you know how sharp she is. It's almost impossible to hide anything from her."

"So, there's nothing we can do?" Silas asked, feeling a little numb and light-headed. Had he really been living without a care in the Americas, immersing himself in his studies and having fun with his friends, when all the while his family was inching nearer and nearer to destitution?

Elton hesitated. "Actually, now you are home, I have an idea to put to you. I don't think you'll like it, though."

"It doesn't matter. I'll hear it. I'll do anything to help my family and our business, Elton."

Elton had a strange look on his face. "Well, I'm glad to hear that. Silas, have you thought of marriage?"

Silas frowned. "Well, I suppose I'll marry one day. I haven't given much thought to it, no. Why?"

"There is a tried and tested way of fixing one's finances very quickly," Elton said quietly. "And that is marrying a rich woman."

"Well, I suppose it would be convenient if I fell in love with a woman rich enough to solve our problems, but—"

"I'm not talking of love, Silas," Elton interrupted. "I am talking about actively looking for a rich woman, or an heiress, or a lady with a large enough dowry to get us out of trouble, and marrying her."

Silas was struck speechless for a moment. "I am not a fortune hunter, Elton!"

Elton sighed, leaning back in his seat. "I knew you wouldn't like it."

"You want me to marry a woman for her money? That's terrible, Elton!"

"Is it? You just said you'd do anything to help your family," Elton countered.

"I meant anything that is morally right."

Elton rolled his eyes. "So, you didn't mean *anything*."

"I can't believe we're discussing this."

Elton leaned forward again, resting his elbows on his desk.

"Look. You said yourself you'll probably marry sooner or later, correct? And you aren't currently in love with anyone, are you?"

Augusta's face, blurred by time, flashed into Silas' head, but he purposefully put her out of his mind.

"No."

"And you don't intend to mistreat your wife, or be unkind to her?"

"Of course I don't!"

"Well, then, what is the harm of marrying a woman who can save our business? Knowing she saved all of us might make you love her more over time than if you'd married some peaches-and-cream Society belle. Lots of women would be happy with a man like you, Silas, and not all marriages are based on love. In fact, most of them aren't. Not every couple are as lucky as Uncle Charles and Aunt Helen."

Silas bit his lip, mulling it over. Much as he hated to admit it, Elton had a point. Rich women were targeted by fortune hunters and ended up losing their money anyway to men who pretended to care for them but turned out to be rakes, gamblers, and cruel men.

At least I'm not one of those men. I'd care for a wife as a husband ought to.

"It just feels so mercenary," Silas said, after a few moments.

Elton shrugged. "It is mercenary. I'm sorry, Silas, I hate to suggest something like this. But the fact is that we need some money to tide us over, and I don't know where that money is going to come from. Now you're home, I hoped . . . well, I hoped you might take matters into your own hands."

That sentence, so innocently meant, sent a shiver down Silas' spine. It was his responsibility to take matters into his own hands, wasn't it? He was the oldest son. He needed to do *something*.

"You've given me a lot to think about, Elton." Silas said honestly. "I . . . I'll think about what you've said. I'll consider it seriously, I promise."

Elton nodded. "Thank you. In the meantime, I'll keep exploring other avenues of revenue and possible future investments—although we can't afford any more mistakes. I'm sorry I don't have any better news for you."

"That's quite all right." Silas stood up, smiling faintly. "I came here to hear plain, cold facts."

Elton got to his feet too, laughing quietly. "Well, you'll certainly get those from me." He extended his hand, and Silas took it. "It's good to see you home, Silas."

***

"Oh, and how was Cousin Elton, Silas?" Eliza asked over dinner.

Even though he had no reason to feel guilty, Silas felt an odd twinge of guilt roll down his spine anyway, as if he'd been somehow misleading his father.

"He's doing well," Silas said briskly, concentrating on his soup. "We had a long talk. Lots to think about."

Charles said nothing, and Silas wondered whether he'd been indiscreet. The truth was, he'd been mulling Elton's advice over and over in his head all afternoon. He hated the idea of marrying a woman under false pretences.

Because that is what it would be—false. One couldn't simply approach a woman and outline the plain, cold facts, making it clear that you wanted to marry her for her money, and not expect to be slapped in the face.

You would deserve it, too.

But try as he might, Silas couldn't think of anything else to do. The world of investing tended to make people poorer rather than richer, and if Charles had already made a few bad decisions, they couldn't afford any more.

But where would he even *find* a rich woman? There were heiresses and women with large dowries aplenty during the Season, but that was over until next year. Now what?

Silas had thought of marriage occasionally, but it had always had more to do with his abandoned childhood friend than anything else.

Of course, they hadn't exactly been friends by the time Silas left. Augusta must have felt so shocked and betrayed when he'd kissed her like that, and naturally, they hadn't spoken since.

He missed her. They'd been such good friends, and Silas was sure he'd been in love with her. He hadn't been in love since, so he had nothing to compare it to. He wondered what sort of lady she'd grown into. A mature, intelligent, dignified young woman, no doubt.

"Oh, that reminds me," Helen said, dabbing her mouth with a napkin. "The Radfords have invited us for supper tomorrow evening."

Silas choked on his soup.

"Ah, they're back in town?" Charles said. "How nice!"

"Yes, Eliza and I ran into Dorothy and Augusta in town. They're preparing this year's poor baskets, I believe. It was so nice to see them again. It's been a few years since they spent Christmastide here, isn't it?"

"They're a busy family," Charles acknowledged. "Still, it will be nice to catch up, don't you think, children?"

Silas didn't answer. He was too busy staring down into the murky depths of his pea-green soup (What sort of soup was it again? Pea and ham? Leek and potato? He really couldn't remember), and trying not to think about Augusta.

She'd been a quiet girl, but not due to shyness or nerves. She was quiet and calm, composed at all times, except for those few mad days when they were young and she'd gone racing through the meadows alongside him, screaming and wild. He could still remember her like that, bits of grass stuck in her hair and her cheeks flushed with exercise.

Then, of course, Augusta had started to grow up, and didn't go racing around the meadows and climbing trees anymore, not with him or with anyone else. If he was honest with himself, Silas would admit the kiss had been born out of desperation. His Augusta was growing up, and the social divide between them was getting wider and deeper. Augusta was, after all, the daughter of a duke. Silas was a merchant's son—and a failing one at that.

"Silas, are you quite all right? You're letting your soup go cold," Helen commented, waking Silas out of his stupor.

"Sorry, Mother, I'm quite tired. It's been a long day," Silas said, forcing himself to smile. He scooped up a spoonful of soup and swallowed it. It tasted like dishwater all of a sudden.

"Well, you need to take care of yourself. Doesn't he, Charles? You work entirely too much, Silas."

Silas smiled vaguely. He wondered if he could claim a

31

headache before supper at Rasbury House tomorrow. No, it might seem too suspicious. What if Augusta remembered the incident and guessed he was being a coward?

Was there really any hope she might have forgotten? Silas fought the urge to groan and lay his head down on the table.

Either way, Augusta wasn't going to bring it up at the table. Probably not, at least.

It won't be as bad as you think, Silas. You and Augusta might find yourselves good friends, just like before. That idea lifted his spirits a little. Buoyed by the idea that he might be about to reconnect with his oldest and dearest friend, Silas was able to finish his soup, and embark on the main course with gusto. He was even able to manage a pudding.

Chapter Five

The drawing room was a quiet and peaceful place, only the sound of Augusta's scissors snipping through the fine gold silk they'd chosen to embellish that year's Christmas greenery decorations. Dorothy liked to decorate the greenery a little differently each year, and Augusta loved it. Christmas was a time for tradition, certainly, but what was the point of tradition if it never let one experiment with anything new?

They'd used gold silk five years ago, though. Augusta could remember seeing the sparkling shapes pinned to a kissing bough, rustling above her head. The scene came rushing back, every bit as vividly as when it had happened.

Young Augusta eyed the kissing bough with surprise as it hovered above her head, wielded by an uncertain young man. It wasn't really used very often—theirs was a family Christmastide, and there wasn't a lot of kissing, except between her parents and Mr and Mrs Mitchell.

The Mitchells were with them that year, laughing and joking in the next room. She remembered lingering at the drawing room window, staring down the drive in barely suppressed excitement, waiting for the Mitchells' carriage to appear, knowing Silas would be inside. Even a few days apart from him felt like an eternity to Augusta. Thank heavens their families were friends in a small town, though—she had excuses to see Silas most days.

But now Silas was standing too close to her in the hallway, holding a kissing bough over her head, looking determined and terrified all at once. He'd shot up in height over the past year, towering over by at least a foot.

"You have to give me permission," Silas said, waking Augusta up from her inspection of the kissing bough above her head.

Augusta chewed her lip, eyeing the half-closed drawing room door, only a few feet before her. She was old enough to understand the repercussions of kissing young men freely.

"I don't know," she said honestly.

Silas considered it. "It's bad luck if you say no."

33

Augusta narrowed her eyes. "I believe we make our own luck. Kissing you might bring worse luck. What if you have bad breath?"

Silas was fighting back a laugh, she could tell, but was trying to stay focused on his task.

"I *am* serious."

"So am I."

There were voices coming closer to the drawing room door now, and Augusta suddenly realised they would be interrupted at any moment. Silas apparently thought the same thing, and his nerve broke.

He dived forward, briefly slotting his lips against hers. It was the oddest thing that had ever happened to Augusta, having someone else's face so close. His lips were soft, and tasted faintly of Christmas pudding, and he did not have bad breath.

Silas darted back, his face an interesting shade of scarlet, and Augusta found herself raising her hand to her lips, utterly shocked at the fact that she'd just had her very first kiss ever.

Then, the drawing room door opened, and Augusta's mother appeared. Silas had put the kissing bough down somewhere, so Dorothy didn't seem concerned in the slightest.

"Ah, there you are, Silas! Your parents are leaving. Hurry, or they'll go without you!"

Silas opened and closed his mouth like a fish, and it was suddenly all too much for Augusta. She turned tail and raced away down the hallway, keen to find some privacy to calm her fluttering heart and mull over what had just happened.

She didn't know what she intended to do or say about that kiss. She wasn't entirely sure how she felt about it, only that it made her feel giddy and happy.

When she returned, Silas was gone. She never saw him again.

"Come now, Augusta, are you wool-gathering?"

Augusta flinched, nearly ruining the pattern she was cutting out. "Goodness, Mama, you quite startled me!" she said, laughing.

Dorothy chuckled. "You were a million miles away. Penny for your thoughts, then?"

Augusta's smile faded. She wasn't sure her mother would

34

want to pay a penny to hear that her daughter was dreaming of a stolen kiss from five years ago. A kiss that had meant so much to her, but clearly meant nothing at all to the other participant.

"Oh, nothing much," Augusta said, falsely bright.

"Come now, don't try and fool your old Mama. I know *exactly* what you were thinking about."

I doubt that very much, Mama.

"And what's that, then?" Augusta asked, setting aside the stack of cut-out gold silk shapes.

Dorothy sat down beside her, beginning to sort through them.

"You're thinking about your wedding, of course. I don't blame you. When I was engaged to your father, I thought of our wedding *constantly*. There was so much to do, and I was so determined that everything should be perfect. And, of course, my head was simply full of your father. I used to wander around in a daze most days; it drove my poor mama quite mad."

Augusta swallowed hard, trying to fight back the lump that had leapt into her throat. She hated it when her mother compared her marriage to her father to Augusta and Ambrose's relationship. Augusta was uncomfortably aware that their situations were not at all the same. Dorothy and Charles had been deeply in love. Augusta and Ambrose were not.

But that didn't *matter*, did it? Love was pleasant, but not necessary. Augusta had no intention of being unmarried for much longer—Society was far too harsh on single women. She was no spinning woman, able to earn the name "spinster" from her talent in spinning that allowed her independence. She was a Society Lady, and Society Ladies got married.

But that didn't change the fact that Augusta had just been dreaming about a stolen kiss from a man who was not her fiancé. Ambrose was a good man, and Silas was clearly not interested in her at all. So, why was she still thinking about it?

Perhaps it was a good thing the Mitchells were coming over for supper. Augusta would be able to see Silas face to face. Perhaps he'd aged, and she wouldn't find him attractive anymore. Perhaps he'd ignore her, or be coldly polite, and she'd know exactly where she stood.

Yes, that would be much better. A little clarity on the matter was just the ticket. Augusta would know how to feel about him then, and she could get on with the important matter of her wedding and her future—both of which relied on her *fiancé*, Ambrose.

"I don't worry much about the wedding, Mama," Augusta said briskly. "I know you'll help me organise everything. I don't mind about things being perfect, not as long as everybody has a good time."

"You're such a sweet girl. Don't forget to enjoy *yourself* on the day. It will be your wedding, after all. Have you discussed it much with Ambrose."

"No, not much," Augusta answered vaguely.

Not much? Try not at all.

Dorothy tutted. "*Men.* They couldn't care less about any of it. Well, not to worry, dear. We can start getting you fitted for a wedding dress after Christmastide, and I'll start on the invitations soon. I know we're cutting it a little fine, but nobody wants to think about invitations before Christmas. They'll just be put away, and people will forget to respond."

"I think if they forget about my wedding altogether, I don't particularly want them to come," Augusta remarked.

Dorothy chuckled. "Such fire! You must write up a list of people you particularly want invited, and Ambrose should do the same. Do you know when Ambrose will be arriving?"

Augusta was starting to feel that she wanted to stop talking about Ambrose.

"No, Mama, I'm afraid not."

"Well, that can't be helped."

The door opened and the butler stepped inside.

"The Marquess and Marchioness of Avilwood, Your Grace."

Augusta gave a shriek.

"Timothy! Timothy's here, Mama!"

"So I can hear," Dorothy said, laughing.

Augusta leapt to her feet, running towards the door just as Timothy and his wife Caroline swept in.

Timothy was a tall, thin man of about twenty-seven, dark haired and blue-eyed, with a few silver streaks at his temples indicating that he'd inherited his mother's tendency to go grey early in life. Augusta privately thought it looked dashing.

His wife Caroline was a year or two older than her husband. She was a mild-mannered woman with unflappable good sense and the kindest nature Augusta had ever known, but she had never been considered a beauty. She had very pale-yellow hair and almost invisible eyelashes and eyebrows, and teeth that never quite fitted behind her lips.

None of that worried Timothy in the slightest. He and Caroline were a match made in heaven, as the saying went, and one of the happiest couples Augusta had ever known. Augusta had often worried about who her sister-in-law would be. She only had one brother, and he was very dear to her. A malicious sister-in-law could drive a brother and sister apart.

Caroline had no intention of doing such a terrible thing. After Augusta threw her arms around Timothy and was swung around in a circle, she embraced Caroline next.

"It's lovely to see you both," Augusta said, grinning so widely her cheeks started to ache. "I've missed you."

"I can't believe we weren't in town for the Season," Caroline mourned. "We missed your *engagement party*, Augusta. I was so terribly sorry."

Timothy snorted. "I was sorry to miss it, Augusta, but I was *not* going to travel down from Edinburgh."

Augusta rolled her eyes. "I didn't expect you to, don't worry! Besides, you're here now."

"Can we meet this mysterious fiancé?" Timothy asked, a mischievous gleam flickering in his eyes.

Augusta hesitated. "He isn't here yet."

"What? It's almost Christmastide."

"He had some business to finish off. You know how it is."

Timothy didn't look as if he agreed at all, but Caroline hurried to smooth things over.

"I'm sure he must be a very busy man. I daresay he's simply miserable, having to stay in town while you're up here."

Augusta thought of how Ambrose's face had lit up at the prospect of staying in London and found she didn't quite agree with that sentiment.

Dorothy stepped forward—she'd hung back to laugh at Augusta and Timothy's exuberant reunion—and kissed her son and daughter-in-law.

"Now, we are having the Mitchells around for supper tonight," Dorothy said. "I'm so glad you have managed to get here in time. You'd better hurry and change; they'll be here at any minute!"

***

"You must be looking forward to seeing him again, miss," Betsey said, lacing up Augusta's evening gown.

Augusta glanced up sharply, intending to catch Betsey's eyes in the mirror, but the maid had her gaze turned down at her task.

"Yes. Well, I suppose so. Five years is a long time, and it will be nice to catch up. But we weren't really very close, Betsey. I daresay he hasn't given a second thought to me being here."

This time, Betsey did look up, and her expression was one of bewilderment.

"I . . . I was talking about Lord Firnsdale, miss. Who were you talking about?"

Colour rushed to Augusta's face. It made perfect sense—she and Betsey had been talking about weddings before Betsey paused to help Augusta into her dress. Naturally, the "*him*" she was talking about would be Augusta's fiancé, not the man she'd been thinking about all day and hadn't seen for the past five years.

I can't afford any more slip-ups like that! It would look singularly odd if I did something like that in company. What if it got back to Ambrose, and he thought I was carrying a torch for Silas Mitchell? Which I am not.

Augusta cleared her throat, fiddling with her cuffs. She didn't say anything, and Betsey tactfully let the subject go.

She'd chosen a sage-green dress, not quite suitable for a proper soirée, but easily good enough for an informal family supper. There was frothy lace at the neckline (square, a little old-fashioned, but flattering) and at the sleeves, which ended just above the elbow. Augusta decided not to bother with gloves that evening, since it was just family and close friends. She'd chosen a jade jewellery set Timothy had got her as a present years ago, knowing how much his sister loved green things.

Her hair was twisted into a simple knot—not that anything concerning Augusta's profusion of hair could ever be *simple*.

Augusta knew she was dragging out the dressing process, hoping to postpone the moment she entered the parlour and looked Silas in the face for the first time in five years.

Was it too late to pretend she had a megrim? No, they'd never believe that. Augusta didn't get megrims, and she didn't faint or swoon or have the vapours. Maybe life would be easier if she started having fits of the vapours when things got tricky.

Betsey stepped back. "You're all done, Miss."

"Should I do my hair a different way, do you think?"

Betsey looked surprised. "But . . . but you said you liked it, miss, when I was doing it. It'll take too long to change it. Do you want to change it?"

Augusta sighed. "No, it's fine, Betsey. Thank you."

There was nothing for it. She'd have to go downstairs. She would be strict with herself, though. She would absolutely not think about Silas Mitchell any more than she had to.

Chapter Six

It was dark by the time the Mitchell family piled into their creaky old carriage and set off for Rasbury House. Nerves were twisting in Silas' stomach, more powerfully than he'd felt for a long time.

The carriage door closed, and they started on their way. It was too late, then. They were going, and Silas had lost his opportunity to take the coward's way out, duck out of the carriage and back into his home.

The carriage was designed to carry four people at the most, so the five of them were quite a squeeze. Helen and Charles sat on one side, with the three children crammed in shoulder-to-shoulder on the other seat.

"Stop elbowing me, Colin," Eliza hissed.

"I'm not doing it deliberately. It's Silas, he's taking up all the space."

"I am *not*. Look at how I'm shoved against the door. Does that look like a lot of extra space to you?"

"Ow! Colin!"

"Stop whining."

"I am *not* sitting in the middle on the way home."

"Children, please!" Helen chastised. "Let's compose ourselves. We haven't seen the Radfords for years, and I'd like us to make a good impression. Dorothy and Augusta will be powerful friends for you to have during your Season, Eliza."

The family fell silent as the carriage rattled on. There was a light covering of frost outside, but no snow yet. Silas guessed there would be soon enough, though, probably within the next few days. Almost certainly before Christmas.

His nerves hadn't settled. He was going to see Augusta for the first time in five years, and he was frankly terrified.

Would she be happy to see him? Would he be happy to see *her*, after all this time?

Worst of all, of course, Silas couldn't tell anyone how he felt.

He'd briefly considered confiding in Eliza or Colin and rejected the idea almost immediately.

His siblings were nice, but they'd hardly handle that sort of secret well. Besides, Silas didn't know how his and Augusta's kiss would impact her reputation now.

I really must stop thinking about that kiss!

He didn't know what had spurred him to lift the kissing bough above Augusta's head and ask her permission for a kiss, aside from his underlying worries that that they were growing apart.

As a child, Silas had always thought he would stay in Rasbury Village his whole life and would one day start working for his father. He'd tend to the orchards his grandfather had started, and if he was lucky, he'd marry Augusta one day.

That was a silly idea, looking back. The Duke and Duchess weren't proud or snobs, but they probably hoped for a little better for their daughter than a merchant's son. And besides, that had been back then, when the Mitchells were a rich and powerful family of relatively good breeding, before their financial problems had arisen.

Silas assumed the Radford family did not know about his family's recent misfortunes. No doubt Charles was keen to keep it that way.

The carriage ground to a halt, and Silas realised with a jolt that they were there. He peered out of the window, and saw Rasbury House towering over them, lights glowing in the windows, seeming to reach up to the skies.

A footman opened the door, and the rest of the family sighed in relief, keen to disentangle themselves from the small carriage. Silas got out last, feeling as though he were leaving his last safe place.

Calm down, Silas. You're among friends. These are old family friends. There's no need to be nervous.

Unfortunately, telling oneself not to be nervous doesn't actually do much to help one's nerves. The Duke and Duchess stood at the top of the stone stairs, eager to greet them as they disembarked from the carriage.

Was the house larger than Silas remembered? Places you remembered from your childhood were supposed to seem much smaller than before, but it seemed to him that Rasbury House had grown.

"Welcome, welcome!" the Duchess said, smiling at them as they ascended the stairs. "Patrick and I have been looking out for you. It has been entirely too long. It's freezing out here, come inside at once before we do our introductions!"

Despite his nerves, Silas was relieved to step into the warm, well-lit hallway, the large front door shut firmly against the chilly night air. A deferential footman helped him out of his hat, coat, and gloves, and Silas turned to find the Duchess looking at him, round-eyed, her hands pressed to her mouth.

"Oh, my goodness, Silas!" she exclaimed. "You're so tall, so manly! You're quite the gentleman now. Isn't he, Patrick?"

The Duke chuckled, stepping forward to shake Silas' hand. "You can hardly be surprised the boy has grown, Dorothy! It's good to see you, Silas. We've been looking forward to seeing you again. And how Colin and Eliza have grown too!"

Greetings and pleasantries were exchanged, and Silas was able to stand still for a moment and catch his breath. It was just the Duke and Duchess. Augusta hadn't come out to greet them. Was she waiting in the parlour or drawing room?

Perhaps Augusta wasn't home at all. No, that wasn't right, Silas knew she was in the village. But perhaps she wasn't going to join them, and nobody had mentioned it to him. Well, why should they?

Silas couldn't decide which made him feel worse—coming face to face with Augusta after all these years, or not getting to see her at all. He briefly considered asking about her but decided against it. It would be too pointed. It might look strange. He'd just have to wait and see if Augusta appeared.

"Come on through to the drawing room," the Duchess said once they were all divested of their outdoor things. "Oh, we have a surprise for you—Timothy and Caroline are at home!"

Charles and Dorothy exclaimed in delight, and they all followed the Duke and Duchess through the cavernous, immaculately decorated hallways. Had they changed since Silas was here last? For the life of him, he couldn't remember.

He vaguely remembered Timothy as the Marquess of Avilwood. Caroline must be his wife. They'd been married for around four years, which would mean Timothy had been married when he was the same age as Silas was now. That was an odd feeling, as Timothy had always seemed very mature and grown-up to Silas, being a full four years older. When one is young, four years is a very long time. Silas was in the Americas by then, but he remembered receiving a letter about it from his mother.

He stepped into the large, brightly lit drawing room. It was a real withdrawing room, designed for comfort and family time. Games and entertainments were scattered everywhere in the form of abandoned board games, books, work, and more. Two figures rose from the sofa as they entered, and Silas vaguely recognised the man as Timothy Radford. He didn't recognise the woman, but introductions were soon made all round.

There was still no Augusta. Silas' heart sank, his disappointment more powerful than he could have imagined.

So, she wasn't going to join them. Perhaps she'd received an invitation somewhere else, or simply didn't feel well.

Perhaps she *did* remember the kiss and had no intention of coming face to face with Silas again and had formulated some handy excuse.

"Now," the Duke said, clapping his hands. "I for one want to hear Silas' adventures. Did you know, Caroline, that Silas has been studying in the Americas for the past four or five years? It was a truly marvellous opportunity, although it required his poor family to give him up for that time."

"I did not know that, how interesting! Oh, do tell, Mr Mitchell."

Silas laughed self-consciously. "Well, I was only studying, so I'm afraid my adventures were few and far between. What few adventures I have I'll save for the dinner table, if you don't mind, when everyone is feeling more genial and good-humoured."

That earned him a laugh, and the Duke clapped him on the shoulder.

"Timothy, weren't you and Silas close friends when you were young?"

Timothy chuckled. "Unfortunately not. I was four years older and fancied myself quite the man. You're thinking of Augusta, Father. She and Silas were thick as thieves."

The Duke laughed. "Of course, how could I have forgotten!

We must tell Caroline some of those stories. Miss Eliza, Mr Colin, have you heard about some of the japes your brother and Lady Augusta got up to?"

Colin's eyes lit up in glee at the prospect of embarrassing stories relating to his older brother.

"I haven't, no, Your Grace. What sort of japes?"

"Stealing apples from Mr Havisham's orchard, for one," the Duchess chimed in. "The poor man used to come storming up here at least once or twice a week when there was fruit on his trees, complaining about that wretched pair stealing his fruit. Patrick and I were quite at our wit's end, and poor Mr Mitchell was absolutely tired of apologising to poor Mr Havisham."

That story earned a laugh, and Silas began to feel himself relaxing. If Augusta wasn't coming, at least he could try and enjoy himself among old friends and family. The only person present whom he didn't know was the Marchioness, Lady Caroline, and she seemed perfectly pleasant and likeable.

As if he'd conjured her by his thoughts, Timothy spoke up.

"Where *is* Augusta, Mother?"

"Oh, don't tell me. She went up to dress at a reasonable time, and Timothy and Caroline went up at the same time. They were down at least half an hour ago, so I'm not sure what Augusta is about."

"That isn't like her," Timothy observed. "Augusta was never a girl to spend hours over dressing."

"She's probably started reading a book and got carried away, you know what she's like." The Duchess started talking about some other topic, some gossip-worthy titbit that had happened before Silas's arrival and which, frankly, could not have interested him less.

All he could think about was that Augusta was coming. She was the reason they were waiting in the drawing room and not going into the dining room yet. Augusta would be downstairs at any minute.

All of Silas' nerves came surging back. He wished he could sit down and steady his wobbly legs, but nobody had been invited to sit down yet. It wasn't a slight, it was simply that they were all standing together, talking animatedly, and apparently nobody else had thought of sitting down yet.

He wanted a glass of water, a sip of wine, even some of that unbearable port his father liked so much. Silas clenched his hands into fists at his sides, his palms horribly damp. *Augusta is here. Augusta is coming.*

"Mr Mitchell?" a soft voice asked, a small hand coming up to rest on Silas' shoulder. He found himself looking down at the Marchioness, Lady Caroline. "Is everything all right? You've gone pale, and you look rather ill. Would you like me to fetch someone?"

Silas went beet red at the thought of being coddled like an invalid, as if he'd gone into a swoon.

"No, no, I'm quite all right, thank you. I think the travelling home has taken more out of me than I thought. I've had plenty of time to recover, but I still feel rather weak. I'll be quite well, I promise."

Caroline nodded, her eyes still concerned. "Shall I see if I can fetch you some food or water? Oh, you must sit down, Mr Mitchell. Your health is important."

Silas had to chuckle. "My health is quite untouched, but my pride is taking something of a dent."

She smiled at that, understanding flashing across her face. "Ah, how could I forget? Gentlemen hate to be coddled. Well, don't worry, Mr Mitchell, we'll be going in to eat soon, and then you should recover your strength."

Silas opened his mouth to say something he hoped would be witty and interesting but was interrupted by the drawing room door opening and closing. He turned around to find that someone had let themselves in, very quietly and unobtrusively.

"Ah, Augusta!" the Duchess said. "There you are! I was starting to wonder where you'd got to."

It was her. Just like that, Augusta was there again. Silas found himself staring at her, probably rather rudely. She looked beautiful, so much more beautiful than he remembered. The Augusta he remembered was shorter and thinner, with a pretty but childish face. This Augusta was full-grown and womanly, her face perfectly set and entirely composed and dignified. She wore a pale-green dress, and a memory stirred, informing Silas that green had always been her favourite colour when she was younger.

Her gaze raked over the guests, recognition flashing. Slowly, inexorably, her eyes came to rest on Silas.

There was a half instant of silence, which to Silas seemed to last minutes, *hours*, and he wondered how the others couldn't notice it. He had to say something, anything, but his tongue simply refused to work.

Had it really been five years? It felt like no time at all. Everything had changed between them, but at the same time, not a thing had changed.

She hadn't changed.

"Mr Mitchell," Augusta said, and even her voice was different, deeper and more cultured. "Silas. It's good to see you again."

Chapter Seven

Augusta knew she'd left it too long. Wouldn't it have been better to be settled in the drawing room, in her own territory, when Silas arrived? Instead, she'd wasted time dawdling in her room, and everyone was already assembled in the drawing room by the time she got downstairs. Then, it was almost as if Augusta was the newcomer.

She was pleased at how composed she sounded when she looked at Silas. The gawky, grinning boy of her imagination was long gone. Five years had changed Silas more than she could have imagined—he was stronger, broader about the chest and shoulders, and his face was chiselled and handsomely formed, his hair neatly styled in a way the eighteen-year-old Silas had never bothered about.

Did he see any differences in her? Most likely.

"Lady Augusta," Silas said, making a neat bow.

"Oh, come on, Silas. We've known each other for so long, I'm sure we can settle for Augusta by now."

Silas straightened from his bow, and his expression was unreadable.

"Of course. It's good to see you again."

Augusta eyed him curiously. Was he remembering the kiss? *Did* he remember it? If he really had drunk too much champagne, he may not remember it at all.

Wouldn't that be ironic? Spending years agonising over a kiss from a boy who didn't even remember stealing it.

"I'm glad you could join us at last; we thought you must have gotten lost," Patrick said, grinning. "It isn't like you to be so vain over your appearance, Augusta."

There were a few chuckles at his joke, and Augusta smiled good-naturedly.

"Betsey had trouble with my hair. I haven't made us late for dinner, have I?" Augusta privately winced at the lie, but it wasn't as if Betsey would actually get into trouble.

"Not at all, my dear. I don't believe it's quite ready yet. We're taking a little time to catch up—it's been far too long, don't

47

you think?" Patrick slipped an arm around Augusta's shoulders, turning to face the room. "We're all agog to hear of Silas's adventures in the Americas."

Silas smiled at that, and Augusta's heart, to her mortification, did a little somersault. He had no right to look so handsome when she smiled, and she had no right to find him so handsome. She had a fiancé.

But finding other men handsome is hardly a betrayal, is it? One acknowledges that one's fiancé is not actually the most handsome man in the world.

Augusta tried to fix a picture of Ambrose in her head, but it quickly fizzled out before the newer, brighter image of adult Silas, who was tall and strong and handsome, but also so undeniably *Silas,* replaced it in a way that Augusta simply couldn't explain. His expressions, his mannerisms, even the words he used reminded her so strongly of her childhood friend, she began to feel rather overwhelmed.

He's here. He's back. Now what shall I do?

It was apparent that Silas didn't intend to offer only icy politeness, and Augusta felt like a fool for ever thinking so. In an intimate supper with a group of this size, any unfriendliness or cold politeness would be noticed at once.

So, if Silas was kind to her, it didn't mean anything. It didn't mean he remembered the kiss, or that he harboured real feelings for her—neither back then nor now.

Even if he felt something for me then, that was five whole years ago. Of course, his feelings would not be the same. Of course they wouldn't.

Her whirlwind thoughts were interrupted by the door opening and the butler tactfully announcing that dinner was served. There was a general sense of excitement at that, and Augusta turned to the door.

Someone cleared their throat at her side, and she looked up to see none other than Silas himself.

"May I escort you to the dining room?" he asked, smiling.

Augusta swallowed. "Of course," she managed.

She took Silas' offered arm, threading her arm through his. The movement sent thrills down her spine and tingles up her arm. She felt intoxicated, almost giddy.

Ambrose never makes me feel like this!

Augusta closed her eyes, desperate to fight off the traitorous thought. She was marrying Ambrose. She had decided.

"I can't help but admire all the lovely decorations," Silas was saying, gesturing to the heavily decorated hall. "You and your family have always had the best decorations. Tell me, do you still make them all yourselves?"

Augusta smiled weakly. "Yes, mostly. Mama helps, of course, and sometimes I rope in my poor maid, if she's not too busy. We enjoy it."

"Well, I'm looking forward to a proper Christmas celebration. It wasn't the same in the Americas."

"I can imagine. Are you glad to see your family and friends again?"

Silas glanced down at her, a smile spreading across his face. Augusta didn't meet his eye. She couldn't. She didn't know what she'd see in his face.

"Very," he said simply.

They entered the dining room, and Augusta regretfully unwound her arm from Silas's. It didn't much matter where they sat, as they were all arranged around a small dining table, to allow for more intimate dining conversation. Everyone would be able to speak to each other, and it would be easy enough to serve themselves rather than getting the poor footmen to do it. Augusta ended up sitting opposite Silas.

Now was the time for Augusta to compose herself. She was uncomfortably aware that she was out of sorts. She was flushed and caught her mother shooting concerned glances her way. They would assume she was feeling ill, of course, and a small, cowardly part of Augusta wanted to do that—feign illness and escape upstairs to the safety of her room.

A much larger part would never allow Augusta to do such a thing. She wanted to stay there, with Silas looking so strangely at her across the dining table, to enjoy the unusual and intoxicating feelings he inspired.

Wrong. It's wrong. I shouldn't feel this way about another man. I'm engaged. I am engaged, to a perfectly nice man who appeared in time to save me from spinsterhood and a life of loneliness. I ought to be grateful to him, not concerned with a childhood sweetheart. Not that he was my childhood sweetheart, of course! Besides, for all I know, Silas has some young lady over in the Americas he's going to ship over any day now, just as soon as he breaks the news of their engagement to his parents.

That last idea wasn't a pleasant one. It left a sour taste in Augusta's mouth, as if she'd eaten something just a little bit off. She had no right to feel a flare of jealousy against what might well be an entirely fictional young woman, but there it was. They were friends once, and it had been a sweet, wholesome friendship, the innocent friendship of children. Augusta didn't want to sully it with uncalled for feelings of jealousy.

She shifted in her seat, vaguely aware of conversation washing over, aware that her mother kept looking at her more and more curiously during the meal, and so did Silas. Augusta concentrated on her food, even though it tasted like sawdust, and the wine tasted sour and pungent. She was hungry, but somehow, the rumbling of her stomach wasn't quite connecting to her mouth and brain. She was moving food around on her plate rather than lifting it to her mouth, and people were going to start noticing soon enough.

What's wrong with you, Augusta? Where is that famous composure of yours?

The sharp ting of a knife on glass cut through the muddle of Augusta's thoughts. She glanced up to see her father rising to his feet, clearly intent on making a speech. Around her, conversation died down, and people glanced over at Patrick, expectantly waiting.

"Good evening, my dear friends," Patrick began. "I just want to thank everyone for coming tonight. I am delighted to have my son and his delightful wife here—Timothy and Caroline—and, of course, our dear old friends, the Mitchells. Charles, Helen, it has been far too long. I have missed your company. Now, aside from thanks, I would like to propose a toast to something that may come as a surprise to the Mitchells."

There was a murmur of good-natured interest, Mr and Mrs Mitchell exchanging curious glances. For once, Silas wasn't looking at her. He was watching Patrick, sipping his wine, lazily interested.

With a sinking heart, Augusta realised what her father was about to say.

"First of all, I'd like to mention how wonderful it is to have you all around me for the Twelve Days of Christmas. Unfortunately, this will be the last Christmastide our dear Augusta spends with us. Next Christmastide—and I think this will be a surprise to you, Helen and Charles—Augusta will be married to the Earl of Firnsdale, who is unfortunately not able to celebrate with us just yet. So, let's raise a toast to my daughter's engagement, and let's make the most of her last Christmas at home."

There were murmurs of surprise, and Mrs Mitchell threw a smile at Augusta, mouthing *"Congratulations"* across the table. Eliza smiled at her, looking thoroughly impressed. No doubt she thought Augusta was doing well for herself, snagging an earl. Timothy and Caroline were smiling at her too, but Augusta couldn't look at them. She couldn't look at Silas, either.

She was vaguely aware that she was smiling shyly, as a lady ought to when something like an engagement was announced. Inside, however, Augusta wanted to get up and run. The announcement seemed to make it all so *real*.

That's just plain silly, Augusta. Was it not real before?

Silas wasn't home then.

She had nothing to say in response to that.

"You're engaged, Augusta?" Mr Mitchell whispered. "Congratulations, my dear!"

"So, shall we all raise our glasses and toast to my little girl— my dear Augusta, whom the older ones in this room have known as a baby—getting engaged to a good, eligible man, and beginning her new future." Patrick was a little misty-eyed as he looked down at his daughter. Augusta was misty-eyed too, but for a different reason. All around her, glasses raised in the air, preparing to toast a future that Augusta was becoming ever more certain she did not want.

Too bad it was far too late to say so.

Then, in the hush following the toast, there was the sound of shattering glass. Everyone jumped, and heads automatically turned towards none other than Silas.

51

Chapter Eight

Silas' glass slipped out of his hand before he realised what had happened. The delicate glass shattered immediately, of course, splattering wine everywhere. Colour rushed into his face, and he felt like the clumsiest fool in the world.

"Oh, I am so sorry!" Silas gasped. "I . . . I don't know what happened. Do forgive me."

A footman hurried forward, dustpan and brush at the ready. Silas couldn't quite believe what he'd done, or what he'd just heard.

"Don't worry about it, my boy! Quickly, fetch Mr Silas Mitchell a new glass, so he can toast along with the rest of us," The Duke said jovially, not seeming at all upset that Silas had inadvertently ruined his speech.

A fresh glass was set down, and wine poured into it. Silas didn't want to drink. He was sure that if he toasted along with the rest of them, it would land on his tongue like acid.

Augusta was engaged. Augusta was getting married. To an earl, who sounded like a fine man, approved of by the Duke.

Silas should have known. Of *course,* Augusta was getting married. This would be, what, her third Season? He was amazed that she hadn't been snapped up sooner. Or perhaps she was just choosy and had waited as long as it took to find a decent man.

Which only meant that this wretched Earl of Firnsdale must be a truly marvellous sort of fellow.

She must love him very much. Silas was shocked at how much his heart ached at the thought. It really *ached*, like a physical pain. How odd. It was as if someone had put his heart in a vice and was now slowly but surely twisting the clamp.

Everyone lifted their glasses, and Silas lifted his too, more from an automatic reflex than from any conscious decision. He drank, along with everyone else. The wine tasted sour, leaving a bad taste in his mouth and almost burning as it went down his gullet.

Silas set his glass down firmly, resolved not to finish it. He felt sick, and none of his food—which had looked so appetizing before—could tempt him.

She was getting married. She was getting married, and that was that.

What did you expect? Did you think she'd wait for you? For you? You were friends once—when you were children and didn't know any better. It's safe to say that your friendship ended the day you stole that kiss from her. She must have been disgusted.

Silas desperately tried to distract himself, looking around for conversation. But everyone was talking to Augusta, congratulating her, asking her questions. Just then, Eliza was asking Augusta how she'd met the earl.

It wasn't a very good story. He was just a business acquaintance of the Duke's, who'd been invited over for supper one day, and the two took a shine to each other. Not the most romantic of stories.

But then, Augusta hadn't been one for unleashing her feelings at any given moment. She'd been composed and restrained, even as a sixteen-year-old girl. Why should she have changed since then?

She wasn't looking at Silas, either. That was a little odd. It was a small table, so you had to quite go out of your way *not* to look at someone. A quick glance around, however, told Silas that nobody else found it odd, or had even noticed.

He wished, not for the first or last time that evening, that he had never come at all.

Why? You would have found out sooner or later. Why prolong the inevitable?

"Now, not that I don't love hearing about my sister's engagement," Timothy said jovially, when the conversation flagged, "but I've heard enough about weddings to last a lifetime. We can always discuss it later—poor Augusta is quite tired of hearing about her own engagement, I think! Now, Silas, I believe you promised us all a few tales of your adventures."

Silas cursed to himself. The poor Marquess could not have chosen a worse moment. But now everyone—including Augusta—was looking at Silas. He had to say something; there was no two ways about it.

Silas dredged up the vestiges of his Society manners, pasted on his brightest smile, and turned to his dinner partners.

53

"Well, it's funny you should ask, as I had a few interesting adventures on the ship journey home . . ."

Silas began to talk. A switch had been turned, and suddenly he was very keen to let everyone know what a wonderful time he'd had in America. He told a few stories, embellishing more than a few. The squall they'd encountered on a short sea journey in his third year became a full-blown storm that had nearly wrecked the ship. He mentioned a close run with what could have been pirates on his way there, ignoring Eliza's narrowed eyes, no doubt remembering his prior claim that there hadn't been so much as "a sniff of pirates".

Some of his stories were accurate, though. He'd seen some beautiful sights, and he described them as best he could, bemoaning the fact he was no artist. He discussed his studies, the people he'd met, the food he'd eaten, the places he'd seen. As he spoke, Silas was aware of Augusta watching him intently, just like the others. He avoided her gaze.

His stories seemed to go down well. Silas was modestly aware that he was a good storyteller—he didn't ramble on, he read the room, and his stories were never boring. He kept his listeners hooked and intrigued, and always left them wanting more.

Silas very, very badly wanted everyone to think he'd had a wonderful time, and that his studies in the Americas had been a wonderful experience. That was mostly because he was starting to believe exactly the opposite.

If he hadn't gone to the Americas then perhaps things would have ended differently with Augusta. Perhaps he could have handled their financial crisis more efficiently—or, even better, stopped it from happening at all.

You're a fool, Silas. You think staying in England would have helped? Going to the Americas gave you an edge, but even now, you'd never be a match for Lady Augusta. Are you mad? She's marrying an earl. Do you think she'd look twice at you?

He raised his voice just a trifle to drown out the nagging voice in his head. It didn't work.

Silas finished with a story about one of his American roommates, a jovial, tubby young man who'd got up to all kinds of hilarious antics. One story in particular tickled the others, and they all roared with laughter.

Silas didn't laugh.

He smiled, of course. It would have looked very strange to sit there blank-faced while the others laughed. But the laughter just washed over him, and Silas felt numb and disconnected. He couldn't laugh. His smile made his face ache and felt like a mask. He wasn't sure what drew his gaze across the table to lock eyes with Augusta, but he found himself staring at her. She'd hardly touched her food too. Her glass of wine sat untouched.

Something passes between them, something that fizzled like electricity, quick and invisible.

At least, Silas could have sworn it did.

Either way, he noticed one thing in particular.

Augusta did not laugh either.

Chapter Nine

She had no real right to be angry, Augusta knew it. Silas had gone on to lead his own life, as he had the right to do, and that was that. She shouldn't begrudge him his experiences, any more than he should begrudge her choice to marry Ambrose.

But *trully*, it made Augusta's blood boil to hear Silas' stories. It didn't help that she felt a generous dose of envy too—he'd been out there, seeing the world and having a wonderful time, while she was being laced into corsets and forced to spend hours getting ready for silly, pointless social events that were always too crowded and too hot.

She was fairly sure that some of Silas' stories were exaggerated—he'd always had a knack for telling a tall tale when they were children—but he wasn't exaggerating the joy he'd felt at seeing new places and enjoying new, unique experiences. The dreamy look on his face was real.

Augusta's heart clenched, and she didn't want it to. She needed to stay calm, detached, and level-headed, at least until Ambrose arrived and reminded her of her duty. She shifted in her seat, clearing her throat, and wondered if she could force herself to eat something. Anything, really.

She had planned to let her mind wander while Silas spoke, politely hearing his words but not really listening to them. Despite her determination, however, Augusta found herself being lured in. She could picture the raging seas, the ship being tossed around like a toy on the huge waves. She could see the sights Silas painted for them so eloquently, smell the scents on the air, hear the noise of the crowd. For a moment, Augusta was tempted to close her eyes, to better immerse herself in the scenarios, but she just recollected herself in time.

A quick glance around the table confirmed that everyone else was thoroughly falling under Silas' spell. When he finished his last story, there was a moment of silence, everyone waiting for him to start the next tale. Silas speared a piece of chicken, popping it into his mouth, and smiled around at his captive audience.

"No more stories? Oh, come now, Silas!" the Duke boomed

out. "Oblige us with one more."

"That's hardly fair, Papa," Augusta found herself speaking up. "Silas has obliged us with plenty of tales tonight."

"Quite right, Augusta," the Duchess said, smiling approvingly at her daughter. "Thank you for sharing those stories with us, Silas. I do hope you'll tell us more about your adventures another time. I imagine that four years' worth of travel has left you with a lot to think about."

Silas chuckled. "Yes, but to be frank, I spent a lot of time thinking about what I'd left behind."

There were noises of agreement and sympathy, but Augusta stared down at her plate, suddenly grappling with a wave of anger.

He had spent time thinking about *he'd left behind*? Did Silas have any idea of what that meant?

Augusta had thought of him every single day for goodness only knew how long. She'd turned down perfectly good marriage offers because she was in love with someone else—someone who did not love her in return, someone who had left the country, with no intention of returning.

I have wasted years of my life on a foolish boy and silly dreams. Now, that *is regretting what you left behind,* Augusta thought. She pasted a thin smile on her face and said nothing, however.

The Duke clapped his hands for attention. "Oh, before I forget, I have an idea for something to do after supper. Who fancies a game of Snapdragon?"

There were murmurs of excitement, and the Duke glanced around the table, his smile widening.

"We have always played Snapdragon on Christmas Eve, as a tradition. I can't think of a single year when we haven't played it. Of course, it isn't Christmas Eve, I know, but there's no reason why we can't also enjoy a game tonight. What do we all say?"

In general, everyone seemed to agree.

***

After supper, the guests gathered in the drawing room, waiting for the servants to set up the game table.

Augusta watched their preparations, lost in a feeling of

57

nostalgia. There was a particular bowl they always used for the game—large and shallow, big enough for half a dozen people or so to crowd around. There was also a smaller bowl of treats and a bottle of brandy. There weren't raisins this time but candied fruits, which Augusta liked better. Almonds could also be used, but on Christmas Eve, the Duke always insisted on playing the game "properly" by using raisins.

The brandy was poured into the bowl and the raisins added. A servant lit a match, and *whoosh!* The surface of the brandy was alight with blue, flickering flames. Some of the candles were dimmed, and the drawing room looked very eerie, with that bowl of fire sitting in the middle of the table.

There were various *oohs* and *aahs*.

"Well, who's playing?" Timothy asked, laughing.

"Not me!" the Duchess said, shuddering. She glanced over at Mrs Mitchell, who laughed and shook her head.

"Nor me," Caroline and Eliza said in unison.

"Just the gentlemen, then?" the Duke grinned, rolling up his sleeves. "You ladies can cheer us on."

"I'll play," Augusta said impulsively. She knew Silas was looking at her but was determined not to meet his eye. "I'd like to play."

"Very well, Augusta," The Duke said, nodding. "You can go first, then. Ladies first, after all. Are we all in agreement?"

Of course, they were. So, Augusta ventured towards the blazing bowl of brandy.

The aim of the game was to grab as many raisins—or, in this case, candied fruit—from the bowl of blue flames as possible. August knew from experience that the game never resulted in burns—that the brandy was always salted, to make the flames less hot.

And possibly to discourage people from drinking it afterwards.

Augusta eyed the burning bowl and darted her hand in before she could think too hard about what she was doing. She came up with a handful of candied fruits, hot and burning her hand.

"Well done, Augusta!" Timothy crowed. "That's three. Well done! Now, who's next?"

The game went on, with people huffing and wincing as they snatched the hot candied fruits and hotter brandy. Augusta stood back, waiting patiently for her turn.

"We should go out together for some event or other," Timothy said to Silas, who was wincing and shaking his hand after his turn. "It's too late in the year for picnics, of course, but we could try something else."

Silas paused, glancing at Augusta quickly then away. "I should like that."

"You ought to bring your siblings, too. I'll bring Augusta if she wants to come. How does that sound?"

"I like it. What activity do you suggest?"

Timothy paused, thinking. "Sledding, perhaps? We haven't gone sledding in a long time. It's a good Christmas activity, too. Assuming we have snow soon enough, of course."

Silas nodded. "That sounds good. Lady Augusta, will you be joining us?"

August tensed up. It was natural for Silas to address her, but it still felt strange.

"I imagine so," she said, lightly and casually, as befitted such an informal family gathering. The Mitchell family were more or less *real* family by now, in any case.

Timothy grinned at that, slipping an arm around his younger sister's shoulders.

"There we are! It'll be a fun little outing, don't you think? Augusta, do you remember when you and Silas built that terrible little sled yourselves? You stole nails, wood, and a rusty old hammer from one of the gardeners and appeared with that ridiculous creation at the top of March Hill. Do you remember?"

Augusta did remember. She remembered Silas's excited face, eyes bright, full of ideas for making their sled. They were going to paint a name on the side and had fought over what colour to paint the sled. Silas had wanted yellow, and Augusta had wanted green. They'd settled on stripes by the time of the first snows.

What a glorious day that had been. Augusta had woken to find snow blanketing the countryside, and her heart had skipped a beat.

They had been too impatient to wait to paint the sled, of

59

course. Augusta and Silas had dragged the sled to the top of March Hill, all bare wood and splinters. It was terribly dangerous, of course, but Augusta and Silas were no older than ten or eleven, and it had seemed like a marvellous idea.

Augusta had sat behind Silas, who gripped the thin leather reins in small, childish hands. There'd been a moment of pause, with the steep, unbroken slope of March Hill spooling away underneath them, and Silas had glanced over his shoulder at Augusta. She still remembered how pink and round his cheeks had been, how his breath had clouded and hung in the air.

Then, he'd smiled.

"Are you ready, Augusta?" Silas had asked, his voice high and childish, nothing at all compared to what he sounded like now.

Augusta had beamed. "I'm ready." She had meant it with all her heart. Silas hadn't even needed to ask her twice.

He pushed off, and they went rocketing down the hill, screaming all the way. The uneven sled tipped over, of course, and they rolled and slid at least half of the way to the bottom. But it hadn't mattered . . . because they had been giggling and laughing together, breathless and giddy.

"I promised it would be the best ride of your life!" Silas had crowed, getting to his feet and brushing snow from his clothes. "Do you want to go again?"

Augusta had grinned up at him. "Of course, I do!"

But that was in the past, with the old Silas. Augusta smiled coolly at the new Silas, who was looking at her expectantly, even hopefully.

"No, I'm afraid I don't remember," she said bluntly.

Silas' face fell. Augusta saw it clearly before he turned away, clearly pretending to watch the game unfold. Timothy glanced between them, his brow twitching with confusion. Augusta cleared her throat.

"Go on, Timothy. It's your turn again."

Chapter Ten

Augusta woke feeling groggy. She'd had a poor night's sleep. It was a pity because she had a long, busy day ahead of her.

She'd woken early, too—Betsey hadn't arrived yet. Augusta lay in bed for a minute or two longer, thinking over the events of the previous night.

She wasn't entirely sure why she'd lied about not remembering the sledding incident with Silas. Why had she done it? Was it to show Silas she didn't care about him anymore, that he was no longer important to her, and therefore the happy memories they'd made together were to be forgotten?

Well, she hadn't forgotten them. Augusta had taken out those memories like a precious trinket year after year, polishing them up, looking lovingly over them. Keeping them fresh in her mind.

Fresh for what, she couldn't have said.

She wasn't going to sleep any more that morning, she realized, and Betsey would be along any minute, in any case. Augusta sat up, groaning, stretching, and yawning, and climbed out of bed. She had intended to go over to the curtains and sweep them open, letting in the morning sun.

Instead, Augusta found herself wandering over to her writing-desk in the corner. She sat down and reached for a small drawer at the back of the desk. She opened it to reveal her little trinket-box.

Like most girls her age, Augusta had made herself a trinket-box when she was young, during her schooldays. She had filled it with all kinds of sentimental nonsense—dried flowers, leaves, acorns from a walk, only to realise that its significance had been lost to the ages. A tiny straw doll that someone had made her nestled in the corner, along with other knick-knacks that seemed entirely incomprehensible to Augusta now.

She'd kept the trinket-box, of course, and there were a few more significant items inside it now—a copy of the invitations to Augusta's coming-out ball, scraps of ribbon from favourite bonnets, paper flowers she'd made with a close friend during her first Season.

And, of course, there was the little golden apple.

It was heavier than one might expect, the surface rough and pitted with age. Augusta picked it up, turning it over in her palm. The golden apple was designed to hang on a Christmas tree, a faded gold ribbon tied around its thick stem. It had been part of the Christmas ornaments to be taken out every year in their house. There were several boxes of them, and the Duchess's favourite part of the season was to take out those boxes and set the ornaments in their places all over the house.

Augusta eyed her reflection, distorted, in the reflective surface of the apple. She remembered looking at the set of golden apples on the tree. There'd even been a tiny golden apple hanging on the kissing bough which Silas had held over her head that year. She remembered looking up at the kissing bough and seeing the light twinkling off the tiny ornament.

Was this the same one that had hung from the kissing bough? Augusta couldn't remember, but she didn't think so.

After the kiss had been stolen and the Mitchells had left, Augusta had gone searching among the Christmas greenery for a souvenir. She didn't know what had impelled her to do so, only that she felt as if she needed to have some memory that Silas had really been there, had really pressed his lips to hers.

At the time, she hadn't known she would not see Silas again for five years. If she had, of course, things would have been different. Very different.

A younger Augusta had glanced nervously over her shoulder, making sure her parents weren't about to catch her. Like the proverbial Jack Horner, she had withdrawn her hand from the greenery with a golden apple clutched in her fist. It had felt like a real treasure. Thrilled, Augusta had gone racing upstairs, the golden apple hidden in her pinafore, to secrete it away in her trinket box.

And that was where it had stayed.

Once Augusta had found out that Silas had gone, left the country altogether, with no intention of returning anytime soon, the golden apple had taken on a different kind of significance. At first, it had been a souvenir of a missed opportunity, a cherished hope. As the years had passed and hope faded, it had become something bitter, a reminder of wasted time and heartache. It had been a childish infatuation, that was all.

Still, the vivid memories and dreams were still burned into Augusta's mind. She'd thoroughly believed that she and Silas would get married. It was silly to think about it now, but Augusta had never doubted it for a minute. She would marry Silas. She'd never considered the possibility of marrying anyone else.

That was why your first two Seasons were so disastrous. You still thought you were going to marry Silas, didn't you?

Augusta couldn't even remember the last time she'd taken the golden apple out to look at it. She sighed to herself, rubbing a thumb over the shiny surface. The rough material of the apple dragged at her skin—the ornament was designed to look beautiful, not to be held. There were faded spots around the bauble, from where a younger Augusta had clutched and rubbed at it, unable to stop associating the trinket with Silas and her lost first love.

Silly, really.

There was a knock at the door, and Augusta jumped.

"Who is it?" she called, her voice a little higher than it should have been. She slipped the golden apple back in her trinket box and closed up the drawer.

"It's me, miss," Betsey said, sounding a little bemused.

"Oh. Of course. Come in, Betsey."

Betsey nudged open the door, a laden breakfast tray clutched in her hands.

"Goodness, miss, you're up early."

Augusta smiled faintly. "I couldn't sleep."

"I'm not surprised. That game you like to play, Snapdragon, is it? It would give anyone nightmares."

Augusta chuckled, despite herself. "Snapdragon isn't as dangerous as you think, Betsey."

Betsey placed the breakfast tray down on the dresser and went to throw open the curtains.

"Those are flames, aren't they, miss?" she retorted. "How can that not be dangerous? Will you be taking breakfast in bed or at the dresser?"

"At the dresser, I think. I'm already awake," Augusta said, wincing at the pitiless stream of morning light. She got up and moved over to her breakfast tray. It was laden with a heartier breakfast than usual—rashers of bacon, fried eggs, boiled eggs, fried bread, toast, orange juice, jam, butter, fruit, and more. "Goodness, Betsey. You've outdone yourself this morning. I'll eat until I'm sick."

"I thought you'd need it," Betsey observed, moving over to the bed to straighten the sheets and vigorously plump up the pillows. "You've got a long day ahead, miss."

"You're right there, Betsey," Augusta murmured, taking her seat. The food smelled delicious, and she was hungry. She'd barely eaten a thing last night, what with her engagement being announced, and Silas just sitting there, looking at her. Now, everything felt a few shades better in the reassuring light of day, and her appetite was back with a vengeance.

"Will you need me to come with you this morning, miss?"

"I don't think so, Betsey. We have to visit the vicar and his wife this morning, to make some decisions about the poor baskets. A lot of boring discussions, I'm afraid."

***

Downstairs, the Duchess was already in a flurry of excitement and activity. She was well-known as a kind, generous mistress, and was well loved among their tenants and the residents of the local town and villages. The Duchess's motto was, "What should a Christian do?" The honest answer (ignoring some of the more fiery and old-fashioned sermons from the pulpits of England) was, in short, whatever they can.

The Duchess donated money to good causes, passed on old clothes and shoes to whoever might need them, intervened in petty disputes, and often sent her own doctor out, at her own expense, when the people of her town were sick. In short, she did whatever she could, and Augusta couldn't help but burst with pride at her mother's charitable endeavours.

Another thing that boosted the Duchess's popularity was her lack of vanity and boasting. She did far more to help people than most other men and women of her rank, and yet she didn't feel the need to boast about it. She never mentioned her acts of kindness, and certainly didn't expect people to feel perpetually grateful.

"Good morning, Augusta. Nice of you to join us," the

Duchess said, raising her eyebrows. Augusta only smiled at her mother's jibe. She could see how excited the Duchess was already, pink spots burning on her cheeks. She loved to be useful and to think of the families receiving their Christmas poor baskets.

Footmen were carrying stacks of the baskets out to the carriage, carefully tying them on the roof. The carriage itself was already mostly full of the baskets. The baskets were full of whatever goodies and supplies Augusta and her mother could think of, and the contents varied every year.

"If you're ready, Augusta, we ought to get going," the Duchess said, peering inside her reticule. It was packed with spare ribbon and what looked like several bags of candied fruit.

"I'm ready, Mama."

"I don't want to be late. You know how the Vicar feels about punctuality."

Augusta suppressed a smile. From what she remembered of the vicar and his wife—one Reverend Alexander White and his wife Doris—they couldn't care less about punctuality, often running late themselves.

They were a young couple, not quite out of their twenties, and had only moved to the parish a few years ago. The Duchess had besieged them, of course, outlining her plans for improvement and the ways in which the poor and needy of the parish could be helped. The vicar had been taken aback by her enthusiasm but delighted at the lengths to which she was ready to go. He had been more than happy to take up the old vicar's practice of distributing the yearly poor baskets, and Mrs White had even offered to help make them up. In short, the Duchess and the vicar got along famously despite being opposites in personality and of different ages.

Augusta squeezed into the carriage beside her mother, trying to push aside the baskets to make room for herself.

"Careful, Augusta! Don't crush the baskets!" the Duchess reprimanded.

"I can't sit down, Mama."

"Oh, don't be silly." The Duchess banged on the roof of the carriage with her stick, and they were off. Augusta very nearly toppled into the stack of baskets beside her, finally managing to crush herself into the narrow space between the door of the carriage and the baskets.

"Couldn't we have brought another carriage, Mama? Or a cart or something. There really isn't room for all of these in here."

The Duchess tutted. "That would be very wasteful. At this time of year, we should be thinking about how we can use our excess to benefit others, not ourselves."

Augusta sighed. She had a feeling that if it hadn't been quite impossible, the Duchess would have insisted on the two of them carrying all of the baskets to the vicarage.

Thank goodness for small mercies! Besides, if she was busy with the poor baskets and her mother's endless errands, she wouldn't be thinking about Silas.

Although, of course, now Augusta was thinking about Silas. She pressed her lips together, glancing out of the window at the scenery. It was a fine day, crisp and cold but not icy. There'd been no snow yet, and Augusta was thankful she wouldn't have to have to go sledding with her brother and the Mitchell family just yet. Sledding with Silas would be too poignant a trip down Memory Lane, and Augusta hoped to avoid it as long as she could.

The odds were not in her favour, though. Grey snow clouds edged at the blue sky, and Augusta guessed they would have snow soon, probably in the next few days.

That meant the sledding would go ahead, then.

Wonderful.

The Duchess, who'd been entirely happy and silent until then, suddenly sucked in a brief, horrified gasp.

Augusta flinched. "Mama? What is it?"

"Oh, Augusta, I'm such a fool. You'll never guess what I've forgotten."

"Not the poor baskets, obviously," Augusta muttered, slowly but surely losing the battle for space with the stack of baskets beside her.

"I was supposed to bring a basket of baked goods to the vicarage. There'll be a few people there, you see, and it means that dear Mrs White won't have to worry about cooking for us."

"Oh, I see. I'm sure she won't mind if you just explain . . ."

"No, no, Augusta, I made a promise. We'll have to stop by the bakery first." The Duchess banged on the roof of the carriage, and it slowed to a stop. The coachman jumped down, poking his head through the window.

"What is it, Your Ladyship?"

"Stephen, I've been a fool. We need to pick up some baked goods, so we'll need to drop by the bakery before the vicarage."

"Certainly, Your Ladyship."

He withdrew, and the carriage trundled on. Augusta sighed.

"We'll be late, Mama. I thought you said the Vicar is very keen on punctuality."

"Oh, if being late means he can have a pastry in his hand, I'm sure he'll forgive me," the Duchess said, pragmatic as always.

Augusta suppressed a smile. "I must agree with you, Mama. Luckily, I don't have any pressing arrangements this afternoon."

"Propitiously indeed," the Duchess agreed.

Chapter Eleven

The carriage jolted terribly, and Silas banged his head on the side of the window. He swore, rubbing his forehead.

"You oughtn't use that sort of language, Silas," Eliza said primly. She sat opposite him on the threadbare carriage seat, looking through the horribly long list of things Helen had sent them to collect in town. Silas deeply regretted offering to come along. Eliza was initially going to go alone, but Silas hadn't liked the idea of his poor younger sister travelling alone, carrying all of those parcels and boxes.

Besides, he'd done nothing but stare at ledgers all day, and it was starting to give him a headache. He didn't know what he'd expected from Eliza—an endless flow of prattling gossip, perhaps? So far, she'd done nothing but review the list and take notes. Silas fidgeted in the uncomfortable carriage seat, wishing they had the money for a new one.

They didn't, of course, and even if there was any spare money around, there were a hundred things it should be spent on before a new carriage. This one worked well enough, and that was all that mattered.

"Don't fidget, Silas. You're distracting me," Eliza said, still not looking up.

Silas sighed. "Distracting you from what? You must have memorised the contents of that list by now. What on earth could possibly be so interesting?"

"More interesting than you, you mean?" Eliza asked, shooting a knowing look up at her brother. "I always like to check over the list. Mama sometimes forgets that we already have something at home, and we really can't afford to buy twice."

That sobered Silas up nicely. It was an unpleasant reminder of their difficult financial circumstances, and the fact that even Eliza knew something was wrong and was working to tighten their metaphorical belt.

"Oh," Silas murmured.

Eliza looked up properly, folding the list and putting it away. "I'm glad you're home, Silas. I really am. I was so young when you left—it feels like a lifetime ago. Mama and Papa missed you so much. Now you're home, it feels like things should start to get better. That's when things got difficult, actually. When you left. Not that it was your fault," Eliza added hastily. "It was just bad luck."

Silas smiled weakly. "I'm glad to be back."

"Are you?" Eliza eyed him closely, and Silas had the oddest feeling she was taking him in. He fidgeted under her unwavering stare. He wasn't used to that sort of frankness from his younger sister. She'd certainly grown up a lot since he'd left.

"Yes, I am."

Eliza nodded slowly. "What do you think about Augusta's marriage?"

Silas froze. "What?" he managed. "What did you say?"

He'd heard her perfectly the first time, of course. Silas just wanted a few seconds to gather himself and think of something to say. He certainly hadn't expected that question from his little sister.

Eliza narrowed her eyes at him. "I said, what do you think about Augusta's marriage? Well, it's just an engagement at the moment. I saw how shocked you looked."

Silas swallowed hard. Eliza was still looking at him as if she could see everything he was thinking. Or perhaps he just wasn't as subtle as he thought he was.

Silas' throat didn't need clearing, but he cleared it anyway.

"It was a surprise," he admitted. "But of course, I'm very happy for her."

Eliza snorted. "You're a bad liar."

"I'm not! Besides, why wouldn't I be happy for her?" Silas said, wounded.

"Oh, everyone knew you were smitten with her when you were young."

Silas paused, staring at Eliza in horror. "Really? Everyone knew?"

"Yes. Well, I knew, at least. I don't know about everyone. Frankly, I'm surprised Augusta waited so long to get married. From what I hear, she was a fine success in London. I was going to ask her if she had any more tips for my coming out. But I definitely remember how close you two were. Papa always said you were thick as thieves. I suppose he hoped you'd get married one day."

Silas' mouth dried up. "What, me and Augusta? Lady Augusta? Hardly."

Eliza shrugged. "Well, the Duke isn't exactly a snob. So long as you were good to Augusta, I don't think he would have minded."

"You don't understand the way the world works, Eliza," Silas said, trying not to sound pitying. But it was the truth. Eliza seemed to think that just because the Duke and Duchess were on good terms with the Mitchell family, they'd be happy enough to see their only daughter marry their eldest son.

It just wouldn't be allowed. Silas hadn't had much to offer Augusta before their financial difficulties had occurred, and he certainly didn't now. Besides, she didn't even seem to like him very much anymore. She was engaged now, and of course, that meant she was firmly off the table. But even if she wasn't engaged, Silas could never have pursued her. He wasn't sure he would have had the courage, not even if he'd stayed in England.

Augusta was going to be a countess. She deserved the best, and no doubt this Earl of Firnsdale suited her down to the ground.

Eliza was quiet for a few minutes. "Perhaps I don't understand," she admitted. "Papa keeps saying so. In a nice way, of course, but the gist of it is still there. Still, I always thought you and Augusta would get married one day."

Silas had to turn and look out of the window, collecting himself. Eliza didn't mean to be unkind, but she might as well have just stabbed him right in the heart.

Don't be so dramatic, Silas. Haven't you had long enough to get over Augusta? Time heals all wounds, remember?

It seemed to be dragging its heels when it came to this particular wound. Silas shifted in his seat, clearing his throat.

"Oh, I don't think so, Eliza. We were like brother and sister."

Eliza wrinkled her nose. "No, you weren't. Remember, I am your sister, Silas. You definitely did not treat Augusta like you treated me. You were such close friends. It was a pity that you moved away. Did you miss her when you left?"

Every day. Every day, it was like a physical ache in my chest. It hurt, far more than you could ever think a separation ought to hurt. I felt like part of me had been torn away.

Silas shrugged. "A little, I suppose. I missed everyone, of

course. I missed Mother and Father the most, of course, and you and Colin. I was thousands of miles away in a strange country, all the way across the sea. It's natural I'd miss my family and friends."

He wasn't convincing Eliza, that much was clear.

I'll have to tread carefully from now on. This isn't the naïve little girl I left behind all those years ago. Eliza's a young woman, and she's sharper than me, by the looks of it.

Eliza only scrutinized him for a long moment, then shrugged, turning back to survey her list. Silas was only too glad to change the subject.

"So, I forgot to ask. Where are we going?"

"We're just going into town to pick up a few things," Eliza answered. "The greengrocer, the baker's, the tailors. Mama is putting new aprons for the servants in their Christmas hampers, along with a few treats."

"Can we afford that?" Silas asked, frowning.

Eliza shot him a disapprovingly look. "Not really, but I think our servants deserve it, don't you? We don't pay as highly as other households, but the work is every bit as hard. We ought to reward their loyalty as much as we can."

"Of course, of course," Silas answered, feeling chastised. "So, the tailor's first, then?"

"Actually, I think we'll pass the baker's first."

Silas sat back and watched the scenery flash by. The town itself had changed, even in the brief time he'd been away. It was bigger, with more people. The once quiet market square was full of shoppers, even though it wasn't even market day. There were plenty of horses and carriages on the roads, ranging from fine carriages to old farm carts pulled by enormous carthorses. There were a few love riders, slouching in their saddles, far above the crowded streets. There were new shops—the tailor's shop was new, he thought—and there were newer houses visible on the horizon. It wasn't the sleepy town he'd left.

What is it they say about going home? That you can never go home again once you've left because it's all too small and sad. It's not at all the same.

He felt a pang of nostalgia for the quiet streets he'd once known. No doubt, this new commerce was good for the town, of course. Silas knew he really ought to keep up with the times.

I'll have to wake up to the way the world is now. I need to bring our business and finances into the modern world, or else we'll suffer. Time to look to the future.

"Are you all right, Silas?" Eliza asked, cutting into his thoughts. Silas glanced up to find her looking curiously at him. "You seem very preoccupied."

Silas smiled weakly. "I was just thinking how much the town has changed since I left. I hardly recognise the place."

Eliza nodded, smiling. "Just wait till you see the modiste's. She's a real Frenchwoman, and the styles and materials she uses are spectacular. I can't believe we put up with old Mrs Harris's outdated fashions. She had the ugliest bonnets you've ever seen, the sort that hadn't been seen in London for decades, I suppose. It was all the sort of stuff Mrs Harris liked to wear. Good enough if you're a widow or an older woman who just wants comfortable clothes in the same style of one's youth, but nobody wears that sort of thing anymore."

"What happened to Mrs Harris when the French modiste arrived?" Silas asked, feeling a pang of sympathy for the sour-faced old woman, who had apparently made the most unfashionable dresses in the county.

Eliza shrugged. "She was already thinking of retiring, and of course, everyone went to Marie's shop. She's a little more expensive than Mrs Harris was, but it's worth it."

"I'm sure," Silas said.

The carriage lurched to a halt.

"We're here," Eliza announced. The coachman opened the door, and Silas climbed down first, feet slipping on the cobbles. They were oddly slick, the ground icier than he'd realised. He helped Eliza down next.

"We'll be back in an hour," Eliza told the coachman, who gave her a nod and climbed back onto his perch. Silas took his sister's arm, trying to prevent them from being jostled by passers-by. Now he was down on the pavement, it was even more apparent how crowded the streets had become. Shoppers moved along elbow to elbow, some poor unfortunates fighting against the stream.

Some gentlemen nodded and smiled at them, stepping aside to give Eliza, the lady, a little extra room, but just as many just shouldered on past. Silas squeezed Eliza's arm grimly. She seemed entirely unaffected by the crowds, standing on her tiptoes and craning her neck to peer over their heads.

"Ah! There is the baker's, just up ahead."

"Mr Tallis?"

"No, a new baker. Mr Everett. He's very good. Come on, Silas, we haven't got all day."

Silas allowed himself to be towed along, taking in the new sights and sounds. He had to admit, the old baker—like the unfortunate Mrs Harris—had not exactly been a stunning practitioner of his craft. He had made rock cakes that had the texture of actual rocks and bread that seemed to go stale the same day it was made. There'd been unpleasant rumours about Mr Tallis supplementing his flour and pastries with other, less edible ingredients. No one went so far as to accuse him of using flour mixed with chalk dust, but Silas wouldn't have been surprised if he had.

As they approached the new baker's shop, the mouth-watering scent of freshly baked bread and pastries spilled out of the open door. Silas sucked in a breath, sniffing the air like a dog.

Well, not all of the changes are for the worse, then. Eliza grinned up at him.

"We could buy some pastries for ourselves, to eat in the carriage on the way home."

"Eating in the carriage? How decadent," Silas teased.

"Mr Everett makes the most delicious pies."

"Well, I am certainly tempted. Pies it is, then."

There was a queue snaking out of the front of the baker's door, and Silas' heart sank at the length of it. They joined the queue, and Silas was relieved to find it moved along quickly. Soon, they were just outside the door.

"Goodness me," he muttered, and Eliza winced apologetically. "Yes, he's very popular. Lots of people come here for their luncheon."

There were finely dressed people in the queue, obviously rich landowners and possibly nobles, but there were also commoners and servants too. Mr Everett's prices must be acceptable to rich and poor alike, then.

Silas caught a flash of colour out of the corner of his eye in the shop window, and automatically turned to look, and he froze.

Augusta was standing inside the baker's shop, staring out at him. The Duchess was behind her, talking to a man with a flour-dusted apron behind the counter.

Not entirely sure what to do, Silas waved his hand tentatively at Augusta.

Chapter Twelve

Augusta wondered if she might faint. Or be sick. Or both, which would be horribly embarrassing. Nobody would ever talk about anything else beyond the time when Lady Augusta, daughter of the Duke and Duchess themselves, had swooned in the baker's shop.

Terribly embarrassing.

She'd been thinking about Silas, much to her chagrin. It was hard not to, and Augusta had just been thinking how annoying it was to have him on her mind all the time again. Had there really been a time when she thought dreamily about him all day, every day? Had she really spent so much time imagining him returning home from the Americas to barge into whatever ballroom Augusta was currently dancing in, just to sweep her aside and propose marriage? Augusta suppressed a smile, remembering how she'd imagined the jealousy on the other girls' faces.

Of course, none of them would actually have been jealous. Eighteen-year-old Silas was nowhere near as broad and handsome as he was now, and he was just plain old Mr Silas Mitchell, after all. But a younger Augusta had never thought of that.

And then, just as Augusta was remembering one particularly vivid fantasy where Silas swept her away off a balcony and onto a waiting horse (they naturally rode into the sunset afterwards), she glanced up and saw the man himself. Silas Mitchell. Standing there, outside of the baker's, staring at her through the glass with a mixture of surprise and horror.

That was when the nausea and the dizzy feeling had crept over Augusta, and she sucked in a sharp breath and turned to her mother.

"Mama," Augusta said brightly. "Silas and Eliza are outside."

The Duchess turned, craning her neck. "Oh, so they are!"

"Friends of yours?" Mr Everett asked cheerfully. "I'll serve them first."

He waved, catching Eliza's attention, and gestured for her to come to the front of the queue. There were some faint murmurs of protest from the people in the queue, but not very many. Mr

Everett and his shop boy served their customers quickly, and they rarely ran out of the old favourites. The Duchess was an important customer, and Mr Everett was keen to butter her up.

Eliza hooked her arm through her brother's elbow, towing him along into the shop.

"Hello, Your Grace, hello, Lady Augusta!" Eliza breezed, all unpolished, charming country manners.

She'll do well in the Season, Augusta thought. But she only smiled and nodded, glancing over at Silas. She couldn't ignore him, not here in the middle of Mr Everett's shop.

Silas was still staring at Augusta, and Eliza cleared her throat. When that didn't work, she jabbed a sharp elbow into her brother's ribs. That brought Silas back to himself. He blinked, coming back down to earth, and smiled at them both, echoing his sister's greeting.

"It's wonderful to see you again, Augusta," Silas said politely. Too politely. It didn't sound natural.

"You, too," Augusta said mechanically. Eliza stepped up to the counter to place her order, which left Augusta and Silas standing together.

An awkward silence descended, and along with it a sudden wave of misery.

Silas and I never had awkward silences. Their time together had been full of inside jokes and rapid, honest conversation. Whenever they were quiet, it meant something.

Usually, it had meant they were scaling a particularly tricky part of the tree they were climbing or some other similar escapade. As they got older, it had meant that one or both of them were scheming mischief.

That had usually been Silas if Augusta remembered correctly.

She'd never experienced that sort of easy friendliness with anyone else. It hadn't taken Augusta long to write it off as a childish phase, telling herself that adults never quite felt comfortable with each other, not without years of knowing each other, or through marriage. She certainly didn't feel as comfortable with Ambrose. In fact, there were long, protracted silences whenever she and Ambrose were together, with Betsey for a chaperone. Augusta often found herself racking her brains for conversation topics.

She couldn't tell whether Ambrose was bothered by the silences or not. Augusta was, and it was always a huge relief to know that somebody else would be coming along with them on their outings.

When Ambrose did talk, he mostly focused on himself. He enjoyed card games, but always seemed reluctant to play with Augusta. If there was a card table or billiard room at a social event, it was guaranteed he would be there.

Augusta frowned to herself, suddenly realising she didn't know of any of Ambrose's other hobbies. He must have other hobbies and interests, but he'd never told her about any of them. Even the card playing was something Augusta had worked out for herself rather than hearing it from her fiancé.

Perhaps Ambrose just wasn't a man with a lot of free time. He'd told her enough about his business for her to know it kept him occupied for most of the week. Perhaps he wanted them to find shared hobbies and interests together.

Am I going to marry a man with whom I have nothing, nothing at all in common? Panic seized her throat at the notion, and she took a few deep breaths.

Stay calm. That's your forte, Augusta. Calm, rational, unruffled Augusta. Sensible Augusta, who made a good decision to prevent being an old maid. You thought this through, didn't you? Ambrose is the best choice for you. Perhaps if you'd married someone else during your first or second Season you wouldn't be so dissatisfied with Ambrose. And whose fault is it that you didn't marry anyone during your first and second Season? That's right: Silas's fault.

Thus, fortified against her feelings returning, Augusta turned to Silas with a bright smile.

"It's good of you to accompany your sister into town, Silas."

Silas looked equal parts thrilled and terrified that she was talking to him.

"Well, I haven't seen much of the town since coming home. It seemed like a good opportunity. So, are we going to meet this fiancé of yours?"

Augusta swallowed, fighting to keep her face blank. "He's arriving soon. I'm not sure when. He is such a busy man."

"Oh, I'm sure," Silas answered at once, but Augusta knew

what he was thinking. He was thinking that it was a poor man who wouldn't keep his fiancé company over Christmastide, especially not with such a warm welcome waiting for him at his future in-laws' home.

Silas, of course, let out no hint that he thought anything of the sort. He was a gentleman and a kind man, after all.

With impeccable timing, Eliza turned back from the baker's counter, laden with boxes of pastries and baked goods.

"Here, Silas, can you carry these?" she asked, shoving the boxes at him without waiting for a reply. Augusta had to smile—Silas had fallen neatly into his role of put-upon older brother. Eliza turned to Augusta, smiling brightly.

"Did Timothy—that is, Lord Avilwood—say anything about going sledding? They say it's likely to snow tonight, so perhaps there'll be enough for us to go sledding tomorrow or the day after," Eliza asked hopefully.

"I'm afraid I haven't seen Timothy today, but I imagine he's keen to go sledding as soon as there's enough snow," Augusta answered.

"Oh, that's good. We're all going, aren't we? You too, Silas?"

Silas chuckled. "I believe I was one of the first people Lord Avilwood asked. Not to sound full of myself, of course. I just so happened to be there."

Eliza sighed, shaking her head. "You're coming too, aren't you, Lady Augusta?"

Augusta swallowed. She'd agreed to the sledding expedition, of course, but she was quickly starting to realise what a terrible idea it really was.

In fact, spending any time with Silas was a terrible idea. Augusta felt his presence as if it burned her. Her gaze kept getting drawn to him all the time, regardless of who else was there or who else was talking. She'd never once felt that way with Ambrose. And now, able to compare them to each other, Augusta realized with a sinking heart that she wasn't out of danger yet. Had she ever been?

Now Silas was back, Augusta was as drawn to him as she had ever been. There was a rift between them now; things were not the same. But that didn't stop her wanting with all her heart to leap across that rift and *make* things be the same. She wanted them to be as close and friendly as they'd been all those years ago, but things couldn't go back the way they were. Not even if she wasn't engaged to Ambrose . . .

But you are! You are engaged to Ambrose. Good, faithful Ambrose, who's in London right now, no doubt thinking about our wedding and our life together, rushing to get all of his work done so that we can be together as soon as possible.

That didn't sound *very* much like Ambrose, but that wasn't the point. The point was that Augusta needed to stay far away from Silas Mitchell.

At that moment, however, Eliza was looking up hopefully, and Augusta was uncomfortably aware she'd agreed to go sledding.

"Of course," Augusta said weakly, smiling. "I'll be going sledding."

Eliza gave a squeak of joy, jumping up and down and clapping her hands.

"That's wonderful! You and I must ride in a sled together. Assuming you don't mind, of course?" Eliza added, visibly realizing she was being too forward and ought to be more ladylike and demure. Augusta liked Eliza all the more for her flashes of spirit, and she gave her a genuine smile.

"It would be lovely, Eliza, although we'll have to see how the sleds are divided up," Augusta said, smiling. "It'll start to really feel like Christmastide, you wait and see."

Eliza dimpled and bobbed a curtsey. "It was wonderful to see you both. Silas and I have a few errands to run before we return home, so we'd better leave now. Is there anything we can help you with first?"

"No, thank you, but it's very kind of you to offer," Augusta replied. "I'm sure I'll see you both soon."

"I have no doubt of it," Silas said, smiling, she thought, a trifle nervously. Augusta flashed him a quick, uncertain smile and turned away. She wanted him to leave. He was making her feel all fluttery inside, alive with memories she thought she'd tucked neatly away long ago coming back to haunt her.

Silas took the hint, and she heard him slip quietly out of the bakery, flanked by his sister. Augusta composed herself. She might be able to fool most people with her smooth, polite Society mask, but the Duchess was never fooled. If her mother had known about her little infatuation with Silas, what might she think now, if she saw Augusta getting flustered and blushing over him when she had a fiancé in London? A perfectly good fiancé too.

Augusta straightened her back, drawing back her shoulders and lifting her head. Good posture was the first step to composure. She took in deep breaths, willing the colour to leave her face. She told herself not to so much as consider Silas Mitchell anymore. Why should she need to think about him, ever? She would think of worthier men instead, like Ambrose.

Solid, reliable Ambrose. He might not be the most thrilling man in the world, but he'd proposed when Augusta was facing the horror and embarrassment of old maidhood. She ought not to forget it. Silas, on the other hand, had been all too happy to leave her behind. It was also worth remembering that Silas was surely not in love with *her*.

Yes, yes, there'd been that stolen kiss, but surely, it had been just another of his childhood shenanigans. Augusta was sure Silas didn't even remember the incident, and *she* was certainly not going to remind him. No, it was better for all involved that the kiss should pass out of memory. Silas almost certainly thought of her as another younger sister. Just like Eliza.

Yes, that was it. Just like Eliza. Very dear to him, but with no trace of romantic feelings. As it should be, really. Augusta cleared her throat, impressing that thought in her mind. *Just like a sister. A childhood friend.* Any romantic relationship existed only in Augusta's head, and it would only serve to do her damage. Going after Silas would result in embarrassment and a broken engagement, not to mention a loss of reputation. Her parents would disapprove, and she'd lose what traces of Silas' friendship remained. No, Augusta would do well to rein in her feelings now before it was too late.

The Duchess turned back from the counter, laden with bags and boxes.

"Goodness, this is ridiculous," she puffed, and Augusta darted forward to take some of the boxes.

"Come on, Mama, the carriage is just outside. We'll be terribly late for the Vicar's, you know."

The Duchess sighed. "I know, I know. It was pleasant to see

Silas and dear Eliza, wasn't it?"

Augusta smiled wanly. "Very nice."

Chapter Thirteen

Silas and Eliza stepped out of the bakery. Silas couldn't quite help himself from turning to look back, but Augusta had already turned away from the bakery window, and all he saw was a glimpse of her skirts.

He turned back with a sigh, and caught Eliza looking at him, a sharp, mischievous sparkle in her eyes Silas did not like at all.

"Don't you dare say anything," he said. "I would rather not hear your thoughts."

Eliza shrugged. "Whatever you say, dear Brother."

Silas snorted, rolling his eyes, and nudged her. "Also, I think you've bruised my ribs."

"Well, if you hadn't been mooning at Lady Augusta like a slack-jawed idiot, I wouldn't have had to elbow you."

"You are a terrible sister."

"No, a terrible sister would have let you just stare at the poor girl until you started drooling and made her disgusted with you forever."

"I regret giving you money for those pies now. Maybe I'll eat them both myself."

Silas went to slip the packet of pies into his pocket, and Eliza squealed in outrage, trying to grab them out of his hand. Laughing, he lifted the packet above his head, and she tried vainly to jump for them.

"Silas Mitchell? I can't believe it is you!"

Silas and Eliza froze. He slowly lowered the pies from above his head and turned to find a lady and a gentleman approaching. It took Silas a few moments to recognise the gentleman.

"Howard Spencer! Well, I'll be! How long has it been?" Silas exclaimed.

"Longer than I'd like to recall." The gentleman laughed. He was of average height, smaller than Silas, and a little pudgy around the middle. He had fair hair curled into unnatural ringlets and kept in place by too much pomade, and watery blue eyes, with a round, good-natured face. "You remember my sister, of course?"

"Miss Georgiana, of course." Silas made a bow. "Do you both remember my sister, Eliza?"

Introductions and the appropriate pleasantries were quickly exchanged. Silas was aware that Georgiana Spencer's eyes were fixed firmly on his face.

He wasn't entirely sure how old Georgiana was—twenty or twenty-one, perhaps? The fact she was traipsing around the town with her older brother indicated she wasn't married. Well, that and the calculating, determined way she was eyeing Silas up and down. She barely glanced at Eliza.

Silas had mostly been friends with Howard, and his memories of Georgiana were of a small girl in pinafores with golden ringlets and a habit of throwing tantrums. The adult Georgiana was small and dainty, with a perfect little doll face, blue eyes, and immaculately arranged golden hair. Her dress was much more expensive than anything Eliza could have afforded. Silas was briefly aware of Georgiana's gaze flicking to Eliza, taking in her shabby dress and pursing her lips in disdain. The gesture was gone in a moment, but Eliza drooped a little, her hand tightening on Silas' arm.

"I do like your bonnet, Miss Eliza," Georgiana said, her delicate, pretty smile not reaching her eyes.

"Thank you," Eliza answered smiling shyly, hopefully.

"Yes. It was a great favourite among the matrons of London, I think. Five years ago, wasn't it? It's so very odd to see the style on a young woman. I daresay you're one of those young ladies who doesn't worry too much about clothes and fashion. I do envy you— I care entirely too much about what I wear."

Eliza's smile faded.

Silas wondered briefly what the consequences would be if he pushed Georgiana Spencer into the muddy puddle behind her.

"Well, well, how are you both?" Howard asked jovially, seemingly unaware of the brief moment of dislike that had passed between the two ladies.

"Quite well. Glad to be home, you know," Silas answered. Eliza was uncharacteristically quiet, and he was suddenly eager to get her away from the Spencer siblings as soon as possible, especially Georgiana Spencer.

"Ah, of course, the Americas!" Howard turned to his sister and offered a brief explanation. "Silas Mitchell here lived in the Americas for several years. Studied there, didn't you?"

Silas inclined his head. Georgiana's eyes widened, and her lips pursed in a clearly well-rehearsed expression of surprise and interest.

"Oh! How fascinating! You must have such wonderful stories to tell." Georgiana affected the carefully cultivated, fluting tones that told of an expensive finishing school and an elocution master. It was the sort of voice that acted like a mask, preventing the speaker's real feelings from revealing themselves whenever they spoke.

"I enjoyed my travels very much, yes," Silas answered, flashing a tight-lipped smile. He turned to Eliza, smiling fondly. "I'm glad to be home. I missed my family."

"I always think a truly loving family would never stand in a son's way when it comes to travel and gaining life experience," Georgiana said smoothly. "Family is a nice thing to come home to but ought not keep one from living one's life."

That sounded like something she might have read in a book. Silas was tempted to ask her but remembered his manners at the last minute.

"Oh, don't fear, Miss Spencer. My family would never prevent me from travelling. I chose to come home."

Georgiana smiled coyly. "Oh, do call me Miss Georgiana. Miss Spencer was my sister."

"Oh, yes, Jane, wasn't it?"

Georgiana's smile dropped when Silas had the audacity to recall her older sister.

"Yes. Jane. She's been married for three years," came the abrupt answer.

Silas nodded. *Then, that makes you Miss Spencer, doesn't it?*

"Well, it's been lovely to see you both, unfortunately, Eliza and I have a list of errands as long as my arm. The greengrocer's, the tailor's, and so on. We'd better get going, otherwise we'll be here all night," Silas said lightly and was sure he heard Eliza sigh with relief.

Georgiana shot a pointed look at her brother, and Howard cleared his throat.

84

"Just a moment, Silas. Would you fancy coming around for dinner, say tomorrow evening? We can have a proper catch up then."

Silas paused, waiting for any excuse to come to mind. But nothing did, and he was forced to accept, grimacing inwardly. Howard grinned, oblivious to the tense atmosphere.

Georgiana smiled too.

"How lovely, Mr Mitchell! I do so look forward to seeing you."

She batted long, golden eyelashes—another practiced movement that had probably been rehearsed in front of a mirror, Silas supposed. It was entirely wasted on him. He smiled weakly and mumbled their goodbyes.

Then, at last, they were allowed to continue on their way, Eliza hanging tightly on Silas's arm.

"I didn't like her," Eliza whispered when they were at a safe distance. "I don't know what it is about her. She isn't at all like Lady Augusta."

"You can say that again," Silas answered grimly.

"Miss Spencer made me feel so small and ugly. Are there going to be other ladies like that during the Season?"

Silas glanced down at his sister and sighed. "I'm afraid so."

***

The carriage rolled to a stop in front of the Mitchell house just in time for Silas to see a man climbing down from his horse. It took him a moment or two to recognise Elton, out in the open instead of hunched behind a desk. Elton looked as though he'd much rather be doing his accounts in his comfortable office rather than bouncing around on the back of a horse.

He glanced over, watching Silas and Eliza climb down from the carriage.

"Cousins, hello," Elton greeted them. "Silas, could I have a word with you, please?"

"Certainly. Eliza, can you handle the rest of things?"

Eliza nodded, organizing the packages with the help of a footman and having them all taken inside. She'd been oddly quiet after her meeting with Georgiana Spencer. It worried Silas to see how easily his clever, confident sister could be made nervous. She'd have to toughen up once her Season started.

"What is it, Elton? Should my father be in attendance? He's out today, but—"

"No, no, it's you I came to see." Elton eyed the disappearing Eliza. "Can we talk somewhere privately?"

"Of course. Come into the study."

Five minutes later, after Helen had determinedly invited Elton to stay to tea, the two men were sitting down in the study. A footman placed a tea tray on a nearby desk and left, closing the door. Elton sighed, crossing one leg over another.

"Have you thought any more about my suggestion for solving your financial difficulties? I recall you found it distasteful."

"Marrying a rich woman for her money? Yes, Elton, I still find it distasteful. I don't argue with your logic, only your moral judgement."

Elton chuckled. "To be blunt, Silas, you're no longer in a financial position to enjoy the luxury of moral judgement. You need to find money, and quickly, and marriage is a time-honoured way of doing that."

Silas narrowed his eyes at his cousin. "And you're here because there's been some sort of development, aren't you?"

Elton inclined his head. "I believe you knew the Spencer family well, once upon a time?"

"I did."

"Well, Howard Spencer's parents are dead, and he has inherited the entire estate. He's a wealthy man. He has a younger sister still unmarried, Miss Georgiana Spencer."

Understanding dawned, and Silas sucked in a breath. "Absolutely not, Elton."

"You don't know what I'm going to say."

"Were you going to say that I should marry Georgiana Spencer?"

There was a silence.

"No," Elton managed, "I was going to say that you should *consider* marrying Georgiana Spencer."

Silas rolled his eyes. "Well, of course, that's entirely different. No, Elton, I won't marry Georgiana Spencer. I met her again earlier this afternoon, in town. She was a spoiled and unpleasant child, and she's grown into a spoiled and unpleasant adult."

Now it was Elton's turn to roll his eyes. "For pity's sake, Silas. Georgiana Spencer is nearly twenty-one and the last of the Spencer girls. Her brother is terrified she'll end up a spinster. He's probably afraid he'll end up caring for her his whole life. Things like unmarried sisters living in a house tend to put off prospective brides. He's rich, so he won't care about your financial straits, and Georgiana will come with a huge dowry. What's more, you're an old family friend. The sort of person any man is happy to see a sister marry. It would be perfect, Silas."

"Yes, except I don't like Georgiana Spencer at all."

Elton leaned back in his seat. "Why not?"

"I beg your pardon?"

"How long did you spend with her today? Five minutes? Ten?"

"Thereabouts," Silas muttered lamely.

Elton shrugged. "That's not enough time to judge a person's character, is it? Besides, let me tell you, ladies act differently around eligible gentleman. I daresay Miss Spencer thought she was charming. At this age, she'll start to feel desperate. What woman wants to reach twenty-one and find herself unmarried?"

"I wasn't aware life began and ended with marriage."

"For ladies, it does. We both know a woman's value drops dramatically after she turns twenty-one."

Silas got up abruptly, moving over to the tea-tray on the desk. "For pity's sake, Elton, we're discussing human women, not cattle."

Elton pursed his lips. For a few moments, there was only the sound of Silas pouring out two cups of tea, adding milk and sugar, and bringing the teacups over to their seats.

"I'm just being realistic," Elton said quietly. "I daresay Miss Georgiana would be keen to marry you. You're a personable young man, and with her dowry injected into the business, we can turn our finances around. It can be done, Silas, but not without that money. In return, she gets a very nice husband and is settled for life. I haven't met her myself, but I've heard she's a beautiful woman. Is it true?"

Silas sighed. "I suppose so, but that's hardly important."

"Don't be ridiculous. Of course, it's important. Are you going to see your friend again? Mr Spencer, that is."

"Howard? Yes, they've invited me over to dinner tomorrow night."

Elton brightened. "That's perfect. It sounds as if Miss Georgiana is already making a play for you."

"I certainly hope not."

"Promise me you'll keep an open mind, Silas." Elton leaned forward, dropping his voice. "You aren't doing this for yourself. Marrying for money is exactly what it sounds like. You don't have the luxury of marrying the woman of your choice. I know that isn't fair, and you can't be compelled to do anything. But you want to help, don't you? This would help tremendously. There's no reason you can't fall in love with your wife after the marriage, but finding a rich woman—and finding her quickly—*must* be our priority here."

Silas was quiet for a few minutes, staring into the depths of his tea.

"Is there really no other way?" he asked quietly. A vision of Augusta flashed in his mind, but he firmly pushed the image away. Augusta couldn't help him now. Wouldn't help him now. And he couldn't blame her.

Elton shook his head. "Not that I can think of. You won't be the first or last man to marry a woman he doesn't love to save his family."

"Saving my family. What a way to put it." Silas said, laughing awkwardly.

"Well, it's true." Elton shrugged. "This will finance Colin's studies at university and provide Eliza with a good dowry. It'll get us out of debt and save the business. I don't exaggerate when I say that you marrying Georgiana Spencer would save us all."

Silas swallowed hard. "I'll think about it," he promised, his throat suddenly dry as a bone.

Chapter Fourteen

The snow started to fall on their carriage ride home. Augusta watched the flakes fall to the ground, lazy and slow. It wasn't heavy snowfall by any stretch of the imagination, but the snow was already starting to lay. A day or two of the same, and there would be plenty of snow for sledding.

Augusta closed her eyes. She was thinking about Silas again despite her determined efforts to put him away from her mind. Part of her wished Ambrose would arrive, but she knew deep down it wouldn't help. She'd just find herself comparing Ambrose and Silas, and it would not be a favourable comparison.

"Augusta?" the Duchess asked gently, startling Augusta out of her thoughts. There was more room in the carriage now, thankfully, since all the baskets had been delivered at the vicarage.

"Hm? What is it, Mama?"

The Duchess pursed her lips. "You seem out of sorts today. You weren't yourself at the bakery, and you hardly said a word at the vicarage. I daresay the Vicar and poor Mrs White thought it very odd."

Augusta blushed. "I'm sorry, Mama."

"I don't want apologies, Augusta. I want to know what's wrong." The Duchess spoke gently and leaned forward to place her hand on Augusta's. "London is a strange place. I feel as though my family are strangers and my dearest friends aren't to be trusted. You've been out of sorts for a while, I think, and it's time we settled down and talked about what is troubling you. I'm your mama, Augusta. I can help."

No, you can't. Nobody can.

She forced herself to smile back at her mother and patted her hand. "I'm quite all right, Mama. But thank you."

The Duchess narrowed her eyes. She wasn't convinced, not one bit.

"Is it about your marriage to Ambrose?"

A cold feeling spread through Augusta's limbs. She was suddenly afraid she would lose everything—Ambrose, her future as a countess, as well as Silas.

She would have nothing left except a lonely future as a spinster, full of regret and bitterness.

"Why would you think of something like that, Mama?" she managed. An evasive answer, but she needed to say something. No answer would be the worst answer of all.

The Duchess pressed her lips together. "You don't seem excited about your marriage. You have shown hardly any interest in the arrangements, and you simply don't seem interested in poor Ambrose at all."

Augusta shifted in her seat, rearranging her skirts.

"I'm not madly in love with Ambrose, Mama," Augusta said carefully. "It's a quieter, comfortable sort of thing. You know I've never been a romantic."

That last part wasn't true, but the Duchess nodded. "Well, you are a very sensible sort of girl."

It was probably supposed to be a compliment, so Augusta smiled. "Well, I'm very happy with Ambrose. I really am, Mama. You have no need to fret."

The Duchess wasn't satisfied. She sat back on her seat with a sniff. "You aren't yourself, Augusta."

"It's London," Augusta tried again. "We were there for so long. You know I don't like the city. It's taken it out of me, that's all. My spirit. I'll recover now I'm home, but all that smog and noise has taken a toll."

The Duchess considered that, chewing the inside of her cheek.

"I suppose you're right," she conceded. "But, darling, if there is any problem with you and Ambrose, you'll tell me, won't you?"

Augusta imagined telling her mother that she had nothing in common with Ambrose, that she didn't like him in the slightest. She imagined her mother's face falling, the disappointment showing clearly before she pasted on a smile and started to reassure her daughter. She'd tell Augusta it was quite all right, that they would support her and help her find a way out of the engagement.

But Augusta would have seen the disappointment, the annoyance, just for an instant. The knowledge that Augusta had been so close to a respectable, safe marriage, only to duck out at the last moment because . . . because why? Because she didn't feel love raging inside her the way novels had told her to expect it to? The Duchess wasn't to know that Augusta had felt the pangs of love before and knew what it felt like.

More importantly, she knew what it did not feel like. Mild dislike and resignation were not love. It was not even friendship.

But Augusta said none of those things. Instead, she smiled.

"You worry too much, Mama."

The Duchess broke into a relieved smile. "Well, I won't deny I'm happy to hear that. There's no call for you to marry someone you don't like, of course, but it is so good to see you about to marry such a suitable man. Ambrose is delightful, and of course, you'll be a countess. I don't think I was ever prouder of you than the day when you told me you intended to accept Ambrose's proposal." The Duchess sighed happily, turning to look out of the window at the falling snow.

I have fooled her! It was the first time the Duchess hadn't seen through one of Augusta's attempts at deceit.

Or perhaps she just saw what she wanted to see. Either way, the conversation was over. Augusta settled back to watch the snowflakes fall and listen to the Duchess talk about the poor baskets and some of the Vicar's suggestions for the following year.

What have I done? What am I doing? Is it too late? I think it might be. It's too late to go back, so I have to press on to the end.

Augusta's life spread out before her. A wedding day, with Ambrose as the groom, and Augusta fighting not to see Silas Mitchell in his place. A long, tedious marriage to a man for whom she could barely feel a passable amount of affection and respect. They had nothing in common now, so there was no reason to suspect that would ever change. Perhaps there would be children, and they might provide a happy spark in an otherwise monotonous life. And through it all, there would be the constant rankling of regret, imagining what her life would have been like if things had only been different.

If she had only been able to marry the man she wanted to marry.

If only. What a horrible phrase.

When they finally reached home and Augusta climbed down from the carriage, she smiled weakly at her mother.

"I think I'll go and lie down in my room for a while before supper, Mama. I'm very tired."

The Duchess nodded. "Very well, but don't forget Timothy and Caroline are joining us for dinner."

Augusta had forgotten. She swallowed hard and pasted on a smile.

"I won't forget."

***

Betsey bustled into Augusta's room shortly before it was time to dress for supper.

"Did you sleep well, miss?" she asked, taking out a shimmering emerald evening dress from the wardrobe. It was usually one of Augusta's favourites, but she couldn't face the idea of wearing anything so fine that evening.

She hadn't slept at all, in fact. She'd lain on top of her bed, staring up at the ceiling, and had resolutely tried to think of neither Silas nor Ambrose.

She'd failed on both counts.

"Well enough," Augusta lied smoothly. "Not that one tonight, Betsey. Can you take out the grey muslin?"

"Of course, miss. It's not so pretty, though, is it?"

"No, but it's an old favourite, and it's only supper with my family."

Betsey bobbed a curtsey and replaced the emerald dress, taking out the grey one in its place. Augusta got up numbly and moved over to her dresser. She watched her reflection with dull, disinterested eyes while Betsey began to style her hair.

It occurred to Augusta in a resigned sort of way that she couldn't go down and face her family in her current mood. They'd notice at once that something was wrong, and Augusta was very afraid she'd suddenly break down and burst into tears, maybe even doing something terribly embarrassing like admitting she didn't love Ambrose but loved Silas instead, all in one breath.

Augusta breathed in, consciously smoothing out her expression into something placid and composed. Much better.

"I can see what you're doing, miss," Betsey said quietly. Augusta glanced up at her.

"Doing what?"

"Putting on your mask. You know, where you tuck all your feelings behind a wall and become the famous unruffled, sensible Lady Augusta. That's what they all call you. I've seen you do it a hundred times before, but never before you go down to have supper with your family."

Augusta bit her lip. "Today isn't a good day, Betsey."

"Can I do anything to help?"

Augusta smiled affectionately at her maid. "No, Betsey, you can't. But thank you for being so kind. Sometimes . . . sometimes I just have to go somewhere in my mind and keep everything calm. It makes me feel better, as if I can control things."

Betsey nodded. "I understand, miss. Now, would you like the sapphires or opals to go with your dress?"

Shortly afterward, Augusta descended the stairs, feeling a little more composed. She caught a glimpse of herself in the long hallway mirror and noticed that while she was paler than usual— the grey dress did her no favours—she didn't appear to be disturbed or upset. So, she felt confident enough to go straight into the parlour, where the rest of the family were waiting.

Timothy and Caroline sat close together, and Augusta noticed they kept exchanging happy, knowing glances. They are in love, she thought enviously.

Timothy cleared his throat, getting to his feet and glancing around. "Well, you took your time, Augusta. I thought you weren't going to join us."

Augusta raised her eyebrows, settling in a seat. "Supper won't be served for another ten minutes or so. I'm actually early."

Caroline tutted at her husband. "Don't be so hard on poor Augusta. You look lovely, Augusta."

"So do you, Caroline," Augusta answered automatically, and then was surprised to realise it was true. Caroline's pasty skin was lit from within by a kind of glow. For once, there was colour in her cheeks, and she was smiling more widely than she had for a while.

There was an expectant air around the pair, and Augusta leaned forward in her seat. Her brother and sister-in-law had news to impart, that much was clear.

Timothy cleared his throat again, attracting the attention of the room. He stood beside his wife, and Caroline reached out and took his hand.

"Well, Mother, Father, Augusta……… Caroline and I have some news. We've waited for a while to be sure, as we've had some disappointments before, but now we think it's time to tell you all."

The Duchess gave an exclamation. "Goodness, I'm intrigued. Come on, tell us your news."

Augusta had a feeling she already knew, but she leaned forward anyway, holding her breath.

Timothy glanced down at Caroline one more time and smiled.

"Caroline and I are expecting a baby."

There was a silence, then a flurry of words.

"Oh! How wonderful!"

"You sly things, you didn't breathe a word!"

Augusta didn't say anything, not that she could have been heard over her mother and father. She stared at her brother and sister-in-law, taking in their happy, excited faces. She knew Timothy and Caroline had wanted children for a while, but it had seemed it wasn't going to happen for them.

She should be thrilled. She was going to be an aunt. But all Augusta could think of was the family she'd envisioned having with Silas. When she was younger, she would draw little pictures of the children she thought they would have, along with their names. Louis for a boy, Violet for a girl.

Jealousy and misery sparked in her chest, and Augusta had to swallow back tears yet again.

Then, she came back to herself, remembering where she was and the reality of the recent announcement.

"Congratulations, Timothy and Caroline!" Augusta made herself say, getting to her feet and crossing the room to embrace her brother and sister-in-law. She felt numb, and hoped that if she displayed the right emotions, they would soon become real.

It wasn't working so far.

Timothy almost snapped her spine in a crushing bear-hug, and Caroline kissed Augusta on the cheek.

"You're going to be a marvellous auntie," she whispered.

Augusta wanted to cry again. Caroline was so sweet and

lovely, and Augusta couldn't even summon up some real happiness for her.

"And you'll be the best mother ever," Augusta replied, and this time it was heartfelt.

The Duchess was beaming, and the Duke looked almost on the brink of tears.

"Well, what with Augusta's engagement and your news, this has been the finest Christmastide ever!" the Duke proclaimed.

The butler appeared, looking around at the chaos in surprise.

"Your Lordship, Your Ladyship, supper is served," he announced ponderously.

The Duke threw one meaty arm around his son and the other around his daughter-in-law.

"Let's go through. We've got a lot to celebrate tonight!"

Chapter Fifteen

A young Silas peered nervously up over the low snow-wall he'd made. He was just short of fourteen years old, not quite grown into his long limbs and gawky frame. He scanned the smooth, snow-blanketed landscape, chewing his lip anxiously. There was no sign of her, but Silas knew very well that meant nothing.

As if to highlight his words, the whitish blur of a snowball whizzed towards him, catching him squarely in the face. He went flying backwards, arms windmilling, and landed flat on his back in the snow.

There was a hoot of victory, and the blurry figure of Augusta loomed over him.

If Silas hadn't quite grown into his looks, Augusta was every bit as bad. While some girls seemed almost grown-up at twelve, Augusta was firmly in her pinafores and puppy fat stage. She was wrapped up in so many layers by a doting nurse and an anxious mother that she was almost round in shape. She leapt up and down, raising stubby arms in victory.

"I won! I got you first, Silas! Admit defeat."

Silas sagged, pretending to sigh and look away, but secretly, he balled up a handful a snow in his fist. He threw it in one deft movement, catching Augusta on the forehead. She squealed, and dived forward, a snowball in each hand . . .

"Silas? Silas!"

Silas jerked out of his daydream and turned from the window to look at his mother. Helen raised her eyebrows.

"Wool-gathering again, Silas? You seem to do a lot of that lately."

Silas smiled tightly. "I was only thinking, Mother. The snow is coming down heavily now, I see."

Part of him had hoped it wouldn't snow until after Christmas, then there'd be no chance of sledding at the Rasbury estate.

His prayers hadn't been answered. The snow had started up last night, just a few lazy flakes, but by morning the landscape was blanketed in a thick layer of snow. It was still falling, too, and Silas had spent most of breakfast time sitting at the table and staring out of the window, letting his breakfast go cold. He smiled weakly at his mother and applied himself to his cold toast and congealed eggs.

Helen didn't smile back. She eyed him curiously, chewing her lip.

"Are you quite well, Silas?"

"Oh, yes."

"I know you wanted to go to the orchards with your father, but he was right to insist you stay here. You'd feel terrible if you missed sledding at the Rasbury estate."

Silas didn't bother to point out that the only reason he'd asked to trudge through the snow in the orchards alongside his father was because he wanted to miss the sledding at the Rasbury estate.

He didn't, of course, and only shovelled a forkful of rubbery eggs into his mouth. He'd gotten lost in daydreams of snowball fights he'd once had with Augusta . . . before he'd ruined everything between them with that ridiculous kiss. If he could only take it back . . .

Silas hesitated, pausing for thought.

Would I?

Would he take back the kiss, even knowing that he would be off for the Americas only a few weeks later?

Silas found he didn't regret the kiss, not one bit. He regretted upsetting Augusta, of course, and regretted the loss of their friendship, but the kiss? No. Wouldn't this have all happened anyway, regardless of the kiss and his trip to the Americas? Augusta would have had a coming out, would have attended a London Season, while Silas would have had to stay behind. Maybe she would have chosen Ambrose anyway, and Silas wouldn't even have his memories and travel and the helping hand of his education to console him.

"Silas? I'm talking to you! Goodness, you are dull this morning," Eliza said sharply, and Silas's daydreams were interrupted once again.

Silas blinked, desperate to wake up and concentrate. It was going to be a long day, and he was going to have to pretend to enjoy most of it.

"I'm sorry, Eliza, my mind was elsewhere."

Eliza sighed, leaning forward to spear another piece of toast. "Yes, obviously. If you're so out of sorts, maybe Colin should drive the dog cart."

Colin brightened up. "Oh, yes, could I? It's only a short drive from here to the Rasbury estate, and I'll be as careful as you like. Do let me drive, Silas. The dog cart is very easy to drive."

Silas pressed his lips together. "Absolutely not, Colin. You're not a good driver. Do you think I've forgotten when you ran that chaise into a tree?"

Colin flushed. "That was ages ago."

"Not long enough. Besides, it'll be harder to drive today, what with the snow and everything."

"I would have thought it would make it easier," Eliza countered, shooting a sympathetic look at her younger brother. "There won't be many people out driving."

Silas said nothing. For two years before he'd left, when he was seventeen and eighteen, he had been allowed to drive the dog cart to Rasbury. The dog cart was better for driving through the snow, with its high wheels, sturdy build, and bouncy springs. However, it wasn't particularly easy to manoeuvre if the driver didn't know what they were doing. The snow was deeper than Silas had seen for a while, and getting to the estate was going to be tricky. Silas, of course, knew the route blindfolded, but Colin seemed the type to try and take shortcuts across fields.

Silas shook his head. Seeing Colin's face fall, he relented a little.

"You can set up the cart if you like. If going there isn't too difficult, I'll let you drive half of the way back."

Colin brightened, and Silas felt a warm feeling in his chest. He hadn't been an older brother for so long. In the Americas he'd only had himself to worry about. Perhaps that hadn't been good for him. He'd come home for his family, after all.

And Augusta. The tiny little voice in his head that always made Silas squirm spoke up. Even though nothing would have changed if you'd stayed. You just wanted to see her, didn't you?

In the letters sent to him in the Americas, Augusta had rarely been mentioned. Not out of any malice, of course. It was just that without Silas visiting Augusta so often, the family had had little opportunity to think about her. Helen had been concerned about Eliza, talking about her future coming out and the London Season—they could only afford one, so it had to be a success—and about Colin's education. Helen's letters had been full of love, full of the two youngest siblings' antics and mistakes. Charles's letters had been informative, telling his son about the business and the family. Sometimes there had been scraps of gossip, and the Radford family were mentioned quite frequently.

Augusta, however, was rarely mentioned in more than passing. As the months and years wore on, Silas had stopped reading the letters avidly for a mention of Augusta. He stopped waiting for a letter from Augusta herself. He had plenty to occupy his time—his studies, his friends, the sights he had to see, the business of living. Augusta had never quite left his mind, but she had certainly retreated into a back room, all but forgotten.

If I'd stayed home, Silas had told himself frequently, I would have found myself waving a handkerchief with the others when Augusta set out for London with her family, all pink and excited. Even if, as in his wildest dreams, he had followed her to London and somehow ended up attending the same parties, what then? The Radfords would have greeted him warmly, of course, and Augusta would probably have been happy to see him. Then, she would have scurried off with her fashionable London friends to meet suitable gentlemen. Titled, rich, well-bred gentlemen who flirted with her.

No, leaving was certainly the best thing to have done. Silas cleared his throat, keen to get rid of his miserable daydreams, and pushed away his half-finished plate.

"Well, I'll go and check over the dog cart," he said, determined to be light and entertaining that day.

"You said I could do that," Colin said, looking wounded.

"Oh, yes. Of course, I did. Well, I'll go and get dressed then. Let's not be late. We don't want to keep the others waiting."

Colin apparently saw nothing untoward in his brother's manner, but Eliza watched him go through narrowed eyes. Silas smiled weakly back at her.

* * *

Thoroughly dressed and layered up against the weather, Silas trudged down the stairs, out of the front door, and out to the waiting dog cart. He wore heavy trousers tucked into clumpy snow boots that were too large and unwieldy for anything other than forcing one's way through snow. He had several knitted cardigans on, a heavy wool scarf, and his thickest, warmest coat. Helen had insisted on all three of her children wearing their mittens, but Silas had also brought a pair of thin leather gloves. They wouldn't be very good for keeping out the cold, but they were waterproof and would allow him to handle the reins of the dog cart, and later on, the sled.

Colin and Eliza were already outside, Eliza shifting from foot to foot in the snow, layered up against the cold even more impressively than Silas. Colin was pacing around the cart, ostentatiously eyeing the wheels and springs, checking the harnesses and generally taking his time.

"Can't I get in, Colin? I'm freezing," Eliza complained.

"It's going to be colder than this when we're plummeting down the hills on the sled, Eliza," Colin countered.

Eliza rolled her eyes. "Actually, it'll be warmer once we get going. Moving around warms you up, didn't you know that?"

Colin ignored her, aiming a soft kick at one of the wheels. Silas winced.

Better stop him before he kicks the cart to pieces. Even if I don't want to go sledding, they'll be terribly disappointed.

"Thank you, Colin! Everything looks fine," Silas said, hurrying down toward them. "In you get, both of you."

Eliza and Colin climbed up into the sled, eagerly wrapping the rugs and blankets around themselves. There were several furs and rugs they used when travelling in open carts during the cold weather. Sometimes they'd take flasks of hot tea with slugs of brandy to keep themselves warm—Silas had warm, happy memories of being allowed a sip—just a sip, mind!—of a hot toddy as the snowy landscape bounced past.

Helen stood at the doorway, a shawl wrapped snugly around

her shoulders, and lifted a hand to wave them off. Her three children waved back. Silas snapped the reins, and they were off.

The rush of icy air made colour bloom in their cheeks. Eliza was sitting beside Silas, snuggled up to her older brother for warmth, and Colin was lounging in the back.

"You seem preoccupied, Silas," Eliza said suddenly.

Silas kept his eyes on the road ahead, which was thickly covered in snow. He was experienced at driving in this sort of weather, and the horses were no less familiar with the route, but the going wasn't as quick as it ought to have been. Silas had had too many nasty experiences with potholes, hidden by snow, which had a tendency to catch a horse's ankle or crack a cartwheel.

"I'm just trying to get us there safely, Eliza," Silas answered, flashing a quick smile down at his sister. "You should have brought a flask of hot chocolate for the drive."

"Oh, don't worry, the Radfords are bringing that sort of thing. They're taking servants out with them, you know. It must be nice, to be waited on all the time."

Silas didn't agree but decided to keep it to himself. The scenery skidded by, all frosty, bare trees, smooth white fields, and an idyllic blue sky that was deceptively cold. The sun was out, but despite its brightness the air was chilly.

"Something is wrong, Silas," Eliza continued, her voice dropping low so Colin couldn't overhear. Silas was glad—he didn't want to have to manage Colin's teasing over his apparent melancholy.

I am not melancholic. This is no more than I should have expected. Augusta is to be married, and then, I likely will only see her again at Christmastide, assuming she spends it with her family. Did I think things were going to end any other way?

Something of his thoughts must have shown on his face because Eliza squeezed his arm a little tighter.

"I know you're not feeling as cheerful as usual, Silas," she continued, "but you must try and pretend. This is Christmastide, after all. It's all about friendship and family. We ought to be having fun. It's a season for forgiveness and love."

At that dreaded word, love, Silas' heart clenched. His experiences of love had been so, so painful, not at all the flighty, heady emotion everyone claimed it to be. It hurt, and he couldn't talk about it to anyone.

It wasn't fair. Even now, worries about his family's future and the loss of Augusta weighed on Silas's mind. He wasn't sure how he'd be able to smile sweetly over the next few hours and pretend to enjoy sledding.

But he couldn't say any of that to Eliza, of course. Silas glanced down at her and found his little sister looking anxiously up at him. She nibbled her lip, clearly trying to read his feelings in his face. Silas forced himself to smile down at her.

"Goodness, you are a worrywart. I'm not preoccupied at all. I just have a bit of a headache. Fresh air and fun will clear it right up."

That seemed to convince Eliza, and she beamed up at him.

"Oh, that's good."

They carried on in silence.

Chapter Sixteen

The snow was falling more heavily than ever. Ignoring her mother's insistence that she would end up catching a chill by the window, Augusta stayed curled up in the window seat, watching the snow gather on the panes and pile up in the gardens.

It was perfect weather for sledding.

If only Augusta wasn't so desperate to avoid sledding. Or, more specifically, sledding with Silas.

Augusta slid a little further down in the seat, drawing her knees up to her chest. She was wearing her thickest wool dress in preparation for today's sledding session, along with thick stockings (two pairs), and countless petticoats and underskirts. There was a loose, wide-knitted cardigan covering it all, far too unfashionable and lumpy to ever be worn in polite society, but perfectly suitable for a cold day sledding down a snowy hill. She would wrap herself up in her old winter coat right before they left, and no doubt there would be scarves, hats and gloves to contend with too.

For now, however, Augusta's layers were keeping her quite warm enough. The heat of the room, lit by a roaring fire, contrasted with the cold whiteness outside. They were in the parlour, waiting for the Mitchells' dog sled to appear. Augusta knew the battered old thing off by heart. She remembered Mr Mitchell's determination to "spruce it up", which involved a few licks of paint and a good clean. Even back then, Augusta had guessed they weren't rich enough to buy a new sled.

She'd never thought it meant much. She still didn't. Who cared if the Mitchell family didn't have a new dog sled?

But clearly it meant something to Silas. Why else would he be so keen to go to the Americas and get a good education? Why couldn't he have been educated in London, for instance?

"I wish you'd come away from that window, Augusta," the Duchess said, and Augusta flinched.

"I'm not cold, Mama."

"Yes, but you will be. You'll come home soaked and shivering from sledding today, I warrant." The Duchess put down her sewing and glanced up at Augusta, chewing her lip. "I don't want you to catch a chill, not when you're so close to your wedding. It would be a terrible pity, wouldn't it? Oh, I know you're always so healthy, but that doesn't mean anything, my dear."

"Mama, you worry entirely too much."

"Why don't you consider sitting this one out? It's only one day of sledding."

Augusta kept her face angled away from her mother, out of the window. She closed her eyes, trying to swallow down the sudden tide of misery. Wasn't this the perfect excuse to avoid sledding with Silas? Hadn't she been praying and hoping for just such an excuse to stay at home?

But it felt like cheating, somehow. Augusta couldn't have said why. The idea of giving into the Duchess's suggestion made her feel as queasy as the idea of going sledding with Silas.

"No, Mama, I'd better go. After all, this will be my last Christmastide as a single woman, remember?" Augusta glanced over her shoulder, smiling tiredly at her mother. "I don't want to miss a single thing. None of the traditions."

The Duchess smiled fondly at her, shaking her head and returning to her sewing.

"Well, you have already beaten all of the gentlemen at Snapdragon. I hope all those candied fruits didn't give you a stomach-ache."

Augusta chuckled. "No, Mama."

She wasn't sure what made her glance back to the window, but she found herself looking back outside just then. She spotted the dark shape rumbling and lurching towards the house, and her heart clenched.

"It looks like they're here, Mama," Augusta said, as lightly and carelessly as possible.

"Ah, excellent. I'll go and make sure the flasks and packets of food are ready. You'll all want to fortify yourselves with hot drinks before you go."

The Duchess got to her feet and bustled out into the hall. She left the door open, and a chill draft came whistling into the room. Augusta shivered. The dog sled passed out of sight of the parlour window, but Augusta knew it would stop in front of the

104

door. March Hill was only a short walk from home, and there was no point troubling the poor horses and taxing the sleds when they could simply walk, dragging their sleds behind them.

Augusta got to her feet, picking non-existent bits of dust and thread from her clothes. She heard the front door open, letting in another gust of cold air, and the rumble of voices. Timothy must be greeting their guests. She heard what she thought was Eliza's laugh, and the familiar sound of Silas' voice. She shivered again and told herself it was just the cold.

Augusta found herself standing motionlessly in the middle of the parlour. It was silly, she knew that—why not just go out and greet them? Why forestall the inevitable? Once again, however, Augusta was suddenly lost in a memory.

She wasn't sure how proper it would be to have a snowball fight now that they were grown up. Ladies weren't supposed to do things like that, and snowball fights were entirely too aggressive.

At least, *Augusta* was aggressive during her snowball fights.

She'd probably scandalise her London friends by the suggestion, but out here in the country, things felt different. Right up until their very last Christmastide together, she and Silas had engaged in spirited snowball fights every year, usually several times. They'd come limping home, faces and hands pink and tingling, usually with bruises and swollen cheeks and lips from well-aimed snowballs.

The Duchess had only ever shaken her head fondly and good-naturedly scolded them both. There was no talk about what ladies should or should not do. It had never occurred to Augusta that the way she behaved with Silas was wrong, not until she'd gone to London for her Season and realised that other ladies behaved very differently from her.

Augusta still wasn't convinced she was in the wrong.

I almost always beat Silas at our games. But he nearly always let me win, I'm sure of it. Not the snowball fights, though. I won those fair and square.

She found herself smiling, half happy and half sad, at the memory.

Outside in the hallway, she heard her name spoken.

"Where's Augusta, Mother? Is she coming? Still getting dressed, I bet," Timothy said.

Augusta drew in a deep breath, pasted on a smile, and stepped out into the corridor.

Silas, Eliza, and Colin stood in the hallway, looking clunky in their heavy snow boots and layers upon layers of winter clothes. Timothy was already dressed, chatting excitedly with their three guests. Caroline was not coming, of course, although she hovered behind her husband, looking a little wistful.

All four of them looked around as she approached, and Augusta found herself seeking out Silas's eyes.

It was as if no time had passed. When they were young, she'd always looked out for Silas in every room she entered, seeking him out before she took in any other information about the room. Even during her first Season, when Silas hadn't even been in the country, Augusta had found herself scanning the crowds for his familiar face and laughing eyes. It had always twisted her heart to remember that he wasn't there, that she'd likely never see him in a crowd again.

And now, here he was. Augusta's heart skipped a beat.

Wasn't that a curious saying? One's heart skipping a beat was invariably a bad thing. But that was how it felt—you locked eyes with *that* person, *your* person, and your heart simply stopped for a moment. Your breath was stolen away, and you could do nothing but stand there and take them in, staring, yearning, hoping.

Augusta knew then and there, standing in the hallway of her childhood home, that she was still in love with Silas Mitchell.

She knew with equal certainty that it was entirely too late.

Ambrose was coming. Silas would meet Ambrose, would shake the hand of the man Augusta was going to marry. What would he think? Perhaps he wouldn't think anything. Maybe he'd just smile politely and think Ambrose a decent match for a Lady Augusta Radford and stop thinking about it altogether.

Perhaps he would think Ambrose was a bit of a bore, but if Augusta liked him, then that was good enough. Perhaps he'd feel a pang of regret. Perhaps he'd wish things were different. Augusta wasn't a vain woman, but there had been the occasional moments when Silas had looked at her and she just *knew* he felt something.

That, of course, had been before the kiss, which no doubt he thoroughly regretted. No doubt, his mind had been opened and subsequently changed during his travels and studies abroad. The past was gone, and try as she might, Augusta couldn't get it back.

Then, Augusta realised she was standing stock-still in the middle of the hallway, staring like a sun-struck owl. She smiled and moved forward.

"I was just offering Timothy and Caroline my congratulations," Silas said, his deep voice sending shivers rolling down Augusta's spine. "I hear you're to be an aunt."

Oh, so Silas had been told about the baby. Augusta flashed a smile at Caroline, who was beaming up at her husband with adoration.

"Yes, we just learned the news. We're thrilled, of course," Augusta answered, secretly pleased by how smooth and even her voice was.

"I'm so jealous," Eliza bemoaned. "I've got no chance of being an aunt any time soon. And I think I'd be a marvellous auntie."

"You'd be terrible," Colin said firmly. "You'd let them stay up far too late and get them all excited by eating too many sugary treats."

Eliza nudged him in the ribs, hard.

Timothy chuckled, shaking his head. "Well, now you're here, Augusta, we can get going. Is everyone ready? I think the snow has eased up a little, which is perfect. We want the snow on the ground, not in our eyes, ha-ha!"

Augusta smiled politely at her brother's weak joke. She wasn't entirely sure how it happened, but she found herself wrapped in a few extra layers, her old coat flung over it all, her hands firmly encased in mittens, and a hat jammed on her head.

Timothy, as excited as a child, went hurrying ahead, leading the way to the not-so-distant March Hill. Colin and Eliza went after him, scarcely less excited. The Duke and Duchess would be following along later at a more leisurely pace to watch the sledding.

That, naturally, left Augusta and Silas to fall into step beside each other.

Augusta kept her focus on the path ahead. The snow was deep, ankle-deep even in areas where it had been cleared away to form a path, but mostly at least knee-deep. She struggled along, cursing her long skirts and heavy petticoats, and Silas walked along beside her, seeming content to let the silence fall between them. Augusta wasn't sure whether she was grateful for it or not.

"I haven't been sledding since our last Christmastide together," Silas said suddenly, causing Augusta to nearly lose her footing.

"No?" she said lightly. "Neither have I. There wasn't much cause to go sledding at my grandfather's house, nor in London."

"I can't imagine young ladies are encouraged to sled down steep hills in London. Or to engage in snowball fights."

Augusta had to smile at that. "No, we rather weren't."

"It must have been very dull. I know how you like to win your snowball fights."

"I always beat you," Augusta countered before she could restrain herself. She sensed Silas looking sharply at her but forced herself to keep her eyes on the ground ahead of her and didn't look at him.

She wanted to look at him, though. She very, very much wanted to look at him.

"You remember," Silas said, his voice strangely small. "I thought you'd forgotten all of our adventures together."

Augusta swallowed hard, a lump forming in her throat. She ought to look at him and tell him that she remembered nothing of their childhood japes. Those memories were best left forgotten, safely buried in the past. Augusta's future lay ahead, and the past was the past. No doubt, Silas also had a fine future ahead of him, and clinging to each other wasn't going to do anyone any good.

Then, Augusta made a large mistake. She glanced up at Silas, meeting those large, familiar eyes squarely. Her heart ached, and her throat clenched, and Augusta could no more have lied to him if her life had depended on it.

"I remember," she managed.

Silas' face lit up. "And what about us building that sled together? I know you didn't remember it last time we talked, but I hoped you might have remembered by now. Memories are funny like that, aren't they? Do you remember, Augusta?"

Augusta swallowed hard again. Her throat was getting dry, and she wished she'd drunk some of the hot tea her mother had set out for them to have before they left. Oh, well. Too late now.

"I . . . yes, I think I do remember it. It gave us all terrible splinters."

Silas let out a deep, booming laugh. "Yes, yes! Because we were both too impatient to spend a full day sanding it down. I got splinters through my thickest trousers and coat."

"I put a hole in my woollen petticoat," Augusta said, smiling. "Mama was absolutely *furious*. But it was worth it."

"Yes," Silas said thoughtfully. "It was worth it, wasn't it?"

Chapter Seventeen

She remembered. She *remembered!*

Silas wanted to sing and dance and skip about like a lunatic.

He didn't, of course. He remained walking sedately beside Augusta, thinking how to best deal with this small victory. If it even was a victory, which it really wasn't. All Augusta had done was concede that she remembered their childhood sledding and snowball fights.

It felt like something, though. *Something.*

He glanced down at Augusta, frantically trying to think of something—anything—to keep the conversation going. She was staring down at the snow, concentrating on each footstep. He noticed how her skirts dragged on the snow, getting in the way as she tried to take large steps over deep snowdrifts. They must be tangling around her ankles and calves, and there was altogether too much material. Silas felt almost guilty about moving so easily and simply in his trousers. It was a pity ladies couldn't wear them too. Really, what difference could it possibly make?

"Timothy," Augusta called suddenly, "where are the sleds? We haven't forgotten them, have we?"

Silas was suddenly struck by an urge to laugh at the ridiculousness of that whole situation—making their way to the top of the hill only to find the sleds had been left behind.

Judging by the chuckle that drifted back to them, Timothy found it funny too.

"Not to worry, Augusta. I've had the servants take the sleds up already, so we don't have to haul them up ourselves."

"That'll save us some time," Silas said, eager to start a conversation with Augusta.

He noticed then that Augusta was staring ahead with what looked like a combination of resignation and apprehension. He followed her gaze and realized that she was staring with annoyance at the stile.

Ah. Of course. When they were younger, Silas and Augusta

had leapt nimbly over the stiles when they went sledding together. He didn't think Augusta's skirts had been let down by then—the rite of passage which took a girl from the schoolroom into Ladyhood, whatever that was. It looked absolutely inconvenient to Silas.

Timothy stepped easily over the stile, and Colin followed. Silas watched approvingly as his younger brother turned to help Eliza down.

Then it was their turn.

"Ladies first," Silas said, gesturing for Augusta to go first over the stile, but she shook her head.

"You go first. I think this is going to be a tricky climb for me, and I don't want to hold anyone up."

Silas could have pointed out that he wasn't exactly going to walk away and leave Augusta to climb over the stile by herself, but he said nothing. He quickly climbed over and turned to watch Augusta follow.

She hauled herself up with difficulty onto the first step of the stile, her long, heavy skirts hindering her. Wobbling at the peak of the stile, Silas was suddenly struck by just how high up it was. Determinedly pushing on, Augusta squeezed herself through the narrow bridge of the stile, and that left her with only a long step down into the deep, soft snow.

Silas stepped forward, intending to lift his hand and offer to help her down, but he was a fraction of a second too late. With both of her arms occupied with holding her skirts out of the way, Augusta was left with no way of saving herself when her foot slipped.

She would have tumbled face first into the snow, and Silas just had time to see her eyes widen in panic before he stepped forward to catch her. It was a reflexive action, one he didn't think twice about. He stepped forward, arms out, and Augusta fell forward into his arms, thumping against his chest hard enough to make him stagger backwards. His arms closed around her waist, steadying her.

Then there was a long, tense moment, when Silas realised he had Augusta pressed against him, his arms around her waist, her hands on his shoulders.

In that position, it was nearly impossible not to look into

each other's eyes.

Augusta stared up at him, her eyes wide and clouded with something Silas couldn't read, and he in turn found he couldn't look away, could barely even bring himself to blink.

There was one long second, when the air filled with the silvery clouds of their breaths, mingling and hanging between them.

Then somebody shouted back down the slope.

"I say, Augusta, are you all right?"

Timothy. Silas had never hated Timothy before, but in that moment, he could have killed him.

Augusta abruptly stepped back, smiling tightly and glancing away from Silas.

"I slipped coming over the stile, Timothy. Nothing to worry about. Silas saved me from landing ignominiously in the snow."

"Ah, all right. Let's hurry up, then, we're losing the light," Timothy called back blithely. He continued on his way, and Colin followed him.

Silas felt hot and cold all over at the same time, which seemed rather strange. Augusta avoided his eye assiduously and walked quickly past him, carrying on up the hill. Silas followed her with his eyes and found Eliza standing just a little further up on the slope, staring at them.

Augusta had her head down and didn't see Eliza's expression, but Silas caught it squarely. Eliza looked . . . not *accusing* exactly, but knowing. As if she knew something about Silas, or as if a realisation had just struck her.

With a sinking heart, he thought he knew exactly what Eliza had just realised, and it didn't bode well for him. Eliza's eyebrows shot up towards her hairline, and she turned on her heel, carrying on up the slope after the other two.

Now the last in the line, Silas began to trudge up after them. His senses were alight, and he was uncomfortably aware that he should never have put Augusta in that position—even if it hadn't been his fault.

She was an engaged woman. Silas said it to himself over and over again, a terse reminder that he had no right to have these feelings for her. It wasn't Augusta's fault, but the world in general might certainly blame her. Ladies were always somehow "in the

112

wrong" when it came to tangled matters of the heart.

If Eliza had noticed the moment between him and Augusta, then other people might have noticed too. They had been lucky that only the oblivious Timothy and Colin had been there. What if they'd been out with a party of people, with a gossip-monger or two among them? What if word got around that the engaged Lady Augusta had been seen in close, improper conversation with a man who seemed to entertain feelings for her?

No, Silas would need to be much more guarded in his feelings. He owed it to himself, and certainly to Augusta. With that determination in mind, he doggedly continued up the hill.

Has March Hill always been so steep?

***

They reached the top eventually, panting for breath and sweating under their layers of wool and linen. As Timothy had promised, a handful of well-dressed footmen were waiting at the peak of the hill, a row of battered old sleds lined up in front of them. There were three of the "old faithful" sleds they'd been riding down March Hill for countless years.

Timothy clapped his hands with glee. "Right, so, there are five of us and three sleds. Can I suggest that Colin and Augusta ride together on one, Silas and Eliza on another, and I'll ride alone? What do you say? Just for the first ride down."

There was a murmur of agreement, followed by a brief flurry of activity. Timothy took the smallest sled, seated himself comfortably, gripped the thin leather steering reins and pushed off. Colin helped Augusta onto the sled, both of them alight with excitement, and pushed off next.

That left only Eliza and Silas. Silas waited for half a minute, just to make sure they weren't going to find themselves knocking into one of the other two, and then moved towards the sled.

"Just a minute, Silas," Eliza said, eyes on the two disappearing sleds. "I want to talk to you."

That was unusual. Silas fidgeted from foot to foot, glancing at the distant footmen, who quite clearly weren't listening in. The Mitchell family had only ever had a handful of servants, and Silas had never gotten used to talking freely in front of servants, as if the poor creatures were deaf.

"What is it, Eliza? If we don't hurry, the others will be coming up again. They'll wonder what we're about." He avoided Eliza's direct gaze.

There was no denying that Eliza in particular was almost unrecognizable from the quiet, dreamy young girl he'd left all those years ago. She was a young woman, poised on the precipice of her future, sharp and intelligent, missing nothing and unafraid to speak her mind. As an older brother, Silas was thrilled to find his little sister growing up and becoming so clever, but as a man on the business end of her very intense attention, he couldn't help but feel a little nervous.

Eliza sighed. "I'm not a fool, Silas."

"What are you talking about?"

"I'm talking about you and Lady Augusta."

Silas flinched. He drew in a deep breath, willing himself to stay composed and calm. It wouldn't do for his secret to get out. It would do Augusta damage, too.

"Eliza, I really have no idea what you're talking about."

Eliza trudged around, positioning herself in front of her brother so he had no option but to look at her.

"Yes, you do," she said firmly. "You have feelings for Augusta. I know you do."

Cold fear tingled down Silas's spine. "I certainly don't, and I'd like to remind you that Lady Augusta is betrothed. That means—"

"I know what betrothed means, Silas," Eliza interrupted. "And I know that a betrothed woman's reputation is just as tenuous as it is when she is single. But it's just you and me here, and I didn't say anything about her betrothal. I said you have feelings for her. Am I wrong?"

"Yes!"

Eliza rolled her eyes. "You're a terrible liar, Silas. Just as bad as Papa and Colin."

Silas swallowed hard, gaze flicking around. "I don't know what you mean. I'm not lying."

Eliza folded her arms across her chest. "Let's dispense with the arguments. I know you have feelings for Augusta. I suspected as much before you left."

"Whatever I felt for Augusta before I left for the Americas,

114

it's entirely gone now," Silas argued. "It would be improper for me to have feelings for a betrothed lady."

Eliza shrugged. "It doesn't mean you don't have them."

Silas cast another glance around. They were entirely alone on the top of the hill, the servants having retreated, and there was nobody to save him.

"Eliza," he said, low and urgent, "you must stop this. Augusta is betrothed, and not only that, but she is far above my station."

"Oh, *Silas*. That's just an excuse."

"It is not," Silas said, a hint of desperation in his voice. "The family is kind to us, but that doesn't mean we're seen as equals."

"How can you talk about them like that? The Radfords have always been lovely to us. They invited us out today to go sledding, and they—"

"Lady Augusta is a titled woman. She has a Duke and Duchess for parents. I, on the other hand, will inherit a crumbling business. We're scraping together the money for your Season and for Colin to attend university, and it's very much touch and go at the moment, Eliza. I don't think you properly understand the disparity between them and us. The Duke and Duchess are wonderful people, and I have nothing but love and respect for them, but I suspect they would draw the line at my presenting my suit to their only daughter. Especially when she has an earl in her pocket. Be sensible, Eliza."

Eliza was quiet for a long moment.

"You've been gone a long time, haven't you, Silas?" she said eventually. "You've changed a lot. For the better, of course. But I suppose you think that everyone else has changed, too. I can't help but wonder whether you just assume everyone else sees you in the same way you see yourself."

Silas felt a twinge of annoyance and hurt. Was that an insult? It certainly felt like one.

"What is that supposed to mean, Eliza?"

Eliza shrugged and moved over to the sled. She took a seat on the front, waiting for Silas to climb on beside her.

"I think you should tell Augusta how you feel."

Silas gave a short bark of laughter. "That's a bad idea, Eliza. Besides," he added, still clinging to his deception, "I don't feel anything for Augusta."

Eliza rolled her eyes. "Yes, yes, so you keep saying."

"Even if I did," Silas ploughed on, "it's too late. Far too late."

Eliza glanced over her shoulder at him, and Silas was suddenly struck by how old and wise his sister's eyes were. Had they always been like that?

"It's never too late, Silas," she said quietly.

That was jarring, somehow. Silas swallowed hard, floundering for something to say back to her. Nothing came to mind.

He climbed onto the sled behind Eliza—the others had reached the bottom long ago—and they pushed off.

In an instant, their world was all wind and ice-cold pieces of snow leaping up and sticking to their faces. Silas's stomach dropped as the hill disappeared out from underneath him, the trusty old sled bouncing and skidding over the well-worn slopes. He took the reins, his arms around Eliza to keep her from falling off, and it was as if no time had passed at all.

Silas found himself smiling, the joy coming back in a rush.

Then, the ride ended abruptly and they reached the bottom of the hill. Silas' euphoria disappeared, and the weight and truth of Eliza's words returned, heavy and ponderous.

Now it was time for the long, slow trip back up to the top of the hill.

Chapter Eighteen

Augusta closed her eyes, letting the cool rush of wind wash over her, the cold air chilling her cheeks, catching strands of her hair and tugging them out of the knot at the back of her head.

Sledding had always felt just like freedom.

It never lasted, though. All too soon, the sled was slowing to a stop at the bottom of the hill, with Timothy on his feet and grinning down at her, and it was Colin on the sled behind her, not Silas.

Augusta's heart lurched, but she forced herself to smile back up at Timothy, climbing up from the sled. Now came the long, slow trudge back up the hill, only to sled back down again. It all seemed rather futile when one put it like that.

"How was that?" Timothy asked, grinning. "It's a fine slope today. I wonder what's taking Eliza and Silas so long?"

Augusta glanced over her shoulder, expecting to see the third sled sweeping down the slope towards them. She was a little surprised to see they hadn't even started off yet. She could see the distant figures of Silas and Eliza, seeming to be engaged in a conversation.

"Are they arguing?" Augusta found herself saying aloud. "I hope everything's all right."

"They're probably fighting over who gets to control the sled," Colin muttered.

Timothy squinted up at the sun. "I hope they hurry up. I don't want to leave Caroline for too long. I thought she might want to come sledding if we were careful, but . . . well, we've waited a long time for this baby. She wouldn't hear of me missing the famous sledding tradition, so here I am."

Augusta smiled at Timothy. He was so clearly anxious to get back to his wife. Everyone knew Timothy and Caroline had married for love—a rare occurrence in their society. Some people had sniffed and said that one or the other could have married better, that they ought to have put duty ahead of their feelings, but Augusta knew that deep down, those people were jealous. Wouldn't it be wonderful to marry the person you loved?

Maybe in time I'll learn to love Ambrose like that. Ambrose is . . . nice. But part of her knew she would never love him the way Caroline loved Timothy.

Or the way Augusta loved Silas.

Oh, stop it!

"Ah, here they come," Colin said. Augusta glanced up, just in time to see Eliza and Silas' sled skidding down the slope towards them, slowing to a halt once the slope flattened out. Eliza was laughing, and Silas was grinning. Her own face split into a smile unbidden.

"Well, that cleared away the cobwebs," Silas called, climbing off the sled and grinning around at them all. "Who's ready for another go?"

Everybody, it seemed. The three gentlemen grabbed a sled each, hauling them up the slope behind them, while Augusta and Eliza walked on ahead.

"You ought to come back to our house for tea," Augusta said. "Did Mama and Papa already invite you? Why not stay for supper? Mr and Mrs Mitchell can join us."

Eliza shook her head regretfully. "We would have liked to, but unfortunately, we already have another engagement."

Augusta nudged her playfully. "That's hardly *unfortunate*."

Eliza winced. "The Spencers have invited us over," she said, her voice sounding carefully neutral.

"The Spencers? Howard and Georgiana?"

Eliza nodded. "Silas and I ran into them in town."

"Ah." Augusta understood Eliza's little wince then. Howard Spencer, from what she could remember, was a dull but good-humoured gentleman. His sister, Georgiana, was another story. She and Georgiana had attended the last Season together, and Georgiana's desperation to catch a good husband had been evident. She was one of those young ladies who did not seem to like other young ladies. Perhaps she'd seen Augusta as competition, but either way, the two women had not been friends at all.

Augusta's overriding memory of Georgiana Spencer was of

snide remarks to the ladies and fawning behaviour to the gentlemen. She had loudly proclaimed herself as a lady who "tired of needlework and gossip", and had then tossed her ringlets and eyed the gentlemen to see how this assertion was received. She was fidgety and irritable in female-only company and had a vehement dislike of any lady prettier than her, keen to find a flaw in character or face.

In short, Georgiana Spencer was a tiresome young woman who annoyed the gentlemen she pursued almost as much as she annoyed the other young women who were forced to spend time with her.

It didn't take a great stretch of the imagination to work out what Georgiana's aim was in inviting the Mitchell family to tea. Augusta glanced over her shoulder at Silas, toiling up the slope beside Colin and Timothy. Apparently, Georgiana was as keen as ever to find a husband.

"I didn't much like Georgiana," Eliza said in a rush. "Do you think I'm being unkind?"

"I know Georgiana Spencer," Augusta said shortly. "No, I don't think you're being unkind."

Far from seeming reassured, Eliza started to chew her lip worriedly.

"Are there many people like Georgiana in London? Ladies like that, I mean."

Augusta thought before answering. She wasn't going to give Eliza a sugar-sweet answer and assure her that everybody would be sweet and lovely, but there was no need to scare the poor girl unnecessarily.

"Some." Augusta admitted. "London is a mixture of people—most places are, now. You'll meet people of all kinds, and naturally, some of them won't be pleasant."

Eliza nodded. "That makes sense, it's just . . . well, Georgiana Spencer made me feel so *small* and silly. I didn't like it."

"The best thing to do, Eliza, is to ignore people like that. Truly, I wish someone had said that to me before my first Season. I wasted time trying to make people like Georgiana Spencer like me because I believed there was something wrong with my manners or character. There wasn't. Don't waste your time trying to win over people whose good opinion is not worth having, Eliza. You'll use up your energy and goodwill on those who don't deserve it. You can't expect to like everyone in London—or even most people, for that matter—so spend your time and care on those you *do* like."

Eliza bit her lip, nodding. "I never thought I'd be so anxious about my Season. The closer it gets and the more I hear about London, the more I worry. What if I make a mistake? What if Society doesn't like me?"

"Eliza, you are good-natured, clever, and pretty. Society *will* like you. There are plenty of ladies who won't like you because you are nicer and prettier than them, and there are plenty of gentlemen who don't approve of clever ladies. But you don't want those people as your friends, do you?"

"Certainly not!"

"There you are. Besides, you'll have your mama. If this Season doesn't go well, then there's always next year."

Eliza was quiet for a long moment. "There'll only be one Season," she said quietly, and Augusta suddenly felt like a prize fool. Of course, the Mitchells couldn't afford to finance two Seasons. They had Colin's education to think of as well as Eliza's dowry. Seasons were hideously expensive.

"Well, one Season is more than enough," Augusta said briskly. "You'll be tired of London by the end of it, I guarantee it."

They were nearing the top of the hill now, and Augusta's legs were burning with the strain. She wasn't used to country walking after her long months spent in London. There wasn't much exercise to be had in London, except for daily promenades in the parks and, of course, the incessant dancing at parties. Neither were any real substitute for long, hard treks across fields and hills, certainly not through deep snow.

It was a relief when the slope finally evened out to the summit. Augusta stood for a moment, hands on her hips, catching her breath.

"I do hope you haven't gone soft with London living, Augusta!" Timothy called, cresting the hill after her, sled dragging behind him.

Augusta shot him a Look. "May I remind you that *you* lived in London as long as I did."

"Yes, but I'm not the one huffing and puffing."

Augusta spread out her arms. "Have I not made it to the top of the hill?"

Timothy chuckled. Behind him, Colin and Silas appeared. Silas was a little breathless, but poor Colin was red-faced and thoroughly out of breath.

"I need . . . need a minute," he gasped, and Silas cackled.

Timothy clapped his hands. "Well, I think we ought to mix up our sledding teams. Colin, would you like to take the small sled and go down by yourself? Eliza, would you like to come with me? Silas, I suppose you and Augusta will want to go sledding together again."

Augusta was vaguely aware of a flush rising to her cheeks. She hoped it would look like a blush brought on by the cold wind and avoided Silas' eye.

"Of course," Silas answered, always the gentleman.

"As for you, Augusta, you'll need to squeeze all the enjoyment out of this sledding trip that you can. Once you're married, there'll be no more sledding."

Timothy meant it as a joke, but Augusta's heart clenched. She smiled vaguely, wishing they could all just hop on their sleds and *go*.

She might have known Timothy's thoughtless comment wouldn't be passed over so quickly. There was a pause, then Silas spoke.

"Why would being married prevent Augusta from sledding? You and Caroline enjoy sledding, Timothy, I know that much."

Timothy winced. "Yes, but Ambrose is a very serious gentleman. A bit of a stick-in-the-mud if you ask me. He doesn't sled, or engage in snowball fights or anything like that. No games of Snapdragon when Ambrose is around, let me tell you. He's always got some hideous story of somebody getting burned or cuffs catching on fire, and that entirely takes the fun out of it."

"He sounds very . . . serious," Silas managed. He was looking at Augusta, and she pointedly avoided his stare. She knew what Silas was thinking. How on earth could Augusta marry such a dull gentleman?

Augusta knew the answer, and it wasn't a satisfying one. It didn't seem good enough for her, let alone Silas. Silas had always had the knack of seeing straight through any bluster or hedging, directly to the truth. Augusta had seen him do it before, and no

121

doubt, his skills had only been sharpened during his time away.

She didn't want them directed at her.

"But why should that prevent Augusta from sledging after they are married?" Silas continued, clearly not willing to let the subject drop. "Surely, the Earl won't want to prevent his wife from enjoying herself?"

There was an awkward silence for a moment or two. Timothy met Augusta's eye, cleared his throat and looked away, evidently pretending he hadn't heard. Augusta couldn't bring herself to tell Silas the truth.

Yes, he would. He wouldn't want me to engage in such a "frivolous pursuit"—not his countess. No, there'll be no more snowball fights and sledding for me. No more games of Snapdragon, no more long, gruelling walks through knee-deep snow. Nothing but calmly sewing and reading by the fire, remarking on how heavily it is snowing outside.

Augusta swallowed hard, fighting back a sudden engulfing tide of misery.

"Eliza tells me you are visiting the Spencers tonight," she said brightly. It was better than admitting the truth—that her fiancé wanted to marry the calm, unruffled Augusta he'd met in London, and wanted little to do with the madcap young woman who'd never lost a snowball fight and made ramshackle old sleds that splintered her hands and tore her petticoats.

An odd shadow crossed Silas' face, as if he knew everything she was thinking but didn't say. It was quickly brushed away, however, and he smiled politely.

"Yes, Howard is an old friend of mine. The whole family is invited."

"Well, I hope you have a lovely time. I do hope you're all still coming for Christmas Eve."

"Oh, yes, you must," Timothy put in, all relief now that the uncomfortable subject had been passed by. "It wouldn't be a proper Christmastide without you and your family, Silas."

Silas flashed a genuine smile at that. "I think you'd break our hearts if we weren't invited. It feels very much like the last one, doesn't it? Oh, I know there'll be other Christmas Eves, but this one . . . this one feels special."

"Everything will be different next time," Timothy

acknowledged. "Augusta will be married, and Caroline and I will have a baby. It's rather thrilling, isn't it?"

Thrilling was not the word that sprang to Augusta's mind. She forced herself to look into the wind, hoping it would stop her eyes from stinging. She convinced herself it was the cold, not the sudden, icy grip of misery that had closed around her heart.

This really was the last Christmastide. She had a feeling Silas wouldn't be there for the next one. Eliza might well be married too, and of course, there'd be the baby. Maybe Ambrose wouldn't want to celebrate Christmastide out here in the country. He might insist on staying in London, and Augusta would have to stay with him.

Suddenly, the future looked very bleak indeed, and not even the imminent prospect of another slide down the hill could cheer Augusta up. She found she was very tired and simply wanted to go home.

Chapter Nineteen

The morning's sledding had left Silas feeling tired and cold. He hadn't been able to warm up properly, not even in front of the roaring fire in their parlour at home. He was just beginning to feel more human by the time they all had to start dressing for their evening at the Spencers'.

And now, they were all crammed into the cart, rumbling along the snowy roads towards the distant lights of the Spencers' home. It was dark by now, of course. Stuck between Colin and Eliza, with no room even to stretch out his elbows, Silas wished with all his heart that they could just have had a quiet night at home.

"Stop nudging me, Silas," Colin said unhappily, and Silas stopped, sighing.

The cart rolled up in front of an oversized house, lights blazing in every window.

"I bet that's terrible to heat," Helen murmured as Charles helped her down from the cart.

The front door opened, and Howard stood there, grinning.

"Welcome, welcome! Mr and Mrs Mitchell, it's so good to see you! You must be Colin, and of course, Miss Mitchell. And Silas, you old rogue! Come in, come in, you're letting in the cold!"

They all hustled inside, grateful for at least some semblance of warmth.

Their coats and hats were duly taken, and Howard ushered them through to an uncomfortable and resolutely fashionable parlour.

"Mama and Georgiana will be down soon. You know what ladies are like, after all," Howard said, chuckling at the three gentlemen as if he were letting them in on a tremendous joke. "Still getting ready."

They all smiled politely and sat down on overstuffed armchairs.

The Spencers' parlour was decorated in shades of green that made Silas feel somewhat sick. He knew the shade was fashionable, but that didn't make it any more pleasant to look at. Howard took a seat opposite, chattering about London and hunting and various dull subjects in a good-natured way that, surprisingly, went a long way to making them all feel at home.

Then the door opened, and the two ladies were ushered in.

Georgiana came first, resplendent in a silvery-blue dress glittering with sequins. Her golden tresses were dressed perfectly, all ringlets and little curls around her temples, and she smiled coyly around. She did look very beautiful, and Silas thought that if he hadn't seen the effect Georgiana had on his poor sister, he would have been more impressed. As it was, Colin was immediately dumbstruck. Eliza smiled weakly, the movement not quite reaching her eyes.

An older woman came next, Mrs Ingrid Spencer, Howard's mother. Mrs Spencer was dressed in a violet gown in a style a trifle too old and tight for her, and her hair was an improbable shade of brown for her age. Still, she greeted them all pleasantly enough, and she eyed Silas with an expression that indicated she knew about her daughter's designs. Silas flashed a brittle smile back and prayed for the evening to be over.

He could think of nothing and no one but Augusta, and it made his heart ache.

"Well, shall we go through?" Mrs Spencer said brightly. "Supper is ready, so we had better not let it get cold. I hope you have all brought your appetites!"

***

The Spencers' dining room was cavernous, studded with dark mahogany panelling that was very beautiful and, no doubt, very expensive, but it made the room look dark and unwelcoming. Their places were already assigned. Silas, unsurprisingly, was placed next to Georgiana.

The food was delicious and plentiful, at least. Silas felt guilty about his own bad humour. After all, Mrs Spencer and Howard had clearly tried hard to make them all feel welcome and at home.

The only issue, of course, was Georgiana. Silas could feel her eyes on him as he ate, calculating, appraising. She was just waiting for her moment, he knew it.

"I hear the orchards aren't doing so well," Howard said during a break in the conversation. "Some of my tenant farmers have been saying that all the heavy rains have washed away too much of the soil. Some of them are rather worried. I'm not a man of the land myself, though I know you're much more hands-on than me, Mr Mitchell. Any thoughts?"

Charles swallowed a large mouthful of wine before he spoke.

"It's true we've seen better years for the orchards," he admitted. "The last harvest was . . . well, disappointing. Still, I'm hopeful for the New Year, of course."

"Naturally," Howard said, good humour unabashed. "I really must pick your brains sometime, Mr Mitchell. I'm quite at a loss when my foreman and tenants tell me things about farming. I feel a gentleman ought to know what's going on in his lands, don't you think?"

"Absolutely," Charles said eagerly. "I always say—"

"Goodness, all Howard ever talks about is farming, these days," Georgiana said conspiratorially, distracting Silas from the conversation. "Sometimes I want to scream with boredom."

Silas smiled politely. "I'm sure, but I think Howard is just concerned about taking control of his lands properly. Farming certainly isn't interesting, but it's a gentleman's responsibility to make sure he understands his tenants' needs and difficulties."

Georgiana pulled a face. "That's hardly Howard's concern."

"But it is," Eliza spoke up. "After all, he is their landlord. He'll make lots of decisions that affect his tenants, and it would be terrible if he didn't understand how they suffer or what they go through. I read a book about it not so long ago. Goodness, what was it called again . . ."

Georgiana shot Eliza a glance of dislike. "Goodness, you're quite the bluestocking, aren't you, Eliza?"

Eliza flushed, opening her mouth to defend herself.

"Bluestocking is hardly an insult," Silas said firmly. "As far as I can tell, it refers to a learned woman."

Georgiana stuck out her lower lip. "Mama always says that too much learning doesn't become a woman. We have a different sort of wisdom. Only plain ladies make themselves dull by too much reading." She tossed her curls back complacently, shooting a pointed glance at Eliza.

Colin, sitting beside Eliza, was glancing between the two women. It seemed that even the clueless Colin was realising there was a current of dislike between the two young ladies. Perhaps that had affected his perception of Georgiana as a beautiful woman.

"Good looks are all very well," Eliza rallied, "but I don't think we ladies should be judged only on that."

"Hear, hear," Silas said firmly. Georgiana sniffed disdainfully.

"Of course not. A proper lady ought to have a certain sort of grace in her bearing. Something regal, you know? And lots of accomplishments, of course. Do you pay the pianoforte, Eliza?"

Eliza swallowed. "Yes, but not very well."

"Oh, what a shame. I suppose you won't be participating in any of the musical evenings during the Season, then. What a pity— all the best gentlemen go to those evenings. Do you play the harp? Paint? Draw?"

"No, I don't."

"Goodness, me. You must embroider beautifully, I suppose? Table-covers and little cushions, then?"

Eliza pressed her lips together. "My sewing is entirely functional, I'm afraid. Embroidery is beautiful, but I really haven't the skill for it."

Georgiana lifted a glass of wine to her mouth with a malicious smile of glee. "You don't have the skill for many things, do you, Eliza? Oh, dear. Still, I'm sure you'll do quite well enough during the Season . . . if you don't set your sights too high."

She let out a high titter of mirth, glancing at Silas as if they were sharing a joke. Eliza swallowed hard, shrinking in her seat, and poked at her food with her fork. Beside her, Colin leaned forward with a grin.

"I do like your dress, Miss Spencer."

Georgiana preened. "Oh, thank you."

"It makes you look a lot like a fish, I think. All those little silvery sequins, like scales. Silas, doesn't Miss Spencer look exactly like that trout we fished out of the river before you left home? That huge, fat trout. Goodness, it was huge."

Colin had, naturally, chosen the best moment to say this. The conversation had flagged, and he made his fish comment during a momentary lull in the chatter around the table.

Helen and Charles were visibly horrified. Mrs Spencer looked as though she wanted to tear off Colin's head, and Georgiana went crimson with fury. Howard seemed to want to laugh but didn't dare. Silas managed to change a giggle into a cough, and Eliza buried a smile in her wine glass.

Colin beamed happily around at everyone and spooned some mashed potatoes into his mouth. Everyone except for Mrs Spencer and Georgiana began to talk at once, and the awkward moment went uncomfortably by.

When Georgiana had gotten over her shock at being insulted, she turned to Silas and continued the conversation. She mostly talked about her most recent London Season, espousing the virtues of the city over the country, the social pleasures to be found there, and the dresses she had worn. Silas listened patiently, occasionally trying to speak, only to be spoken over.

He found his mind wandering, and naturally Augusta came immediately to his thoughts. There had never been any awkward conversations like this between them. He didn't remember Augusta ever levelling a cruel word at anyone. She enjoyed the company of other women, and he'd never known her to insult another lady for her own benefit.

The meal eventually ended, and Silas had to smother a sigh of relief.

"I wonder, Silas, if you and I couldn't have a little word in private?" Howard said casually. "I'd be obliged if you could join us too, Mr Mitchell."

Silas swallowed hard. "Certainly," he managed.

***

The ladies retired to the drawing room, and the three gentlemen remained in the dining room. Port was served, of course, and for a few moments, they sipped in silence. Charles was clearly fighting to stay awake. At home they never bothered with the ladies and gentlemen separating after dinner—there was really no point. They all went through to the drawing room together, and Charles always had a nap by the fire.

"It's good to see you after so long," Howard said eventually. "I hear you've had quite an exciting few years—all that travel."

"Yes, I enjoyed the travel. I'm glad to be home, though."

Howard nodded. "I understand. I also hear you're in the market for a wife."

Silas swallowed. "That's quite a crude term, I always think. In the market."

"Goodness, you're still so nice, Silas. What would you have me say? On the hunt?" Howard laughed good-naturedly. "My point is, I know you're looking to be married. I think it's a worthwhile goal, by the way. I don't intend to marry anytime soon—too much to do, and I'm enjoying my freedom far too much—but I think it's a worthy goal."

"Thank you," Silas answered, feeling a little wrong-footed. He knew exactly where Howard was aiming the conversation, and he didn't like it very much. He could only hope Howard would be subtle enough for Silas to pretend he didn't know what the conversation was about.

"Let's cut to the chase, shall we?" Howard said, leaning forward.

So much for that hope, then.

"What do you mean, Howard?" Silas asked, hedging for time. Charles seemed to wake up a little, staring at Silas curiously.

Howard sighed. "I mean that Georgiana likes you. I like you, Silas. I'd be proud to call you a brother-in-law. For whatever reason, Georgiana isn't taking in London. She doesn't want one of those dull old fops, anyway. I'd be much happier to see her get married off to a man I know and like."

Silas cleared his throat, wishing he could sink down through the floor.

"I appreciate the compliment, Howard, I really do. But—"

"I know your business is crumbling," Howard interrupted.

The words rolled across the table, heavy as cannonballs. The colour drained from Charles' face.

"You know?" Silas repeated, his voice hoarse. "How did you find out?"

Howard sighed. "I didn't mean it as an insult, Silas. It's just one of those things, isn't it? You and Mr Mitchell are good business owners. You're good, honest men, and that's why I'd be so happy to see my sister marry into your family. If you marry Georgiana, I'll give you the money to keep your business afloat. Not a loan, a gift.

You tell me how much you want, and I'll do my best to give it to you."

Silas glanced, wide-eyed, at his father. For the first time, he realised that Charles didn't know what to say. It wasn't his fault, of course—the proposition had come out of the blue. Silas was on his own. He would have to reply for them all, and Charles would say nothing.

It was a little jarring for a young man who'd always looked up to his father as the font of all knowledge to see his father speechless.

Perhaps he was just being unfair.

Silas cleared his throat again. He was going to scrape his throat raw at this rate.

"This . . . this is very unexpected, Howard. I know it's a tremendous honour, please, don't think I don't understand that. But . . . well, I think I'm going to need a little time to think it over. Marriage is . . . is a weighty thing, don't you think? I don't want to make any rash decisions."

He wasn't sure what he'd expected from Howard. A blaze of anger, perhaps? The offer to be taken off the table? But Howard only nodded.

"I understand. I'm quite happy for you to think about it, Silas. You've never been an impulsive man, and I always liked that about you. Take some time to think about it, by all means. But not too long, understood?" he added.

Silas swallowed. "Understood."

Chapter Twenty

There was a lot of work to be done. Everyone had gotten up early, Augusta included. Most of the decorations had been put up weeks ago, but there were still last-minute preparations to be made.

Augusta had been assigned to cut out gold silk shapes to hang on the kissing bough. They'd taken to placing the kissing bough on the mantelpiece in recent years. Augusta knew why—because it looked pretty there. It meant nobody would be able to take it down and request a kiss without everyone else seeing.

That was fine. Absolutely fine. There was no reason at all for Augusta's bad mood and irritability. If she was moody, it was only because she was tired, and they had a lot of work to do.

The Duchess kept sailing through the drawing room, where Augusta was working on the decorations, followed by a horde of servants. The Duchess was known as an excellent hostess, so there was a lot of pressure for her to put on the perfect Christmas Eve party. And, of course, this was going to be Augusta's last Christmastide at home, as a single woman.

People kept reminding her of that. Augusta didn't like it.

"In here, I'd like the presents all arranged here. I'm not happy with the way the chairs are set up, so let's rearrange them and open up the room a little, what do think? And over here . . ."

She swept past, Augusta only catching snippets of her conversation. Augusta sighed, wondering if she had enough silk pieces.

Probably more than enough.

She could think of nothing but Silas that day.

They'd gone down the hill together on a sled only once. After a few slides, Augusta had claimed she was tired, and the rest of them were tired enough to agree with her. Was the long, hard slog of dragging oneself and the sled up the hill truly rewarded enough by the slide back down?

At one time, Augusta would have answered "Yes, of course, absolutely!" Now, she wasn't so sure.

By the time they returned home, Augusta had been completely chilled, inside and out. She'd hoped the more time she spent with Silas, the less drawn to him she would feel. It was almost as if she needed to leave Silas behind in order to grow up.

Well, it wasn't working. Augusta thought more and more about Silas, and she was beginning to realise that her feelings would not go away. She could see no future where she left Silas behind.

So, what now? What could she do now? How did she go on to live her life with Ambrose—a life she was looking forward to very much, by the way? She'd fought too hard to avoid being bypassed and put on the shelf to allow her last chance to slip away.

I couldn't have married Silas anyway. Mama and Papa would never have allowed it.

That was a flimsy excuse, and she knew it. The Mitchell family were nowhere near as grand as the Radfords, but that had never stopped Augusta's family from treating them as friends and equals. The Duke and Duchess loved Helen and Charles Mitchell, and in her heart, Augusta was sure they wouldn't have objected to her marrying Silas. Not if it was a love match and they knew Silas would care and love for Augusta. Not if Augusta had wanted to marry him.

It hardly matters. You aren't going to marry Silas. You never were. You're going to marry Ambrose.

At the thought of Ambrose, Augusta suddenly felt so, so tired. He would be arriving soon. Or at least, so he said. She wouldn't put it past him to cry off at the last minute, to say that his work in London kept him far too busy to take even a couple of days off at Christmastide to come up and visit his fiancé and future in-laws.

The worst part was, Augusta wouldn't have minded if he did. She truly wouldn't. In fact, she might even enjoy the celebrations more if Ambrose wasn't there. That wasn't right, Augusta knew it. No fiancé ought to enjoy her husband's-to-be absence so much.

Why couldn't she like Ambrose? He was nice enough, wasn't he? He wasn't Silas, but no other man she'd ever met had measured up to Silas. He was kind, and rich and he was prepared to take care of her and save her from spinsterhood. Why did she find him so boring, then? Why was she so unhappy at the thought of marrying him? That wasn't fair on anyone.

You had a chance to back out. Papa would have let you back out. But you chose to go on, didn't you? You were determined to marry Ambrose and be a countess and avoid being a silly old spinster because Society thinks unmarried women are an embarrassment. So, you chose your own fate, didn't you? You made your bed, and now you have to lie in it. And that's that.

No amount of self-scolding seemed to stick, though. Augusta drew in a few deep, measured breaths. It wasn't for long. She would just need to get through another few days of Christmastide, then the parties would be over. Silas would stop visiting, and she could knuckle down and concentrate on her life ahead. On Ambrose.

"I think we've got enough gold silk patterns now, don't you, Augusta?"

Augusta flinched at the sudden voice behind her, very nearly cutting through the tip of her finger with the horribly sharp scissors. The start had given her a real fright, and she dropped the scissors and silk, drawing in a few deep breaths.

"Sorry," Caroline said, wincing and lowering herself into the seat beside Augusta. "I came to see if you needed help. I didn't mean to give you such a start. I thought you'd heard me coming towards you."

Augusta smiled weakly, staring at her mercifully un-snipped finger and thanking the stars for her lucky escape.

"Well, no harm done. I was wool-gathering, anyway. My head was in the clouds."

Now Caroline had mentioned it, Augusta noticed with embarrassment that she'd cut out dozens upon dozens of gold silk patterns while she was lost in thought about Silas and Ambrose. They had far more than they needed, probably far more than they would use.

Caroline began to sift through the patterns, picking out the ones she liked best.

"These are beautiful, Augusta. Whenever I try to cut out silk patterns, they end up wobbly and odd-looking. People always ask what my patterns are supposed to be."

Augusta smiled politely. "It's just practice. How are you feeling, by the way?"

Caroline placed a hand over her belly. She wasn't starting to show yet, but it wouldn't be long. "Tired and a little dizzy. I'm disappointed over missing the sledding, but Timothy promises I can go next year."

"Well, I can assure you it's fun."

Augusta fumbled around with the gold silk and scissors, wishing she had something to do. She had to keep herself busy. Caroline was looking at her with a strange expression, one that made Augusta feel a little uncomfortable.

"Are you all right, Augusta?" Caroline asked finally.

Augusta cleared her throat. "Of course, I am. Why wouldn't I be?"

Caroline shrugged. "I don't know, but you seem distant. You seem unhappy. Timothy remarked on it last night. He's worried about you."

"Well, he needn't be. I'm fine," Augusta said firmly, not able to meet Caroline's eye.

Caroline didn't push. She wasn't the sort of person to nag and nag until she got an answer. She was quiet and polite, and entirely unassuming.

But she wasn't stupid, and she never missed a trick. Augusta didn't kid herself that she was fooling her sharp minded sister-in-law.

"I know you aren't, Augusta," Caroline said quietly. "If you won't confide in me, I wish you'd talk to somebody. Timothy, perhaps, or your Mama. We all just want you to be happy."

Augusta tried to say, "I am happy", but the words stuck in her throat. Then, the doorbell rang, and the two women flinched, glancing curiously at each other.

"Perhaps it's the Mitchells," Augusta said aloud, but she knew it wasn't. The Mitchells were coming later that night to attend the Christmas Eve party, so there was no reason they'd come along so early.

The girls stayed where they were, half-alert to any summons, when the butler stepped in.

"Lady Avilwood, Lady Augusta, Her Grace would like you to

wait on her in the parlour," he said, all gravity and seriousness.

"Goodness. That sounds impressive," Augusta remarked, abandoning her pile of gold silk shapes and rising from her seat. "Let's go and see what Mama wants."

Augusta heard voices in the parlour. It was odd that someone would choose to visit on Christmas Eve. She couldn't stop herself hoping it was Silas, even though she was sure it wasn't.

And even if it is him, what then? You're only torturing yourself. This isn't going to make you happy, you silly girl.

She glanced at Caroline, cleared her throat, and stepped inside.

A man was standing at the mantelpiece, his back to her. For a split second, Augusta thought it might be Silas.

Then he turned around, and she saw it was Ambrose.

"Ambrose," Augusta said faintly. "What a surprise."

Disappointment clenched in her gut. Her heart sank, and Augusta even felt silly baby tears start in her eyes. She hastily masked her feelings, although not quite quickly enough to escape Caroline's sharp eyes. She was aware that her sister-in-law was looking at her, and Augusta firmly did not let herself look back.

The Duchess sat in her usual seat, grinning conspirationally at Ambrose. "Just a little surprise for you, dear! Did you think you'd have to celebrate Christmastide without your fiancé?"

Ambrose came towards her, a winning smile on his face. "Hello, Augusta. Are you well?" He took her hand, brushing a kiss on her knuckles absently before letting her hand drop. "I've brought Mother. I hope you don't mind."

Augusta's heart plummeted even further into her stomach. She noticed for the first time that a wizened old woman sat on the couch, partially hidden by the Duchess' bulk.

The Dowager Countess of Firnsdale, Susannah Finch, was well-known as a nasty, malicious woman who loved gossiping and complaining about everything and everyone. She exclusively wore black and pearls and had ruined at least half a dozen ladies' reputations over the years, which she considered a badge of honour.

"Lady Firnsdale," Augusta managed, forcing an entirely insincere smile to her face. "What a pleasure to see you."

"I didn't want to come," Lady Firnsdale rasped ill-temperedly. "Country families never celebrate Christmastide properly. It's all about presents and fun rather than a proper celebration. I told Ambrose, I insisted that he should celebrate Christmastide with me, for I do it properly, but of course Ambrose wouldn't be moved. Once a gentleman secures himself a lady, he never minds his mama anymore."

There was an awkward silence after Lady Firnsdale's outburst. Caroline, who hadn't yet had the misfortune of meeting Lady Firnsdale in company, had let her jaw drop a little. She earned herself a glare from the lady in question, and Augusta nudged her.

"Well, we are happy you're here, Lady Firnsdale," the Duchess said as graciously as one could manage under the circumstances. "Ambrose, how was your journey?"

"Oh, terrible. I'm sure you can imagine. Everyone is travelling, keen to get home before Christmas Eve. Mother was terribly shaken and rattled during the trip. Still, we're safely here now, and that is what matters."

He turned to Augusta, reaching out to take her hand. "You seem very surprised, my dear. That's good, I wanted it to be a surprise. You didn't think I'd let you celebrate Christmas Eve alone, did you?"

Augusta wanted to say that she wouldn't have been alone, and it hadn't been a nice surprise at all, and why hadn't he warned her?

She couldn't say that, of course. He'd be hurt and furious. The Duchess and Caroline would be shocked, and the venomous Lady Firnsdale would finally have some real ammunition against Augusta. She didn't like Augusta, solely for the reason that Augusta had the audacity to marry her darling son and would never measure up. Augusta did not like Lady Firnsdale, not one bit. Ambrose had made noises about his mother coming to live with them once they were married. Augusta had no intention of allowing it but hadn't wanted to make a fuss before the wedding.

But now, seeing how easily Ambrose had insinuated his mother into their private family celebrations—to which she had not been invited—Augusta had an uneasy feeling that the subject was not to be open for discussion after all.

What if Lady Firnsdale simply arrived one day and settled

down with no intentions of ever leaving again? Without Ambrose's backing, there would nothing Augusta could do about it.

"Are you all right, Augusta?" the Duchess asked, cutting into Augusta's thoughts. "You look a little troubled."

Augusta swallowed hard, cursing herself for her lack of self-control.

Concentrate, Augusta. It won't do to let your mask slip now.

"I'm just surprised. It's a lovely surprise, of course," Augusta said.

"Of course," Lady Firnsdale repeated testily. "What else would it be but a lovely surprise? What sort of woman isn't happy to see her fiancé?" Augusta ignored her, and thankfully, so did everyone else.

"I'm just a little tired."

"Well, you'd better bear up for tonight," the Duchess said jovially, seemingly reassured. "It's going to be a wonderful party."

Augusta kept the smile on her face, even though her cheeks were starting to ache. "Yes, I'm quite sure it will be."

Chapter Twenty-One

They had a light luncheon that day. There was no point eating a large meal—they were all going over to the Radfords' for a hearty Christmas Eve dinner. Silas remembered the many similar gatherings spent with the family there as if they were yesterday—more food than a person could ever hope to eat, piled up and smelling heavenly. Nothing went to waste, either—whatever food they didn't eat or was left over from the servants' Christmas Eve dinner was packed up and given to the poor. It was well known thereabouts that if you didn't have enough for a proper Christmas dinner, you should go to the Radford estate, and you'd get plenty there.

They were always so kind. So generous.

Silas stayed quiet for most of the luncheon. Eliza and Colin chattered eagerly, both excited about the prospect of a real party. Colin managed to eat at least twice as much as everyone else—the boy had hollow legs—but the rest of them were keen to preserve their appetite for later.

Eliza disappeared hours before it was time to start dressing, keen to make a good impression and look nice. Colin barely waited any longer to go off and start getting ready. Silas had to smile to himself at that—for all his acerbic, cynical wit, Colin was going to be quite the dandy soon enough.

Silas retreated to the drawing room and sat in front of the fire. He had a lot to think about, and some weighty decisions to make. He barely glanced up from the flames when the drawing room door swung open. Charles padded across the carpeted floor—old, threadbare and in great need of replacing as it was—and quietly took a seat beside his son. They sat in silence for a minute or two.

Silas knew exactly what his father had come to discuss.

"Yesterday was rather a surprise, wasn't it?" Charles said at last. "Mr Spencer's proposal, that is. I don't wish to be rude about your friend, of course, but I'm a little shocked that a gentleman

138

would all but offer his sister's hand in marriage over the after-supper port. Even if the man in question is a good friend."

Silas shrugged. "Howard wants to provide for his sisters and his mother. He's very keen on making sure they are taken care of. He loves them dearly. The only problem is that his father has led him to believe the only way to care for his sisters is to find them a suitable husband."

"Hm. Well, even so. I'm sure he wouldn't do anything without his sister's consent, naturally."

"Naturally," Silas echoed. "He's given me a lot to think about, though."

Charles looked sharply at his son. Silas kept his eyes on the fire, not meeting his father's gaze.

"Has he? Silas, are you seriously considering Mr Spencer's proposal?"

Silas closed his eyes. "Yes, Father. I am."

There was a long silence.

"Well," Charles said eventually, "just when I think you can't surprise me anymore. Do you have feelings for Miss Spencer, then?"

Silas shook his head slowly. "I don't like her," he confessed. "I suppose I'd get used to her, and I would certainly take care of her and make sure she had the most comfortable life I could provide. But if I marry her, I'll get her dowry— it's substantial, and it'll do us a lot of good. Howard will pay whatever we need to get the orchards up and running again. Think about it, Father. We can get the business flourishing again. We can pay off our debts, we can put the money into the estate. It'll make a *difference*, Father. Howard mentioned something about a house, so perhaps Georgiana and I would have somewhere else to live. I don't think she'd like living in the family house."

Charles pressed his lips together. "This is a very mercenary view, Silas. I am surprised that you'd be so . . . so . . ."

"So callous?" Silas finished, a little too sharply. "I'm sorry, Father, but somebody has to do something about our fortunes. Do you think my principles will help us when we're bankrupt? When we lose the house, our land, everything? What do you think Eliza's prospects will be like then? What about Colin? Do you think any decent university would accept a young man with no money and a bankrupt family? One of us has to do something, and I have been given the opportunity."

Silas paused for breath after his outburst. He felt guilty, speaking so sharply to his father. Charles had always been a good parent, and Silas had plenty of love and respect for his father.

But he loved the rest of his family, too. His years alone in the Americas had changed him. He was so longer the mild, reserved young man who quietly did what he was told.

He'd learned to take his destiny into his own hands.

My destiny. The thought made him shudder. No matter which way he looked, Georgiana Spencer stood in his future, smiling coyly and smugly at him. Perhaps she'd change when she was married. He'd known ladies in the past who seemed to become different people once they married—for better or worse. Perhaps Georgiana would settle down and become kinder and calmer.

He doubted it, though. Not if she married a man like him. Perhaps love could change Georgiana, and Silas did not flatter himself that Georgiana was in love with him.

"I understand what you are trying to do," Charles said eventually, breaking the long silence which had sprung up between them, "but I don't want to see you make a loveless marriage, Silas."

Silas shrugged. "I'm not sure it matters, not in the grand scheme of things, at least. I'm sorry, Father. I don't mean to be so sharp. But we need money to pay for Eliza's Season. If she marries, we'll have a wedding to pay for. Colin wants to study abroad, he's told me. Eliza wants to travel if she doesn't marry. All of that will cost money—a lot of money. And that's just Eliza and Colin. What about when you and Mother want to retire? What about the orchards? We need money, Father, and we need it as soon as possible. I don't see any other way to get it beyond marrying Georgiana Spencer."

There was another silence, long and painful. Silas gripped the arms of his chair, watching the dancing flames until they blurred. He wasn't sure whether he wanted his father to stay or go. Charles stayed.

"Well, Silas, you aren't a child anymore," Charles spoke after so long, Silas was thinking of getting up and going up to his room to change. "I suppose I can't tell you what to do. You were always a kind boy, always thinking of others. I hoped you would keep that qualities as you grew, but this . . . oh, my dear boy. I don't want you to sacrifice your life for us, Silas. I truly don't. Please, *please* consider well before you make any irrevocable decisions. Miss Spencer may be a pretty girl with an impressive dowry. There may be financial benefits to marrying her. But will you love her, Silas? I don't want you to be trapped in a loveless marriage."

"Father—"

"No, Silas, you must listen to me here. I love your mother very, very much. You all know that. Marrying my Helen was my finest reward, and she has made me happier than I could ever have hoped. I was a lucky man to find her, and I congratulate my luck every day."

"I know, Father," Silas said softly. "You and mother are such wonderful examples for me and the others. We saw how much you loved each other. But I can't afford to be sentimental now. Sentiment won't save our orchards. It won't secure our futures. It just won't, Father. You must see that."

Charles sighed. "I see you've made up your mind, Silas."

"I haven't," Silas admitted. "I know what I ought to do. I'm just struggling to build up the courage to *do* it."

"Well, I hope you'll do the right thing, my boy," Charles murmured, reaching out to place a hand on his son's shoulder. "I love you very much, Silas, and I want you to be safe and happy. More than that, I want you to be *loved*. Promise me you'll consider every aspect before you make a definite decision. Do you promise?"

Silas sighed. "If it'll make you happy, Father, then yes. Yes, I will consider every aspect."

"Good. Your word is quite good enough for me, Silas. Quite good enough."

Silas smiled weakly at his father. He noticed, not for the first time, that Charles looked so much older and so much more tired than he had in previous years. Silas felt the familiar stab of guilt—he should never have left.

But then, I couldn't have stayed either.

"I'm sure I'll come to like Georgiana in time," Silas said aloud.

Charles smiled, a trace of sadness in his expression. "*Like* is not *love*, my boy."

"Aren't the two things similar enough?"

"No, Silas. No, they aren't."

Silas swallowed hard, turning his attention to the fire. He'd been toying with the idea of faking a megrim to get out of the Christmas Eve party. He'd be sad to miss it, of course, but wouldn't it be wiser to avoid Augusta as much as he could? Shouldn't he start being strict with himself now, before she was married? He couldn't imagine her Lord Firnsdale would want to live in the area—he sounded like a determined Town man, judging by what other people had said about him, who didn't particularly enjoy the country. But what if they took a country seat out here? What if he ended up seeing Augusta more than ever after her marriage?

How would he bear it?

No, Silas told himself, I'd better start as I mean to go on. And that means avoiding Augusta, drawing back from our old friendship. Not that they had much of a friendship anymore, anyway. She'd been a stranger to him since his return home, and the realisation twisted like a knife in Silas's heart.

He jumped when Charles got suddenly to his feet. Charles smiled down at his son.

"We'd better get ready, then," he said, and Silas knew then and there that there would be no pretend megrims. He was going to have to go.

For a moment, Silas considered coming clean, telling his father everything. He could tell Charles about his childhood fancy for Augusta, about the stolen kiss under the kissing bough, which had seemed to shock Augusta so much, about the heartbreak he'd suffered when he'd had to leave England for the Americas.

He could talk about how the years had changed him, but not his feelings for Augusta. He could talk about how his heart ached when he saw her, how he yearned for her, how he thought every day about her and knew that he would never get her out of his mind, even though she was engaged to another man, and he was contemplating marriage to another woman.

Silas did not, of course, say any of that. He had the impression that Charles was holding his breath, waiting for Silas to say something. If he was disappointed when Silas only got to his feet with a smile and a nod, he didn't let on.

"You're right, of course, Father. I'll go and get ready," Silas said. He left the parlour quickly before he could say something he would regret.

***

Silas dressed hurriedly, barely thinking twice about the clothes he threw on his back. He wore a deep-green velvet suit, which wouldn't usually be proper for a supper party, but this was an informal Christmas Eve celebration. The only part of his dress needing real attention was tying his cravat.

Silas had never had a proper valet, not even during their wealthier years. The had always lived simply, and aside from the one maid who helped to dress Helen and Eliza's hair, they didn't bother with ladies' maids and valets.

He inspected himself in the mirror.

I look like a proper gentleman. Not quite proper enough for Lady Augusta Radford, though. No title. No tremendous wealth. Nothing outstanding about me. Did Augusta ever think I was outstanding? I doubt it, frankly. She's far too used to mixing with nobles and such.

Silas Mitchell would never be a noble. He was plain Mr Mitchell, and that was all he would ever be. Silas was content with that, but it meant some doors would forever be closed to him.

Augusta's heart, for example. He closed his eyes, fighting back the sudden image of Augusta as a grand countess, distant and cold. A queen of ice on a throne of diamonds. Lord Firnsdale was a blurred figure in Silas' imagination, but he stood firmly between Augusta and Silas, reminding Silas of who he was and where he stood in relation to Augusta.

It was an upsetting image. To distract himself, Silas bustled around his room, brushing non-existent dust and lint off his jacket and tweaking his cravat until the starch threatened to wilt. A sudden tap on the door made him jump.

"Who is it?" Silas asked. It was far too much to hope that it might be someone coming to tell him the party had been cancelled.

The door creaked open, and Colin peered inside.

"You look very fine," Colin said approvingly. "Everyone says you look so much more distinguished now you're home."

Silas cleared his throat. "Thank you. What do you want, Colin? It's not time to go yet, is it?" Silas' heart had begun to hammer. He'd thought he had more time.

Colin shook his head. "I was wondering if you could help me with my cravat?"

"Oh." Silas relaxed a little. "Of course I will. Come in."

Chapter Twenty-Two

Augusta was trying her best not to cry. She confided in Betsey often, but it was just a step too far to admit to her maid that she was so miserable at the sight of her own fiancé, she wanted to burst into tears. No, there was nothing for it— she would have to soldier through the evening somehow. At least there should be no more surprises. Ambrose and his wretched mother had arrived for the duration, and there was nothing she could do about it. Silas would be coming, and the three of them would be required to spend time in the same room together, for hours on end. They would have to make polite conversation and listen to Ambrose's endless stories about London and his business. They'd have to listen to Lady Firnsdale's gripes and complaints, and no doubt some lies and slander masquerading as gossip.

Augusta frowned at her reflection, delicately pinching her cheeks to bring some colour into them. It was no good. She was far too pale, and she looked tired. Betrothed ladies were supposed to *glow*, weren't they? They were supposed to radiate happiness and inner contentment and all that nonsense.

Ha!

Augusta had yet to experience a moment's contentment since agreeing to marry Ambrose. That was no doubt her own fault. You couldn't spend every minute with a man wishing he was someone else, and then agree to marry him and expect everything to be all right.

And now, she was going to have to come face to face with the man she loved, with the man she was marrying at her side.

It's just one night.. One night. A few hours. Don't forget, this will be your last Christmastide at home. Ambrose has already hinted that we'll be spending future Christmastides at his mother's home, or in London. Twice. He's not a subtle man. So, wring every drop of enjoyment out of tonight. Savour it. Times are going to change for you from now on. After Christmastide, your life will never be the same.

Augusta just wished she could believe the change would be for the better.

"Lady Augusta?" Betsey asked tentatively, making Augusta jump. She must have been staring into space. Heaven only knew what her expression was like. She glanced up, meeting Betsey's eyes in the mirror.

Betsey stood by the bed, where she'd laid out the shimmering lavender gown Augusta planned to wear that night. Betsey held a hairbrush in one hand and a handful of pins and ribbons in the other, ready to do Augusta's hair. Now, she looked worried, chewing her lip.

"What is it?" Augusta said, trying to sound light and even a little excited. She *ought* to be excited for the Christmas Eve party.

"You don't look well, Lady Augusta. You look a bit . . . a bit pale."

"I'm just tired," Augusta said, and it wasn't entirely a lie. She was tired these days. Bone tired. Her mask, which she'd worn to every London party and soirée and dance, was getting heavier and heavier. She had to wear it constantly around Ambrose, and it was exhausting.

Betsey pursed her lips, a gesture which Augusta knew meant Betsey didn't believe her. She didn't push, of course, but only came over to lay down the hairbrush and hair utensils.

"Very well, milady. As long as you're quite well. But I've noticed you haven't been yourself at all lately. Not one bit."

Augusta swallowed. "There have been a lot of changes recently, haven't there? Things change so quickly. I can't always keep up." She gave a light laugh, which came off as tense and a little sad.

Betsey picked up the brush again and began brushing through Augusta's hair. She was always so careful—never tugging on knots, easing the brush through Augusta's flowing long hair. She closed her eyes, enjoying the sensation. For a few minutes, the problems of Silas, Ambrose, and Augusta's impending wedding melted away. There was only the gentle, sweeping sound of the brush running through her hair.

"You've got beautiful hair, milady," Betsey murmured. "I say that a lot, I know."

"Only because I have you to help maintain it," Augusta said, opening her eyes and smiling at Betsey in the mirror. "Betsey, I know we haven't talked about this, but you will come with me when I marry, won't you? You can be the official lady's maid to the Countess of Firnsdale. I'd like to have a familiar face with me when I leave home."

She expected smiles, but Betsey only swallowed hard, looking miserable.

"You know I'd love to, Lady Augusta, but . . . well, the Dowager Countess sent her own maid down to the kitchens to find me. She was so snooty, I felt *that* tall, you know. She said my services wouldn't be needed when you marry the Earl, and they were going to hire a proper French maid."

Augusta spun around, her hair swinging out around her.

"*What*? How impertinent! Am I to believe the Dowager Countess has decided this without consulting me?"

Betsey nodded. "The maid said I wasn't to talk to you about it because the Earl and his mother had already decided it all between them."

Augusta pressed her lips together in a thin line. "I see. Well, Betsey, I can assure you it isn't the case. I won't be told who I can and can't have as my *personal* lady's maid. I want you, Betsey. You're my friend, and the Dowager Countess has no right to say otherwise."

Betsey wrung her hands together. "But I won't be as good as proper French lady's maid."

"I don't care. When I marry, Betsey, I'm going to start as I mean to go on, and I won't be controlled by my mother-in-law."

"You might not get much of a choice." Betsey bit her lip, looking a little shocked at the words that had just left her own mouth.

Augusta was quiet for a moment or two. "Thank you for telling me about it, Betsey. Just to be clear, do you *want* to come with me after I'm married?"

"Of course, I do, Lady Augusta! You don't even have to ask."

"Then you're coming," Augusta said flatly. "And that's an end to it."

Betsey did not look reassured in the slightest, bending over the hairpins and shuffling them around. Augusta stared at her own reflection, now pale and angry. She was going to have to have a word with Ambrose about the matter. Not tonight, though. Not during the Christmas Eve party.

When, then?

She bit her lip. She'd find the right time.

"I think I'd like something different for my hair today," Augusta said aloud. "I fancy a change. I don't know what, though."

Betsey's head shot up, and her expression brightened. "Ooh, I've got an idea, milady!"

***

Silas briefly considered flinging open the carriage door and sprinting away over the snow-covered grounds of the Radford estate.

He didn't, of course.

The Mitchell family piled gladly out of their carriage, shivering in the cold air and hastening towards the warm, inviting entrance to the Radfords' fine manor home. Silas followed, dragging his feet.

It's just one evening . . .

The Duke and Duchess were waiting to greet them, of course. They were all smiles, complimenting Eliza on her new gown (how they had afforded it, Silas did not want to know), and asking Colin where he planned to study (somewhere abroad). The snow had started to fall again by the time they all finally shuffled inside. Silas was thoroughly chilled, although he would have happily stood out in the cold for a while longer if it meant not having to see Augusta and experience that miserable, horrible wrench of heartbreak.

People—poets and novelists, that is, who weren't always considered to be *people*, as such—often likened love and heartbreak to a fever, to a sort of delirium. That was nonsense, in Silas's humble opinion. Breaking one's heart was like breaking a limb. It *hurt*, and for longer than you thought it could. It throbbed and refused to heal, and you had to be careful how you moved around and how you lived your life—the slightest wrong move could tug on your injury and make it hurt all over again.

Silas managed to distract himself from his maudlin musings during the short journey from the front door to the parlour. As always, the Duchess had done a wonderful job of decorating. The inside of their home looked like a winter wonderland—silver and gold paper chains hung along the walls, gold silk patterns and greenery, fresh and smelling delicious, had been carefully placed on every possible surface, it seemed. The smell of wood sap and pine filled the air, and the blood-red berries poked out from the holly and mistletoe sprigs, a pleasing counterpoint to all the green.

Ahead of them, Helen was exclaiming something along the same lines, and the Duchess was smiling and gracefully receiving the compliments.

"Oh, we have something of a surprise for you all," the Duke chipped in, pausing at the parlour door. "There are some last-minute guests for you all to meet."

He swung open the door, and Silas, who had somehow ended up near the front of the little gathering, was obliged to step inside first.

Inside, he saw a middle-aged gentleman of indeterminate age and uninteresting looks. The fellow got hastily to his feet when they entered. A shrivelled old woman sat beside him, scowling at the newcomers as if they'd personally wronged her.

"Let me introduce Lord Ambrose Finch, the Earl of Firnsdale, and his mother, Lady Susannah Finch, the Dowager Countess of Firnsdale," the Duke said with something of a flourish.

Silas felt sick. He knew he wasn't *going* to be sick—he hadn't eaten anything for hours. Still, his stomach lurched.

This was Augusta's fiancé. Augusta herself was not down yet.

Lord Firnsdale busied himself with shaking hands and bowing to everyone. His mother sat where she was, muttering rather too loudly about Christmastide being for families, not neighbours who wangled invites. This was obviously aimed at the Mitchells, and the Duchess shot the old woman an angry glare. Aside from that, neither she nor her husband acknowledged the rude Dowager Countess, so Silas took his cue from them.

He wanted to point out that she and her plain-faced son weren't related to the Radfords. Not *yet*.

Timothy and Caroline were there, of course, and the extra numbers diluted the discomfort caused by the presence of Lord and Lady Firnsdale. They all chatted companionably, although Lord Firnsdale never addressed Silas directly, except for when they were introduced. When he glanced around, his eye flitted over Silas, much like it did over Colin. His gaze dwelled on Eliza for a few seconds more than Silas would have liked. He could already feel himself bristling.

This is going to be a long evening.

"As soon as Augusta comes down, we'll go into supper," the Duchess said brightly.

Lord Firnsdale quietly cleared his throat. "Where *is* Augusta, Your Grace?"

"Getting ready, I assume."

"She does not normally take so long." Lord Firnsdale pursed his lips. "I don't approve of excessive vanity in ladies."

There was an awkward pause in the conversation then, and Silas suddenly found himself speaking.

"I don't think taking an extra half an hour over dressing can be construed as *vanity*, Lord Firnsdale."

Lord Firnsdale turned pale eyes onto Silas.

"Augusta is not the sort of lady to fuss over her appearance," he said loftily. "She always looks beautiful and well turned-out, so naturally, she doesn't require hours of preparation. You couldn't be expected to know that, of course, Mr Mitchell."

"I've known Augusta since we were children," Silas snapped. The others had gone back to talking amongst themselves, so the remark was aimed only at Lord Firnsdale. He blinked, obviously not used to being contradicted or spoken to in that manner. His gaze narrowed, and Silas cursed his sharp, hasty tongue.

He was spared from having to make an awkward apology by the parlour door opening. They all turned, and Augusta stood on the threshold.

Silas had often heard the expression "breath-taking", but he'd never truly experienced it before now.

Augusta wore a shimmering gown of pale-lavender, a stark contrast to the neat, demure dresses she normally preferred. The sleeves were as thin as gossamer, and the gown gathered at the shoulders and swept down like a Roman tunic, pulled in at the waist by beading and embroidery. It was beautiful. *She* was beautiful. But the most outstanding thing of all was . . .

"Augusta, your *hair!*" Lord Firnsdale gasped. "It is *loose!*"

Augusta smiled nervously, half-lifting a hand to her head.

Her hair, exquisitely curled and braided, mostly hung loose down her back in thick, glossy ringlets. A dozen shimmering diamond pins glittered in its depths.

"I thought I'd try something new," Augusta said. "As it's just us here this evening. A family gathering."

"You look lovely, darling," the Duchess said, looking to her husband. "Doesn't she?"

The Duke nodded, and Caroline also complimented Augusta on her new look. But Lord Firnsdale had gone quite pale, and his lips were pressed together in a narrow line. Silas fought not to grin.

While he was enjoying Lord Firnsdale's disapproval, he managed to lock eyes with Augusta.

Then, it was as if their gazes got tangled up together. Silas couldn't look away. He couldn't blink. Augusta stood as if turned to a stone.

One of them had to say something. Silas swallowed hard.

"Hello, Augusta."

She lifted her chin, her gaze still unwavering.

"Hello, Silas."

Chapter Twenty-Three

Augusta had nearly lost her nerve on the stairs. Her hair felt strange, heavy and warm around her neck and down her back. It wasn't *improper*, exactly, but she knew she'd cause a stir and offend some of the more rigid matrons if she attended a ball looking like it. Augusta felt she had never looked so glamorous before, and she loved it. Betsey had been fairly beaming with pride when she had finished the new hair style.

It was immediately clear to Augusta that Ambrose did not approve of her appearance. He pressed his lips tightly together, shooting angry little glances at her. Anger rose up hotly inside her. What right does he have to tell me what to do or how to dress?

Soon enough, he'll have every right, the little voice at the back of her head piped up. Augusta ignored it as best she could. Besides, she had bigger things to worry about—like staying composed when Silas's eyes were burning into her. He hadn't taken his eyes off her since she had first stepped into the room, and it was quickly becoming noticeable.

"Right, I believe the time has come to move along to the dining room," the Duchess said, smiling at the company. The married couples immediately paired up, and Colin offered his arm to his sister. Ambrose, unsmiling, offered his arm to Augusta. That left poor Silas to escort the Dowager Countess. Augusta didn't envy him the job of escorting the unpleasant old prune.

They all filed out of the parlour together, heading down the hall to the dining room.

"I don't like your hair like that, Augusta," Ambrose whispered harshly.

Augusta pressed her lips together. "Why not?"

"Why not? Well, it's not entirely proper, is it? You aren't a child—you shouldn't wear your hair down. Are you going to sew your hems up a few inches too? Like a schoolgirl? Why not wear a pair of breeches while you're at it?"

Augusta swallowed hard, fighting back an uncharacteristic

burst of rage.

"I think I look rather nice. Everyone else thinks so too. Mama would have said if there was anything improper about my appearance, don't you think?"

"I have great respect for the Duchess, but she does tend to have rather a lax attitude towards matters of importance. I'm not sure her opinion ought to be greatly heeded."

Augusta had no doubt that her engagement would have ended there and then if they hadn't stepped into the dining room at that very minute. In the hustle and bustle of finding their seats—and Ambrose carefully pulled out Augusta's seat himself, making sure she was entirely comfortable and settled—Augusta's anger faded a little. *I'm just being prickly, that is all,* she told herself.

Besides, it wasn't as if she *could* wear her hair down for more formal gatherings, was it? So it didn't really matter, and it wasn't worth making a fuss about.

Ambrose sat next to her, of course, and Silas took a seat directly opposite. Augusta's heart sank. Now she would have to spend the whole of dinner trying her best not to look at him. She noticed he was resolutely not looking at Ambrose.

Augusta frowned a little, fiddling with her fork. Did Silas not like Ambrose? She was fairly sure there had been something of an atmosphere between the two men when she had entered the parlour. Perhaps Ambrose and Silas just weren't similar enough to get on.

It certainly couldn't be anything to do with jealousy. No, that would be silly. Augusta cleared her throat, smiling up at her guests as the soup course was served.

The Duke cleared his throat, rising to his feet to deliver a speech. Everyone fell silent.

"I'd like to start by thanking you all—family, family-to-be, and our dear friends, the Mitchells, who might as *well* be family—for joining us this Christmas Eve. I'm especially delighted to receive Lord Firnsdale—Ambrose, you will make a marvellous son-in-law, and I couldn't be happier for you to marry my daughter."

Smiling, Ambrose reached over to take Augusta's hand. She didn't realise it at first and missed the gesture before noticing; hastily recollecting herself, she placed her hand in his.

Augusta felt absolutely nothing. No spark, no frisson, nothing that an engaged couple might feel when they touched each other. She might as well have been holding her father's hand, only the Duke's hands weren't so soft and clammy. Her fingers twitched in Ambrose's grip, and she longed to snatch her hand back.

She couldn't. She was forced to sit there, her hand in Ambrose's, throughout the whole speech. Panic began to set in.

How can I marry this man? I can't even stand to hold his hand for a few minutes. I'm going to be his wife. *We're going to live out our lives together. How on earth am I going to manage?*

The speech ended after what seemed like an eternity, and Augusta had the excuse of her cooling soup to pull back her hand. The Duke had chosen a bad time to deliver a speech—everyone's soup was lukewarm, but they were all laughing about it.

Except for Lady Firnsdale, of course. She screwed up her face as if she'd bitten into a lemon, pushed away her soup, and began to loudly complain.

But nobody was really listening to Lady Firnsdale. Conversation broke out, and people began to chatter and laugh. Ambrose ate in silence, however, and Augusta found she wasn't much in the mood for talking. The silence between them dragged on as the courses were served—none of which suited Lady Firnsdale, of course.

She glanced up and caught Silas looking at her again. He averted his gaze, and Augusta wished he hadn't. Her heart was pounding, and she found herself studying the curve of his brow, his strong nose, and his long eyelashes, which swept his cheeks when he looked down. Come to think of it, Augusta didn't think she'd *ever* seen anyone so handsome as Silas.

Ambrose cleared his throat beside her, and Augusta jumped guiltily.

"I apologise for my comment about your hair," he said quietly. "It isn't proper, of course, but it isn't as if you'll wear your hair like that when we're married. And you do look very nice, of course."

Augusta bit her lip. "Thank you," she murmured. The matter of Betsey lingered in the back of her mind, but surely *that* wouldn't be much of an issue. She didn't want to ruin the evening, not after Ambrose had apologised.

Ambrose smiled down at her and shovelled a forkful of beef

into his mouth. He clearly thought the matter was permanently resolved. Augusta felt it wasn't . . . though she couldn't quite explain why.

***

When the last course was eaten and not even Colin—who seemed to have hollow legs—could eat anymore, the Duchess got to her feet.

"Ah, are the ladies going through at last?" Lady Firnsdale exclaimed. "It's about time."

"Oh, no, Lady Firnsdale. We don't stand on ceremony for such small, intimate parties. No point in separating the ladies and gentlemen for such a small party as this, is there?"

Lady Firnsdale's face was a picture of disdain, and the Duchess hastily turned away.

"I was going to say," she continued, "that it's time to decorate the tree! Now, my dear Ambrose, Lady Firnsdale, you won't know that this is our yearly tradition. We always bring a tree indoors, and we wait until Christmas Eve to decorate it, and we like our friends to help us. Will you join in?"

Ambrose was smiling, but Augusta noticed it was a rather fixed smile. "Goodness, I had no idea I would be helping with the decorating. I'm really not prepared."

"Oh, don't be so silly, Ambrose. It's just hanging a few silk shapes and baubles on a tree," Augusta laughed. Ambrose did not laugh along with her.

"Well, Augusta, I'm not sure I enjoy being called *silly*."

"Oh, I didn't mean—"

Ambrose cleared his throat. "I was actually planning to retire early tonight. I rather think the journey has caught up with me. You don't mind, do you?"

Augusta wasn't sure whether the question was aimed at her or her parents. She smiled weakly and murmured, "Of course not."

Not that Ambrose was waiting for her permission. He got up from the table, murmuring his excuses and good nights, and made his escape before the rest of the party even realised what was going on. Augusta glanced subtly around the table. Her parents seemed a little taken aback, as if they'd expected something . . .

different. It wasn't as if it the hour was particularly late, and it was Christmas Eve.

Augusta was a little ashamed to admit to herself that she wasn't disappointed at all. In fact, she felt as though a weight had been lifted off her shoulders. She glanced at Lady Firnsdale and found the woman glowering at her.

"I'll stay," Lady Firnsdale said bluntly. Nobody had asked.

The remaining guests filed through to the drawing room, where the undecorated Christmas tree stood. There were boxes standing beside the tree, full of the gold and silver shapes that Augusta had cut out, along with wooden ornaments, paper chains, and cunning little baubles they'd used for years. Augusta felt the familiar thrill of excitement at the sight of it. This had always been her favourite part of Christmastide, and she and Silas had enjoyed it together many times in the past.

Lady Firnsdale shouldered roughly past Augusta, heading for the armchair nearest the fire.

"Aren't you helping us with the tree, Lady Firnsdale?" Silas called after her, an arch tone to his voice.

Lady Firnsdale settled down in the armchair with a sigh.

"No," she responded briskly. "I can't stand for very long. Besides, in London, decorating the tree is always a job for the servants. Why not sweep your own floors and dust your own mantelpieces, while you're at it?"

Augusta caught Silas's eye and had to turn away and press a hand over her mouth to smother a giggle. Lady Firnsdale was so ridiculous! Without Ambrose there, she was just a silly, unpleasant old woman, not Augusta's prospective mother-in-law.

Eliza dived on the boxes with a squeal, and Colin followed, scarcely less excited.

The Duchess linked her arm through her husband's, chuckling. "I think we'll let the young people have at it this year."

That left Augusta and Silas to decorate the other side of the tree. She glanced up to find him smiling down at her.

"Well," Silas said, "this is familiar, isn't it?"

Augusta smiled back. "Yes, it is."

Chapter Twenty-Four

Silas had been hard pressed not to grin like a lunatic when the snobbish Lord Firnsdale had taken his leave.

Good riddance! He did not like Lord Firnsdale one bit, and the feeling was evidently mutual. Silas had immediately identified the stab of jealousy for what it was, but he was determinedly trying to ignore it. He might feel jealous over Augusta's betrothed, but he had no *right* to. She had chosen Lord Firnsdale, and that was that. Ambrose Finch was the man Augusta wanted to marry.

Although, after seeing the two of them sit in silence for long stretches at a time at the dinner table, one might have been forgiven for thinking otherwise. Silas had watched them covertly, privately shocked to see how long they went without speaking. When he and Augusta were young, they had rattled on endlessly together. They never ran out of things to say to each other. It was just so *easy* to talk to Augusta, but there Lord Firnsdale was, entirely ignoring her. As if he didn't *understand* the treasure he'd earned for himself.

Pearls before swine. Silas entertained himself with a mental image of a pig with Lord Firnsdale's face. The resemblance was striking, or so Silas thought. Perhaps it was the upturned nose, or the ham-like, pinkish hue of Lord Firnsdale's face in the heat of the dining room.

It was a shame the unpleasant Dowager had chosen to stay downstairs, but that couldn't be helped. Silas had briefly considered whether she'd chosen to "keep an eye" on Augusta, but quickly disregarded the thought. What family wouldn't be thrilled to have Lady Augusta Radford join them? They were lucky. Tremendously lucky.

Not that you'd think it, with Lady Firnsdale glowering from the fireside.

They busied themselves with the tree, and for a while, it felt like old times again. Silas could have been ten, twelve, or eighteen, standing beside Augusta, hanging silk shapes and ornaments on thick, sweet-smelling branches. They talked about everything and nothing, and it occurred to Silas that he hadn't seen Augusta smile so widely and so happily in a long, long time. He told a joke—a terrible one, no doubt, and she burst out laughing, throwing back her head in joyful abandon. Her glossy hair hung over her shoulders, and Silas longed to touch it, to let the silky strands slip between his fingers. When they were *very* young and Augusta's hair used to fight its way out of its braids when they were out and about, she would command Silas to brush it and help her plait it again.

Silas had always loved brushing her hair. He still thought about it sometimes. Even back then, Augusta's hair was thick and long. She'd always liked it long, even though it would have been much more convenient to cut it short.

Augusta threw a glance over her shoulder and caught him looking. Silas tensed, braced for a frown or a questioning stare. He'd expected she would turn away at least.

But Augusta kept looking, her eyes wide, her grin fading into something softer and a little . . . surprised, perhaps?

Silas's heart began to pound. He opened his mouth—to say what exactly, he had no idea—but of course, they were interrupted.

Colin dropped a small painted wooden ball he was about to hang on the tree branches. It rolled away, and there was a flurry of squeals and laughter as he and Eliza tried to catch it. The Duchess and the Duke were laughing, while Helen and Charles were shaking their heads, glancing at each other with a chuckle. It was a cosy domestic scene, and Silas had to laugh at Colin, scrabbling to rescue the ornament from under a table where it had rolled.

When the ornament was recovered and restored to its place, the moment was gone. Augusta had gone back to adjusting the ornaments, and the tree was soon more or less decorated.

With one exception, of course.

"Now, it's time for the star!" the Duchess announced, lifting up the ornate, antique golden star that had decorated the Radford Christmas tree for as long as Silas could remember. "Who would like to do the honours?"

"If I remember rightly," Charles said slowly, "it should go to either Silas or Lady Augusta. I recall there was always a long, ongoing battle over who should have the right to place the star on top of the Christmas tree. It was a lively discussion, I can remember that much. A very involved debate."

Silas felt colour rush to his face. Memories of an eight-year-old Silas and a six-year-old Augusta rolling around on the rug of the drawing room, furiously tussling for the right to place the star on top of the tree. It was no use telling them that one could do it this year and one the next year—at that age, a year was an eternity. A year was *never*.

Silas glanced over at Augusta and saw she was smiling down at her feet, no doubt lost in the same memories.

"We haven't fought on the drawing room rug for years, Mama," Augusta said, earning a chuckle from the parents.

"Well, you ought to let Augusta do it," Eliza said. "That's only fair, isn't it, Silas?"

"If I remember correctly," the Duke said, tapping his chin in mock thoughtfulness, "Augusta put the star on the tree at our last Christmas. So, it is Silas' turn."

"We ought to be fair, Papa," Augusta said. "Silas, I insist. You are the guest. I am no longer a child, and I'm sure I can live well enough without doing the honours this year. I can always wait until next year—a year doesn't seem such an eternity to me anymore. You can put the star on the tree."

Silas chuckled. "How shockingly gracious of you. Unfortunately, I must decline. No, I cannot accept your gracious offer."

Augusta narrowed her eyes. "Well, *one of us* has to do it."

"I tell you what, let's flip a coin for it."

She smiled. "All right. We shall let Fate decide."

The others clustered around, already in a silly, excitable mood, ready to laugh over the ridiculous wager of who should place the star on the top of the Christmas tree. Silas took out a coin from his pocket, glancing down at Augusta. There was an odd expression on her face, as though she'd just remembered something sad that had cut through her happiness. She seemed breathless, expectant.

"Heads or tails?" Silas asked.

Augusta drew in a breath. "Tails."

Silas flicked the coin high up into the air, the gold glinting in the light. He snatched it out of the air, slapping it down on the back of his other hand, covering it over.

He lifted his hand, peering at the coin. A flat, carved silver face looked back at him.

Heads.

"Well?" Augusta asked, obviously caring more about the result of the toss than she wanted to let on.

Silas grimaced. "Tails, I'm afraid. You win, Lady Augusta. I concede defeat—the Fates have chosen."

He made an elaborate, flourishing bow, carefully slipping the coin back into his pocket before anyone could see.

There was a smattering of applause, and a few laughs and snide comments. The star was handed to Augusta, and the Duke set up the ladder. Augusta stared down at the star for a long moment, then glanced around at them all and smiled.

She began to climb.

Silas stepped forward, holding the ladder to steady it. Augusta's hand brushed his as she climbed, no doubt an accident. Accident or not, it sent shivers down Silas's spine. He fought to keep his composure and concentrated on not letting Augusta fall. The tree was taller than he'd realised.

Augusta leaned forward, wobbling a little, and Silas' heart leapt into his mouth. She placed the star neatly on the top of the Christmas tree, and leaned back, holding her breath.

It stayed where it was, and they all burst into cheers. Grinning around, Augusta delicately stepped back down the ladder. When she finally planted her feet on the ground again, Silas found they were very close, entirely too close. It wasn't proper.

Augusta's smile wavered, and Silas' breath caught in his throat. Then he remembered where they were, and stepped back, smiling. Augusta glanced around and dropped a theatrical curtsey that earned her a few approving chuckles.

Her gaze landed on Lady Firnsdale, seated by the fire, and Silas watched as the smile dropped from her face like a stone.

Lady Firnsdale's armchair allowed her full view of the tree and the commotion. She was not smiling. Her face was set and grim, her gimlet eyes boring into Augusta with an expression Silas could not read.

Evidently, Augusta could. After a moment, she dropped her eyes and turned away. She'd gone pale, though. He noticed that much.

Lady Firnsdale got to her feet.

"I shall be retiring now," she said, her voice having the same effect on their spirits as a bucket of cold water might have on a campfire. "I think I have seen quite enough."

She made her haughty way to the door, not looking back. They murmured half-hearted goodbyes, but once the door had closed behind her, everyone exchanged curious looks.

"She seems quite a character," Helen said tactfully.

The Duchess pulled a face. "She's awful. Nobody in London likes her. We didn't invite her; Ambrose just brought her. I suppose I can hardly disoblige him; he is our son-in-law to be. I am sorry if she's ruined Christmastide for you and the family, Helen."

"Oh, not at all. It's almost amusing. There must always be a spectre at the feast, I suppose."

The two women laughed over the witticism, and Eliza and Colin began to eagerly talk with the Duke about something.

Silas stepped over to where Augusta stood beside the tree, head tilted back to look up at the star.

"It's beautiful, isn't it?" Augusta murmured. "One always forgets. I'll miss this, you know."

Silas bit his lip. "I'm sure you'll still be able to enjoy Christmastide with your family once you're . . . once you're married."

Augusta sighed. "Perhaps I will. But it won't be the same. It'll never be the same."

"Some changes are good for us. If you're sure you're making the right decision, that is."

Silas cursed himself. He'd gone too far. Augusta shot him a surprised glance, then her gaze slipped away from him.

"Oh, every bride gets cold feet as the big day approaches," she said lightly. "Don't take me too seriously, Silas. I've done a lot of thinking about my future, and I know exactly what I need to do."

"Oh," Silas managed. "Well, that's good. That's good."

Chapter Twenty-Five

December 25th, Christmas Day

Silas had drunk too much mulled wine last night. He opened his eyes groggily, wishing for death. It wasn't the ideal way to wake up on Christmas morning. He could already hear the bustle and chatter of his family moving around downstairs. They wouldn't open any presents until he came downstairs, so he'd better get moving.

He'd lain awake for hours last night, thinking about Augusta. Silas knew he still loved her; he'd known that for a long time.

But how did she feel about him? There'd been moments when . . . No, he shouldn't let his thoughts and hopes run away with him. Augusta was an engaged woman, and there was no getting around it. She hadn't been forced into the engagement. She'd chosen it. So, what else was Silas to think?

He sat up with a groan, closing his eyes and willing his headache to recede. The least he could do was wake up and act cheerfully for his family. His wonderful, kind, loving family, who'd accepted him home with open arms. They didn't deserve to be dragged down by his maudlin demeanour on what was supposed to be the happiest day of the year. He forced himself to get up and splashed icy water from his washbasin onto his face. The cold shocked him awake, and with some food and coffee, Silas was sure his headache would ease up enough for him to be the smiling son and benevolent older brother. He mentally ran through the Christmas presents he'd brought for his family in his head.

It would have been nice if he'd brought presents from the Americas, but he'd left the country months ago, when Christmas was a far-off thought, and of course, it was too late now. Charles had sternly told them all to limit themselves to small, inexpensive gifts.

Silas had bought a beautiful, hand-stitched scarf for his mother, a set of cufflinks for his father, some ribbons and handkerchiefs for Eliza, and a set of leather-bound books for the studious Colin. He'd bought various trinkets and sweetmeats for the servants; they had always been firm favourites in the past.

He hadn't bought anything for Augusta.

Silas had thought about it, mostly whenever he had picked up a pretty necklace or a ribbon that would perfectly complement the colour of her eyes. But he always found himself putting it down again. The two families had never bothered with exchanging Christmas gifts; the Radfords could afford to buy themselves whatever they wanted, after all. No doubt Ambrose would buy Augusta a lovely Christmas present, something he knew she wanted and would love.

Silas closed his eyes, imagining Augusta's excitement when she unwrapped Lord Firnsdale's present, and his benevolent smile as he watched her. The room lurched, and Silas felt nauseous. He opened his eyes and saw himself in the mirror—a pale, miserable spectre.

The spectre at the feast. It's not Lady Firnsdale, though. It's me.

Still, he had at last decided on the perfect present for Augusta, and she wouldn't even know it was from him.

Silas was going to let her go, once and for all.

What was more, Silas had decided to accept Howard's proposal. He really couldn't think of any other way to save the family and the orchards. He would marry Georgiana, and surely, they'd learn to get along well enough sooner or later. He would visit Howard after Epiphany and tell him the news—the man had already been quite patient enough.

Silas had clung onto his memories and hopes of Augusta all the way across a vast ocean, but now hope was gone. and it was time to let it go. Silas drew in a deep breath, pasted a smile on his face, and went downstairs to face his family.

**

"Me next, me next!" Colin exclaimed, as excited as a child. He'd already unwrapped Silas's present and was thrilled over the books. The Mitchell family took turns opening their presents, and it was every bit as exciting for Silas to watch the others unwrap theirs as it was to unwrap his own.

So far, Silas had received a model globe from his father, a

beautiful leather journal from his mother, and a set of boules from Colin. He suspected Colin wanted the boules more for himself than his brother. In fact, they'd already arranged to play a game together after church.

They all had one present left. Colin unwrapped his . . . to reveal a pack of cards.

"From me!" Eliza trilled. "I know yours got all wet and sticky when you spilled your hot chocolate all over them."

Colin laughed, giving the cards an experimental shuffle. "Thank you, Eliza. You open yours next. I think it's from me."

Eliza unwrapped her present to reveal yet another set of handkerchiefs. Silas winced—she'd already received handkerchiefs from him and Charles. But she laughed good-naturedly.

"I'll be drowning in handkerchiefs at this rate! I feel like I ought to have a cold to use them all up. Go on, Mama, and Papa. Yours are both from me, I think."

Charles unwrapped his parcel to reveal a new shirt, and Helen had received an embroidered cushion cover.

"These are beautiful, Darling. Thank you," Helen said, leaning forward to give Eliza a kiss.

That only left Silas. Eliza shuffled closer. "Go on, Silas. Unwrap your last present."

The other three were discussing whether they should smooth out the wrapping paper to reuse next year. Colin had torn his rather badly, and Helen was trying to repair the damage while her husband assisted. Silas decided to quickly open his final present while they were distracted.

Silas lifted it experimentally. It was surprisingly heavy for such a small box. The neatness of the wrapping paper indicated that it was either from Eliza or Helen. He tore off the paper to reveal a small, neat box.

Inside was a small golden star—painted, of course—about the size of Silas' palm. It had a hollowed-out base where it could be placed on top of a Christmas tree.

"It's a Christmas star," Silas said, more than a little confused. "But we already have a star for ours."

"It's from me," Eliza confessed. "It's for you, Silas. For your own Christmas tree next year. Yours and Augusta's."

Silas went very still. "What do you mean, mine and

Augusta's?"

"I see how you look at her, Silas."

"Eliza, please, don't. I don't want to discuss it. Besides, Augusta is marrying someone else."

"I know you have feelings for Augusta. Don't try and lie to me, Silas. I know you do. I peeked at the coin, you know."

Silas blushed. "I don't know what you mean."

"The coin you tossed. I know you let her win. I see how you look at her. Even before you left to go abroad, I knew you loved her."

"We were children."

"And now you're not," Eliza countered. "Come on, Silas. Why did you really come home from the Americas?"

Silas sighed. "It doesn't matter, Eliza. As I've been saying all along, Augusta is engaged. She's chosen to marry Lord Firnsdale, so that's all there is to it."

"Not quite," Eliza said, leaning forward. "I watched them last night. They barely spoke. They hardly looked at each other. Augusta is not in love with Lord Firnsdale. You must see it. I don't even think she likes him very much."

"Well, she's agreed to marry him."

Eliza shrugged. "Perhaps she thought she had no other choice. You could give her another choice, Silas."

Silas was quiet for a long moment. "What are you saying, Eliza?"

"What do you think I'm saying? Tell Augusta how you really feel."

"She's—"

"I swear, Silas, if you say Augusta is engaged one more time, I'll bludgeon you to death with that star," Eliza hissed. "I know she's engaged. But I still think you ought to come clean and tell her how you feel. If she politely turns you down, well, at least you'll know the truth. You can move on. She can marry Lord Firnsdale and be as happy as she can with a man like that."

"What do you mean, a man like that?" Silas asked sharply.

"Oh, you must have noticed how controlling Lord Firnsdale is. He's entirely ruled by his mother too, who is one of the most horrible women I've ever met. I think Augusta will lead a miserable life with them."

Silas chewed his lip. All of these thoughts had occurred to him before, but he'd resolutely put them aside, reminding himself that Augusta was well out of his reach.

Although Eliza didn't seem to think she was. In fact, Eliza seemed to think there was still hope. Her optimism was beginning to rub off on Silas.

"What are you two gossiping about over there? Silas, what was your gift?" Helen called.

"Hm? Oh, a Christmas star, from Eliza," Silas replied.

Helen chuckled. "Very funny, Eliza."

Charles glanced at his pocket watch. "Oh, goodness, look at the time. Right, we'd better all get moving, or we'll be late for the church service. Enough presents, children, let's get ready."

There were a few half-hearted groans, and they all got up, shoving the unwrapped presents back under the tree.

Silas was not in the mood for church. It would be freezing outside the church and boiling within, from all those bodies packed closely together. Also, their pew was directly opposite the Radfords. That meant he would spend the whole service staring at Augusta.

And probably Lord Firnsdale too.

Silas was sure he was only torturing himself with such last-minute hopes. He was like a drowning man clutching at a straw. When would he finally accept Augusta was lost to him forever? Her wedding day? The birth of her first child, with Lord Firnsdale smiling fondly down at his firstborn? Silas closed his eyes, swaying slightly.

"Silas?" Helen asked, a tinge of worry in her voice. "Are you all right?"

Silas' eyes shot open, and he smiled nervously. "Of course, Mother. I'm just a little tired after last night."

"Ah, I see. Well, hurry up and get ready for church."

Silas turned towards the stairs, and was immediately ambushed by Eliza.

"You must talk to her," Eliza hissed.

"I must do nothing of the sort, Eliza. In fact, I think I'd do better to keep my distance and stay away, not interfering."

Eliza eyed him for a long moment. "I can't make you do anything, Silas. Augusta is hard to read. But I'm quite sure she doesn't love Lord Firnsdale, but I can't tell whether she loves you or not. But if you don't tell Augusta how you feel, you will regret it for the rest of your life. I can tell that."

Chapter Twenty-Six

The church service dragged on, as usual. Augusta felt entirely drained after last night's activities. The spectacular Christmas tree, which greeted them all first thing in the morning, only served as a painful reminder.

She kept seeing Silas' face whenever she closed her eyes, grinning and laughing, tossing the coin into the air for the privilege of placing the star on the tree. She was suspicious of her easy win. Had he let her win? Nobody else saw the results of the coin toss. She kept seeing the expression on his face as he looked up at her, his smile fading away and replaced by something softer and more intimate. Augusta swallowed hard, trying for the hundredth time to wrest her attention away from Silas and back to the sermon. It didn't help that the Vicar had a famously dull, monotonous voice. Quite a few of his congregation were smothering yawns.

Also, the Radfords' pew was almost directly opposite the Mitchells', which meant that Augusta and Silas were virtually face to face. He kept averting his gaze. Whenever she glanced his way, Augusta never caught him looking directly at her.

What was worse, Augusta was sandwiched between Lady Firnsdale and Ambrose. Ambrose didn't appear to be listening to the sermon. Instead, he sat like a stone, staring into space. Lady Firnsdale was listening intently, leaning forward so as not to miss a single syllable. Whenever Augusta shifted in the slightest, Lady Firnsdale glowered at her and dug a pointed elbow into her ribs.

Augusta was considering throttling the old lady.

It was a relief when the sermon came to an end. Augusta was all for racing right out of the church and into the carriage, but of course, that didn't happen. Everyone—including the Vicar—wanted to greet the Duke and Duchess, and of course, sweet Lady Augusta and her new fiancé. Everyone queued up to bow and curtsey and shake hands, exchanging pleasantries which all blurred together into one incoherent hum to Augusta.

She felt oddly dizzy and reached out to steady herself on Ambrose's arm.

Ambrose was not there.

Augusta turned to find her fiancé a little way away, arm in arm with his mother, leaning down to escort her out of the church. Augusta felt a little silly. She gripped the front of the pew and closed her eyes, willing the world to stop spinning. Was it an oncoming megrim? Had she eaten too much, drunk too much last night? Augusta breathed in deeply, willing herself not to faint in front of the whole village. She felt sick and hemmed in by all the people.

What was wrong with her? It couldn't be anxiety over her engagement. No, she'd decided once and for all Ambrose was the man for her. She was decided on that.

A firm hand appeared at her elbow, steadying Augusta just in the nick of time. Her eyes flew open, and she found herself looking directly at Silas.

"Silas," Augusta gasped, unable to help herself. "I didn't see you there."

Silas eyed her, clearly concerned. "Are you all right, Augusta? You seem unwell."

"I'm fine. Just tired. I didn't eat much at breakfast, which Mama will no doubt blame for this whole episode. I'd be obliged if you didn't tell her."

Silas nodded slowly. "Far be it from me to deny anything to a lady. I'm glad to see you today, Augusta. Eliza and Colin have been raving about the Radford Christmas ball all day. They can't wait. This will be the first time they've attended, of course. They were too young when I left for the Americas, and I don't believe you've had it since, is that right?"

Augusta smiled weakly. She didn't remember much about the Christmases that had followed Silas' departure. They had lost their appeal after that.

"Yes, I think so. We're terribly excited, too. Everything is ready."

Silas nodded, pausing. He clearly had something else to say, so Augusta waited patiently.

"Do you plan on dancing tonight, Augusta?"

"Yes, of course."

"Well, would you mind saving one of your sets for me?"

A lump formed in Augusta's throat. She fought to keep her

169

voice steady and smiled up at him.

"Of course. I'd love to dance with you, Silas."

Silas smiled, and the world seemed to screech to a halt.

Then, the Duchess appeared in Augusta's line of vision, saying something about leaving, and the moment was gone.

Silas was quickly swallowed up by the congregation, and Augusta was escorted out to the carriages. Ambrose had appeared at her side, tight-lipped. She wondered absently why he was annoyed now. She couldn't quite bring herself to care.

Augusta, Ambrose and Lady Firnsdale climbed into Ambrose's carriage, and the Duke, Duchess, Timothy and Caroline climbed into the second. Perhaps if Augusta's head hadn't been so full of Silas, she would have noticed immediately that something was wrong. As it was, they travelled for a few minutes in silence before she began to realise there was a tense atmosphere in the carriage.

"You and Mr Silas Mitchell seem very friendly, Augusta," Ambrose said tautly.

Augusta blinked. "I beg your pardon?"

"Mother told me about how you laughed and joked with him last night. I don't find it proper, Augusta."

Colour rushed into Augusta's cheeks. "Are you accusing me of something, Ambrose?"

"No woman ought to take that tone with her fiancé," Lady Firnsdale chipped in. Augusta ignored her.

"Ambrose, Silas and I have been friends since we were small children. That is all there is to it. There was nothing improper in our behaviour, and if there was, I'm sure someone would have brought it to my attention."

Ambrose pursed his lips. "I am not happy about you being on such good terms with Mr Mitchell, Augusta."

"Well, it's not as if I'll see him very much after we are married," Augusta pointed out, her own words sinking like a dagger into her heart. "Except for Christmastide, of course."

"No, you certainly will not. And we shall spend Christmastide in London after we are married, Augusta."

Augusta pressed her lips together tightly in case she said something she might regret.

Or perhaps she would regret not saying it.

There was no time to collect her thoughts, however, as the carriage pulled in at the Radford home only a few minutes later. Augusta climbed out of the carriage and went inside, without stopping to wait for Ambrose and his mother. She was too angry for words.

***

"Goodness, Augusta, not dressed yet? The guests will be arriving soon enough," the Duchess said gently, peering around Augusta's bedroom door. "Have you and Ambrose had a squabble? He had a face like thunder when he came inside, and you stalked up here to your room."

Augusta, sitting at her dresser, eyed her mother through the mirror. "I'm not a child, Mama. And I don't like Ambrose dictating who my friends should be. Papa never told you who you could and could not be friends with."

The Duchess came inside, closing the door. She held a neat, silk box in one hand, half hidden behind her back.

"Perhaps Ambrose is afraid of losing you. Once you're married, things will change, I'm sure."

Augusta bit her lip. "But what if they don't?"

The Duchess came closer, looking troubled. "Has something happened, Darling? You can tell me."

Augusta swallowed hard. "No, of course not."

"Are you having second thoughts?"

She shook her head irritably. "No."

Augusta knew she had to put Silas Mitchell behind her. She'd never be happy otherwise. Perhaps that was why she was picking faults in Ambrose's behaviour; she was almost looking for an excuse to back out.

Calling off the engagement will achieve nothing. You'll just be right back where you were before—single, with no prospects.

"Oh, that's good," the Duchess said, with obvious relief. "I am glad, Augusta. You know, I am so proud of you, making this tremendous match. I've been so worried about you—afraid you might never marry, and you'd be sad and alone forever. But then, Ambrose came along, and now, you'll be a countess, and everything will be perfect. I am proud of you."

171

Augusta swallowed hard, wishing she could enjoy the compliment.

"Thank you, Mama," she whispered.

"Now, I almost forgot. I have a present for you."

The Duchess set the silk box beside Augusta on the dresser and stepped back, waiting in anticipation for Augusta to open it.

She opened the box, and drew in a sharp breath, all thoughts of Silas and Ambrose gone.

It was a gold necklace, studded with rubies and diamonds, beautifully polished and set. It would go perfectly with the white-and-red gown Augusta planned to wear that night.

"Oh, Mama!" she gasped. "It's beautiful. Is this Grandmother's necklace?"

The Duchess bent down to kiss Augusta on the temple. "Yes, it is. She gave it to me on my wedding day, just as it was given to her on hers. I was waiting for your wedding day to give it to you. But the other night, I got to thinking. I wondered why I was waiting for your wedding day, as if that will be the greatest achievement of your life. Why hadn't I given it to you when you learned Greek and Latin, or the day you played the pianoforte so beautifully it made me and your Papa cry. Or even when you were a little girl and overheard me saying how much I wanted blackberries, so you and Silas went foraging in the woods to fetch them, even though you came home all scratched. So, I decided I ought not to wait for you to marry Ambrose to have the necklace. It's yours now, and whenever you wear it, so you will know how proud I am of you, always, no matter what else you choose to do with your life. Call it a late Christmas present."

Tears were pricking at Augusta's eyes, and she turned to smile up at her mother.

"It's hardly a late Christmas present. It's still Christmas Day."

The Duchess chuckled. "Yes, but at this rate, it'll be New Year before you get dressed and come downstairs. Now, hurry up! I can't wait to see you wearing the necklace."

Augusta ran a fingertip over the sparkling jewels and found the lump that had formed in her throat made it hard to breathe.

"It's beautiful, Mama," she said, close to tears. "Thank you for giving this to me. It means so much."

The Duchess pulled her daughter close in a hug. "Consider it a reminder to always be yourself, Augusta. No matter what happens."

Chapter Twenty-Seven

Everyone remarked on how beautiful Augusta looked. She replied to the compliments with the proper grace, but they soon became meaningless. Beauty was nice, but it didn't really mean anything. Beauty, as the Duchess often said, was just good luck and a good seamstress.

Ambrose appeared beside her, dutifully offering his arm, and they made their way through the crowds.

"You look very pretty tonight, Augusta," Ambrose whispered, leaning back to gauge the effect of his compliment.

"Thank you," Augusta answered distantly, and Ambrose frowned.

"Thank you? Is that all? Come, Augusta, vanity doesn't suit you. Come, let's sit by Mother."

Colour rushed to Augusta's cheeks, and she allowed herself to be reluctantly steered towards the matrons' chairs, where Lady Firnsdale held court in the centre. The woman eyed Augusta with open dislike as they approached.

"We'll dance the first set together," Ambrose said, almost as an afterthought, settling Augusta into a seat. He sat beside her, leaving Augusta sandwiched between him and his mother once again.

Augusta did not want to sit down. Her legs itched to dance, but the dancing hadn't yet begun. She wanted to walk through the crowd, greeting friends and family members. She didn't want to sit there like a nervous debutante or a bored old chaperone.

But Ambrose had settled himself down, with no hint of getting up again, so Augusta had a feeling she would be stuck there for a while, unless she was rescued. Silence dragged on, and Augusta began to worry that they'd just sit there all night, with her bored stiff.

Suddenly, Lady Firnsdale leaned forward, addressing both Augusta and Ambrose.

"Don't forget, no more than two dances. It'll be improper otherwise," she said, glaring at Augusta.

Augusta sighed. "Do you mean no more than two dances with Ambrose, Lady Firnsdale? I am well aware of the rules."

Ambrose frowned. "Who else will you be dancing with, Augusta?" his brow cleared. "Ah, yes of course." he continued, answering his own question. "Your father, and Lord Avilwood, naturally."

Augusta bit her lip. Now was probably not the time to mention she intended to dance the second set with Silas.

As if she'd read Augusta's thoughts, Lady Firnsdale snatched the dance card from Augusta's wrist. She read quickly, frowning.

"I see Mr Silas Mitchell is dancing a set with you," Lady Firnsdale said, meeting her son's eyes. "Of course, you can't do anything about that now, but I must say, Augusta, I am surprised at you. It is hardly proper."

Augusta set her jaw. "I'm sorry, Lady Firnsdale, but I really don't see how it's any business of yours."

Lady Firnsdale sucked in a breath, and Ambrose's expression hardened.

"Please don't talk to my mother like that, Augusta."

"Yes, but Ambrose—"

With impeccable timing, the orchestra struck up the introduction to the first dance. There was a general murmur of excitement, and couples hurried towards the dance floor. Ambrose took Augusta's hand, towing her through the crowd to take up their positions. As it was the Radfords' ball and Augusta was their daughter, the dancing would not begin until she was on the floor and ready to dance.

Augusta did not want to dance.

"I don't mean to be impolite," Augusta murmured, "but Lady Firnsdale is rather overstepping the boundaries."

"I have no idea what you mean, Augusta," Ambrose said, a fixed smile on his face.

"Did you know that Lady Firnsdale, via her maid, told Betsey—my maid—that she wouldn't be allowed to come with me when I was married?"

"What of it?" Ambrose retorted with such complacency, it took Augusta by surprise.

The dance began, and for a moment or two, Augusta and Ambrose had no leisure to speak. He moved mechanically through the steps, face grim, and stepped on Augusta's hem twice and her feet once.

When they finally were able to speak, Augusta picked up where they had left off.

"What do you mean?" she said, trying her best to stay calm. "Of course, Betsey will come with me after we are married. She's my lady's maid. I shall need her."

"You shall need a lady's maid, certainly," Ambrose countered, "but I'm certain your Betsey is not the best qualified candidate. Mother has thought so for a while, and after seeing the shocking state of your hair last night, I'm inclined to agree."

Augusta almost stopped dead in the middle of the set. Only muscle memory kept her going as a flame of fury lit inside her.

"I am not leaving Betsey at home," she insisted.

Ambrose pressed his lips together. "We'll get you another maid, Augusta. A proper lady's maid. Mother can find one for you."

"I want Betsey."

"Betsey is not a suitable lady's maid for a countess. I'm sorry, Augusta, but there's an end to it. I daresay you won't miss her too much."

Augusta swallowed down another surge of rage.

"Ambrose, I absolutely cannot countenance—"

"Don't make a scene," he said quickly. "We'll discuss this later."

They wouldn't discuss it later. Augusta knew that with absolute certainty. They wouldn't discuss it later, and Ambrose wouldn't budge on the subject of Betsey. Augusta felt strangely numb, as if she wasn't the one controlling her own body through the dance.

Was it a premonition about her marriage, perhaps, suggesting she wouldn't be able to control her life as Ambrose's wife?

"Ambrose, I really can't let this go. Betsey is important to me, and I simply can't leave her when I move away. You must understand."

"No, you must understand," Ambrose snapped, his voice low and menacing. "You are going to be a countess, Augusta. Perhaps you're used to being allowed to run wild, indulged and petted by your parents. Oh, yes, I've heard the stories of your childhood—

climbing trees, snowball fights, sledding, fighting and tossing coins over who gets to place a star on top of the Christmas tree—but all that must end when we are married. I've indulged and obliged you through our courtship, but it's time to grow up now. Do you think I'll allow my wife to go sledding, or dance with another man, even if he is supposedly a childhood friend, or wear her hair down in such a shocking manner, as you did last night? I won't, Augusta. I thought you were more composed and genteel that that. I'm frankly shocked."

Augusta struggled to gather her thoughts, and took a deep breath before speaking. "Ambrose, I don't believe what I'm asking is too much."

"Well, I have said no, so there's an end to it. I hope you'll show more respect to my mother when we are married, too. There is much you can learn from a woman like my mother."

Augusta didn't dare speak in case she ended up shouting. The familiar rage bubbled up inside her, and this time, her famous composure and unruffled exterior struggled to keep it back. She pressed her lips together and concentrated on the steps of the dance, glad to have something to keep her mind off the conflict raging between them.

Ambrose looked annoyed, but also rather smug, she thought. No doubt he thought he'd won the argument. Augusta didn't imagine they would discuss it later. He evidently thought it was settled and would be angry if she mentioned the subject again. Misery flooded through her.

I can't live like this! What am I going to do?

No answers presented themselves. Other dancers swirled past, all chatter and laughter and flowing, colourful gowns. Augusta felt oddly disconnected, as if she were the only one dancing on an empty dance floor. She wasn't used to feeling so numb—she had always prided herself on being a staid, practical person—someone who always had their feet planted firmly on the ground.

At that moment, her feet in her thin dancing slippers were tripping over the floor, as light as air, as if she could be swept up and away at any moment by a stiff breeze. It was the strangest feeling. Augusta didn't like it. To be swept away was to be out of control, or rather, controlled by someone else. Someone who did not have her best interests at heart.

For the first time, Augusta wondered whether Ambrose had hidden motivations behind his marriage proposal. Augusta had accepted him because she thought she would not find anyone else, because she didn't care about love with Silas gone, and because she thought marrying Ambrose would make her parents happy and proud.

Why did Ambrose propose to me?

The dance ended, and Augusta felt an incredible surge of relief. Ambrose bowed as custom demanded, but his face was stony. Lady Firnsdale pushed through the happy couples towards them, mouth set in a thin, wrinkled line.

"I have a megrim, Ambrose," she announced. "I should like to retire. Augusta, smile, for heaven's sake. Nobody wants to see a sour-faced lady."

Biting back a retort to that prize piece of hypocrisy, Augusta did not smile. Lady Firnsdale sniffed, as if smelling sour milk, and turned back to her son.

"Take me to my room, Ambrose."

Ambrose was suddenly all concern. "Of course, Mother. Augusta, would you like to retire with us? We can play cards or read in the drawing room."

"No, thank you," Augusta replied, her voice brittle. "I'll stay down here."

That was clearly not the answer Ambrose wanted to hear, but it didn't seem much of a surprise to him either. He nodded curtly and offered his arm to his mother. The two of them disappeared through the crowd, and Augusta stood where she was, watching them go.

"Penny for your thoughts?" a deep, familiar voice asked at her shoulder, and Augusta jumped. She glanced up to see Silas, and a shocking feeling of happiness and relief washed through her. She couldn't remember ever being so glad to see him.

"Oh, it's you, Silas! I . . . I was miles away."

"Where are Lord and Lady Firnsdale going?" Silas asked.

"They're retiring for the night. Lady Firnsdale has a megrim. She often has megrims when there's something she doesn't want to do." Augusta bit her lip, a little shocked at her own boldness, but Silas only chuckled.

"I see you are not Lady Firnsdale's greatest friend. I don't blame you. I don't think the woman has any friends."

Augusta laughed in relief. "I think Ambrose loves her, but that is all."

"Hm. Well, did you enjoy the first set? I think I saw Lord Firnsdale treading on your feet at least once."

Augusta grimaced. "Yes, I regret wearing such light dancing slippers. My toes are rather sore."

"Well, I can promise you I won't tread on your feet." Silas smiled down at her, extending his hand. "Are you ready for our set?"

Suddenly breathless, Augusta realised the orchestra was already starting up for the second dance, and couples were taking their places. She placed her hand in Silas's before she even knew what she was doing.

"Of course, I'm ready."

Chapter Twenty-Eight

Silas couldn't quite believe he was dancing with Augusta. Had they ever really danced together? When he had left for the Americas, Augusta hadn't been out, and he hadn't been much interested in dancing at balls and parties anyway.

No, Silas was quite sure this was their first dance together.

It was thrilling.

He'd stood up for the first set with Eliza, who was very keen to dance, and they'd been reasonably close to Ambrose and Augusta for Silas to observe them covertly. The pair had been talking earnestly, but hadn't seemed happy at all. Of course, Silas hadn't been close enough to hear what they'd said, but their hard expressions had told him it was likely not very pleasant. Augusta's face had been set and angry and Ambrose white-faced and grim. On top of that, Lord Firnsdale had appeared to be merely going through the motions of the dance. In fact, he had seemed to be somewhere else entirely, and Silas couldn't help but wonder why.

Augusta was clearly rattled. She was pale and kept chewing her lip, a habit she'd had as a child whenever she was upset about something. She'd chew and chew on her lip when she was troubled. The Duchess had scolded her for it numerous times, warning her that she'd make her lip bleed or end up with unsightly scars if she didn't stop. He hadn't seen Augusta do it since he'd returned home, so he hadn't thought about it. But now, he remembered it clearly. Why was she so upset?

Their dance had been announced as a waltz, which he found unusually exciting. He was relieved he'd practised his dancing while in the Americas. He'd been very keen to impress Augusta with what dancing skills he had if he ever had the chance to partner her, though it had seemed unlikely.

"Is everything all right?" Silas murmured in the breathless moments before the dance started in earnest. "You seem upset."

Augusta glanced up at him, as if she were poised to say something. "I . . . I don't think I can discuss it with you, Silas," she said eventually, frowning prettily.

Silas nodded. "I understand. I won't press you—though I'm no gossip. But I want you to know, Augusta, if you need to talk to a friend, I will always be here ."

"Do you think it's improper for an engaged or married lady to have male friends?" Augusta asked suddenly. "I know a single lady might struggle to be friends with a gentleman—people assume certain things, of course, and the gentleman himself might form expectations. But if she's engaged, or married . . ."

Silas frowned. "Only a horribly jealous man would care about such a thing. Surely, a man secure in his wife or fiancée's love wouldn't worry about her being stolen away by another man? I personally think that a woman who can be lured away by another man is not really worth having."

"That's what I think too. I just—" Augusta broke off. "I've been thinking more deeply about things lately. I've had cause to mistrust my own judgement."

Silas leaned down, dropping his voice so they couldn't be overheard.

"From what I know of you, Augusta, it would be a mistake to mistrust your own judgement. I would sooner trust your opinion over my own. That is how much faith I have in you."

Augusta's eyes flicked back up to his face, wide and surprised. She opened her mouth to speak, but at that moment, the music started in earnest, and the dance began.

Holding Augusta in his arms was such a strange, unreal experience, Silas wasn't entirely sure it wasn't all a dream—that he'd wake up in his own bed, and it would be Christmas Day morning all over again.

They said nothing further during their dance, but Silas noticed Augusta had a strange expression on her face the whole time. She seemed miserable and elated all at once. Something was happening between them, some magnetic force pulling them together. Silas felt almost silly for not having felt it before. Did Augusta feel it too? He couldn't tell.

Even if she did feel something towards him, it didn't mean anything, he told himself. Ladies prioritised a good marriage over love any day, and Augusta had always been an intelligent woman, praised for her good sense. Why *shouldn't* she choose Ambrose Finch, Earl of Firnsdale, over plain old Mr Silas Mitchell?

It made perfect sense.

The dance was almost over, and Silas felt an odd wrenching inside him, faced with the prospect of letting Augusta go. Then, the music screeched to a halt, and there were general murmurings of confusion. The dancers faltered and stopped, glancing around. Silas spotted a beaming Duchess standing on a small dais by the orchestra.

"I'm sorry to interrupt all you happy dancers," she declared, immediately attracting everyone's attention. "But I have something interesting to point out. Some of you may have noticed kissing-boughs hanging from the ceiling. If you all stay exactly where you are and glance upwards, some lucky couples may find that they are directly below a kissing-bough. If so, well . . . you all know what to do."

There was an explosion of laughter and chatter, and each couple glanced up. Silas saw Eliza and Colin nearby, laughing at the kissing bough dangling above their heads. Colin tried to squirm away, but Eliza swung an arm around his neck planted a kiss on her younger brother's cheek, cackling as she did so, much to the amusement of everyone around them.

He saw an older couple, both grey-haired, looking up at the kissing-bough and then at each other. They smiled fondly, the lady reaching up to cup her husband's cheek. The gentleman leaned down to press a soft kiss to his wife's lips.

An engaged couple, holding hands, blushing madly, leaned tentatively towards each other, exchanging an affectionate peck. Couples with no kissing-bough above their heads laughed and cursed their luck. There was a round of applause for every kiss.

Silas swallowed hard, looking up.

Sure enough, a kissing-bough hung directly above them, gold and silver silk shapes and paper chains hanging from it and twinkling in the light. He glanced down, and caught Augusta staring up at him, her expression unreadable.

"Well," she suddenly said. "Would you look at that?"

"Just our luck, eh?" Silas said, laughing self-consciously.

Augusta paused, glancing to the side. "Well, it wouldn't be the first time you've kissed me under a kissing-bough, would it?"

182

There was a silence. Silas swallowed hard, trying to speak.

"You . . . you remember that?"

Augusta smiled wryly. "Of course, I remember. That was my first kiss. It's bound to be memorable."

Silas cleared his throat. "You don't seem angry about it."

She frowned. "Why should be angry? It was just a kiss. That's what people do under kissing-boughs."

"Yes, but . . . well, I thought you didn't want to kiss me."

"I was shy. That's not the same thing."

Silas reeled a little. Was Augusta telling him that she'd *wanted* him to kiss her back then? She'd been shy, she said, but not angry at all, as he'd believed for so long. His heart soared. He hadn't ruined everything!

"I thought you were angry with me for it," Silas managed. "I thought I shouldn't have done it, that I'd ruined our friendship."

Augusta frowned, shaking her head. "No, not at all. I was only young, Silas. I didn't know how to respond. When I finally came out to talk to you again, you'd gone. And then, of course, the next thing I knew, you'd gone to the Americas."

A flash of red-hot guilt and regret washed through Silas.

"Oh, Augusta. I'm so sorry."

"You don't have to apologise," Augusta said quickly. "I was angry at you, but for leaving. I won't deny it. But you had always wanted to travel, I knew that too. Studying in the Americas—it must have been a dream come true. I just wish you hadn't left thinking I was angry at you."

Silas felt dizzy all of a sudden. He was vaguely aware that he was holding Augusta's hands in both of his and wondered how they'd gotten there. Had she put her hands in his, or the other way around?

"Well, now I know the truth, I'll always treasure our kiss," Silas found himself saying. Augusta's eyes widened and took a step forward.

"You will?"

"Of course. You were—*are*— my dearest friend. I worried for so long that I'd upset you, that I'd ruined everything. Knowing that I didn't . . . well, it reassures me more than you could imagine."

Had the world stopped around them? Silas felt as if they'd been standing there, in the middle of the ballroom, forever, but also for only a few seconds. They might as well have been the only people in the room.

"Silas, I—" Augusta broke off abruptly. She kept glancing up at the kissing-bough above their head, and he noticed she was chewing her lip again. Silas longed to lean forward and press his lips to hers once more. What would it be like? His memories of their first kiss were coloured by his own embarrassment and worry. He remembered Augusta's face as she'd looked up at him, and the sight of her retreating back as she'd run away with more clarity than he did the kiss itself.

But I can't....

I mustn't...

Silas took a step backwards, bowing neatly and pressing Augusta's hand to his lips.

It would have to do for now.

"I can't kiss you, Augusta," Silas said finally, unable to believe the words coming out of his own mouth. Hadn't he dreamed of this for years? Ever since he'd been old enough to realise he was in love with Lady Augusta Radford, he'd dreamt of kissing her.

Not like this, though.

Silas straightened from his bow, unable to look Augusta in the eyes. He didn't know what he would see there. Relief? Disappointment? Misery? He wasn't about to risk it. Not now he'd finally realised what he needed to do. It was going to be painful enough without that.

"Why not?" Augusta said, trying—and clearly failing—to keep her voice light.

"Because this is a moment you ought to be sharing with your fiancé." Silas said, forcing a smile. "I stole one kiss from you once, and that will have to be enough. I have no intention of stealing anything else from you. I'll keep your friendship and my memories, though. If you don't mind."

Silas looked away, not trusting himself to hear Augusta's response. He escorted her to the edge of the floor without another word. There, he left her, not looking back. He simply couldn't.

Chapter Twenty-Nine

Augusta felt as though she couldn't breathe. She watched Silas disappear into the crowd, until he was entirely swallowed up.

Gone. Gone. Gone forever!

Augusta felt a little dizzy. She wasn't sure if she was going to faint or be sick. Both, perhaps.

Of course, that was not the Lady Augusta Radford way. No, she wasn't about to swoon like a damsel in distress. Augusta glanced around, and she caught her mother looking at her, her face creased into a worried frown. The Duchess mouthed something at her, but Augusta didn't have the time or energy to work out what it was.

I have to find Silas.

No—there is something I must do first.

Augusta hurried off the dance floor, ignoring the curious looks thrown her way. She thought she heard her mother call after her, but she didn't stop. She shouldered her way through the crowds, ignoring the puzzled glances of others.

It was a relief to burst out of the crowded ballroom and into the quieter, cooler hallway. There were a few footmen on duty, and one or two older ladies fanning themselves, taking a break from the crush of the ballroom. Augusta was free to hurry through the hallways, heart pounding. She was looking for the drawing room.

The drawing room was usually off-limits during such a large party. For smaller supper parties and more informal gatherings, the ladies would usually retire to the drawing room after dinner, leaving the gentlemen to their port and brandy. However, since most people were crowded into the ballroom and hall, there was no need to open up the drawing room for general use.

Guests and family, of course, were free to enter. And that was where Ambrose and Lady Firnsdale had been heading when they had departed.

Augusta hardly knew what she was doing. Was she making a

mistake? Maybe. But Augusta knew without a doubt that marrying Ambrose would be the biggest mistake she could possibly make. Even if she wasn't wrong about him and he really was a kind, caring gentleman, Augusta couldn't possibly condemn the man to a loveless life. She didn't love Ambrose. She would never love Ambrose. He deserved to know the truth and have an opportunity to find a true love of his own.

Augusta still didn't know what she was going to tell him.

Ambrose, I'm sorry, but I can't marry you.

We ought to break our engagement off, Ambrose. Yes, I'm sure.

Now, I know I'm leaving this a little late, Ambrose, but I don't think we should get married after all.

Augusta sighed internally. She would just have to hope she could find the right words somewhere along the way. Perhaps Ambrose would understand.

She turned a corner and saw the drawing room door ahead of her; it stood ajar, a sliver of light spilling out into the darkened hallway. Augusta slowed down, trying to think about what she would say—the truth, of course, but there was no need to be entirely tactless. That was when she heard low voices coming from inside. Augusta heard her name being spoken, and she slowed even further, pausing by the door to listen covertly.

". . . I don't like Lady Augusta any more than you do, Ambrose, but let's stay focused here," Lady Firnsdale was saying. Her voice was strong and forceful, not at all what you'd expect to hear from someone with a megrim.

"She's a spoiled brat," Ambrose snapped, in a harsher voice than Augusta had ever heard him use before. She recoiled automatically, shocked. Ambrose thought she was spoiled?

"Oh, for goodness' sake, Ambrose. You were doing so well, why give up now?"

"I'm not giving up, Mother."

"Oh, really? Why kick up so much of a fuss about the girl's hair? If she wants to look like a slattern, let her! And that wretched maid. Why not just say she can keep her maid and then change your mind after the wedding? There's not much she can do then."

Ambrose growled. "May I remind you that you were the one who started all of that? You told the maid she wasn't going to come with us after the marriage."

"Yes, that was a mistake, I'll grant you. I didn't think the wench would go running to her mistress to tell tales. I'm telling you, Ambrose, you need to fix this, and quickly. Just play the loving fiancé for a little while longer, until you get a ring on the girl's finger. Then, all our problems will be over."

Augusta felt as though her throat was closing up. She shuffled closer, leaning forward to listen, holding her breath.

"Mother, I am tired of pandering to her. She's so dull. It's only when that wretched Silas Mitchell turns up that she shows a spark of spirit."

"May I remind you that these are your debts we need to pay off? I'm not the gambler here."

"No, but you spend a fortune on jewels and clothes."

"That's not the same," Lady Firnsdale said with a sniff. "Just go back and make up with the girl. Her parents look on you favourably already, and we're so close, Ambrose. Just a little longer, and all of our financial problems will be over."

Augusta pressed a hand over her mouth, backing away. She'd heard enough. Turning to run, Augusta collided with a small table, and the crystal vase resting on it went crashing to the ground.

Smash!

Augusta didn't dare hope that the occupants of the room hadn't heard. She turned to run, but the door behind her was yanked open, and Ambrose appeared. There was a long, horrified moment when their eyes met, and then, his face broke into an unpleasant smile.

"Ah, Augusta. I must say, eavesdropping is not very ladylike."

Augusta swallowed hard, lifting her chin. "Excuse me."

She turned to leave, but an iron grip suddenly closed around her wrist, hard enough to make Augusta cry out in pain.

"Let go of me!" she hissed. Ambrose hauled her backwards, slamming her into the wall. The impact knocked the wind out of Augusta's body, and she gasped for breath. She glanced around frantically for help, but the hallway was deserted. Virtually all of the servants were busy with the ball. Augusta could hear the distant clamour of music and conversation, but she knew nobody would hear her here, not even if she screamed.

Ambrose bent down so they were nose to nose, grabbing both of her wrists and pinning them against the wall. It hurt, but Augusta wasn't about to give him the satisfaction of wincing.

"Let go of me," Augusta repeated, teeth gritted. "I won't tell you again."

Ambrose smiled thinly. "No, you won't tell me again. In fact, you'll never speak to me like that again, I can promise you that."

"Our engagement is over, Ambrose."

"That's where you're wrong, my dear. You see, I've worked too hard and come too far to see it all slip away."

"You were only ever interested in me for my money," Augusta spat, disgusted and feeling like the world's greatest fool. "To pay off your gambling debts."

"Aren't you clever? Isn't she, Mother?"

Augusta glanced to the side and saw Lady Firnsdale standing in the doorway of the drawing room. She had a sneer of contempt on her face. There'd be no help from that quarter. Augusta tried to wriggle free, but Ambrose only shoved her back against the wall again, tightening his grip on her wrists painfully.

"You cannot treat me this way," Augusta protested, trying to hide the fear and desperation in her voice. She realised—too late, it seemed—that she had no idea who Ambrose Finch really was. "What exactly are you hoping to achieve by this?"

"The thing is, Lady Augusta, our engagement must go ahead. We have to marry if I am to have your money, and I'm not about to let you ruin everything. I don't care what I have to do to you, but we are walking down the aisle together. If you mind your manners and do what you're told, no doubt we'll have a decent enough marriage. Let's start with—"

"How about you start by letting my daughter go?"

A deep voice boomed out down the hallway. Ambrose sucked in a breath, eyes widening at the sound of the Duke's voice. He instantly released Augusta and sprang away from her.

Augusta should have gone straight to her father's side. But the anger churning inside her was too much, and it came bubbling up and burst through her usually composed exterior like lava from a volcano. She swung her right palm, and there was a satisfying *slap* as her palm connected with Ambrose's cheek.

He cried out sharply, stumbling back, his hand pressed to the vivid red mark blooming on his cheek, while Augusta raced over to stand behind her father. There were a couple of footmen heading their way now, their faces grim. She glanced up at the Duke and was a little shocked at the expression of fury on his face.

"Your Grace, we can explain—" Lady Firnsdale began smoothly.

"No, I don't believe you can," the Duke interrupted. "Debts, you say, Ambrose? Well, I'm afraid you won't be paying those off with my daughter's dowry, as the engagement is over."

"She can't jilt me . . ." Ambrose mumbled nasally, rubbing his cheek, flinching when the Duke took a step towards him.

"Get out of my house, you reprobate," the Duke hissed. "If my wife hadn't told me that Augusta seemed upset about something and asked me to follow her— well, I dread to think what would have happened, and in my own house too! One more word from you, you blackguard, and I will take action. Every door in Polite

Society will be closed to you forthwith. I will be informing your creditors of this outrageous behaviour too, and you will be stripped of everything you own. Is that clear?"

Ambrose nodded vigorously.

"Good. Now, get out of my house. You and your wretched, unpleasant mother had better be gone within the hour. My footmen will help you pack." He glanced back at the footmen standing behind them, adding, "Make sure they don't steal anything."

The colour drained from Lady Firnsdale's face.

"But, Your Grace, we have nowhere to go! Besides, it's almost midnight! Surely, one more night—"

"Another word from you and you will be thrown out of my house, and your baggage thrown after you," the Duke snapped. "May I suggest an inn?"

He turned on his heel, Augusta's hand in his, and led her away down the hallway.

"I'm so glad you were there, Papa," Augusta said, feeling badly shaken after her ordeal. The Duke's arm tightened around her shoulder.

"So am I, Darling. So am I."

Chapter Thirty

26th December, Boxing Day

The party was over. Augusta had stayed in the ballroom until late, more to make sure she would avoid seeing Ambrose and his awful mother than anything else. To her disappointment, Silas had already left, apparently claiming tiredness. The footmen and butler confirmed that Lord and Lady Firnsdale had left to seek an inn, and the door had been closed firmly behind them.

That was a relief, but Augusta knew her troubles were not over. She felt like a prize fool. Oh, she knew that cleverer women than her had fallen victim to fortune-hunters, but that didn't really make her feel any better. What might have happened if her father hadn't come along to save her? Or, perish the thought, what if she'd never overheard Ambrose and his mother talking? She would have gone on to marry Ambrose, not discovering his true nature until she was his wife.

Then, it would have been too late, of course. That was the worst thought of all.

Augusta shivered, trying to concentrate on her book. The days after Christmas Eve and Christmas Day always felt strangely hollow. The parties were over, the presents all opened, the festivities wrapped up for another year. The kissing-boughs had been taken down from where they hung above the dance floor and lay scattered all over the drawing-room table. They were still fresh but would soon start to wilt. They couldn't be saved until next year, but the silk shapes and ornaments could. It was Augusta's job to strip the kissing-boughs of their ornaments, but she couldn't bring herself to do it just yet. On her lips, Augusta could still feel the phantom tingle of a kiss she'd never received, and still remembered the haunted expression on Silas' face when he'd turned away.

She'd tried to write him a letter, but couldn't get beyond "Dear Silas". At least half a dozen wasted, crumpled pieces of paper lay scattered around her writing-desk. Eventually, Augusta had given up.

Silas had walked away from her. Shouldn't she respect that? She had been going to marry another man. How could she have expected him to give her a second chance? It hadn't been fair.

Fair did not seem to come into matters of the heart, however. Augusta's heart still ached, longing for something, or someone, she was quite sure she would never have.

Of course, it was all over with Ambrose. The news wouldn't have reached the gossips yet, not unless Ambrose or his awful mother had told them. So far, Augusta had only told her parents. And Timothy and Caroline, of course. Timothy had raged and had to be restrained from charging out into the night and challenging Ambrose to a duel.

Caroline had sat up with Augusta late into the night in the drawing room. She hadn't said anything—no, "Anyone could have fallen victim to a man like that", or "I never liked him", or even "You're better off without him". Her silence was comforting, and Augusta felt herself drawing closer to her sister-in-law than ever.

She knew the Duke and Duchess had been shaken by events. After all, they'd liked Ambrose and had heartily endorsed his request to marry their only daughter. The Duchess had murmured something about letting Augusta down which had almost broken Augusta's heart. As if any of it was their fault!

By the time Ambrose and his mother were ejected from the house, all of Augusta's family knew about the broken engagement. It was difficult for them to keep smiles on their faces and carry on with the party as if nothing was wrong, but it had been necessary to keep up the pretence. Nobody could know yet. A jilted fiancé and a broken engagement—especially so close to the marriage date—would always thrill the gossips. A woman never came away without injury to her reputation when it came to broken engagements. It didn't matter how awful her would-be fiancé was, somehow, it was always her fault. Augusta was sure Ambrose would put on an injured, long-suffering face to the world. She would be subject to censure, disapproval, and plenty of gossip.

She could weather the storm, she knew she could, especially with her parents and Timothy and Caroline backing her up. The Mitchells would side with her, she was certain, and that went a long way to helping her feel better.

Still, she wasn't quite ready to open herself up to all the gossip just yet. She would wait for a while, until everything settled down and she felt more equal to dealing with it. A few days, perhaps. A few weeks if possible.

No, not a few weeks. Augusta's heart sank at the thought of all the wedding preparations that would have to be undone. It would be a difficult month or two.

The drawing room door opened, and Augusta glanced up. The butler hovered in the doorway, looking uncertain.

"Lady Augusta, you have a visitor. I'm not sure you will wish to receive them, and Their Graces are not available."

"Who is it?"

Her question was answered by a dishevelled, red-faced Silas pushing past the butler.

"Sir! I requested that you wait in the hall!" the butler said, clearly offended by the trespass.

"It's quite all right, Bennet, thank you," Augusta managed, rising to her feet. "I am happy to have an audience with Mr Mitchell."

The butler pressed his lips together, bowed and obediently retreated.

That left Augusta and Silas standing facing each other, quite an improper situation, to be sure, and silence descended.

"Hello, Silas," Augusta said, her voice quiet.

"Hello, Augusta. Merry Christmas, by the way. I forgot to say that yesterday."

Augusta smiled weakly. "Thank you. Would you like me to ring for tea?"

"It was going to be your Christmas present," Silas suddenly blurted out.

Augusta frowned. Christmas present? She hadn't received any present from Silas.

"Christmas present? I don't understand."

Silas groaned, running a hand through his hair and ruining the neat style. "I haven't been able to get you out of my head, Augusta. Not for years. I love you to distraction, and that's the truth of it."

"Silas—"

"I know, I know. You're engaged. I know it, Augusta, and my

Christmas present to you was going to be to let you go. I would stop entertaining hopes, let you go on with your own life. You deserve that, at least. Believe me when I say I only ever wanted your happiness, and I am determined not to be selfish. I won't get in the way of your future."

"Silas, I really—"

"You'll make a magnificent countess," Silas continued doggedly. "But the fact is that I love you, and I can't live with myself if I don't tell you the truth. I would marry you in a heartbeat, Augusta, even though I couldn't offer a fraction of what Lord Firnsdale can. I love you, and I always have. I want you to know that."

Silas finally, finally stopped for breath. He stood, his face distraught, clearly worried about Augusta's response.

She drew in a deep breath.

"I am no longer engaged to Lord Firnsdale."

There was a long silence.

"You . . . you're not?" Silas eventually managed. "My condolences."

She gave a short laugh. "Oh, no condolences necessary. He was a vile fortune hunter, and I've had a lucky escape."

Silas's eye flew wide and his jaw set grimly. "The wretch," he exclaimed, balling his fists.

"Yes, he is a wretch. But Silas, that isn't why I broke off the engagement. At least, I didn't know about the fortune-hunting when I decided I could not marry Ambrose." She took a tentative step towards Silas. Her palms were damp, and her stomach churned with anxiety.

"What was the reason?" Silas asked, breathless.

Augusta gave a tiny smile. "Can't you tell? I'm in love with you, Silas. I have been for the longest time. I was so angry when you left for the Americas, and I was determined to put you behind me. Well, I couldn't. I agreed to marry Ambrose because I thought he was a good man who would give me a comfortable life. I was wrong about that, but even before then, I'd realised I couldn't marry him. I couldn't marry him . . . because he isn't you, Silas."

Silas sucked in a breath.

"You . . . you truly mean it? You . . . you love me, Augusta?"

Augusta laughed. "Of course, I mean it, you fool. Haven't you been paying attention all these years? I don't think I've ever not loved you."

"Not even the time I hit you full in the face with a snowball? Or when I made a mud pie on your clean pinafore?"

Augusta gave a gurgle of laughter. "Well, perhaps not then. But most of the time."

Silas came closer, reaching out to take Augusta's hands. "You must know that our family finances are not good at the moment. I can't offer you a title, or a fortune, or anything like that. You must know that, Augusta. I'm no fortune hunter, but there's no denying our situations are very different."

Augusta wanted to grin like a lunatic. "I have enough money for both of us. Although, I think you'll have to convince Papa somewhat—he might be a little nervous about me getting engaged again so soon."

Silas smiled. "Are you proposing to me, Augusta Radford?"

"I don't know. Are you proposing to me?"

"I don't dare let myself dream you'll say yes. I'm half convinced all this is just a lovely dream."

"Would you like me to pinch you?"

"Surely, no!"

They both burst out laughing, and Silas leaned forward to rest his forehead against Augusta's.

"I love you, Augusta," he murmured. "Would you do me the honour of becoming my wife? I can't offer you much except myself and my heart, but those are both yours forever."

"That will do quite nicely," Augusta whispered. She darted to the side, snatching up a kissing-bough and holding it above their heads. She smiled boldly up at Silas, marvelling at how handsome he was.

And he loved her. He had always loved her.

Silas reached out, cupping Augusta's face in his hands.

"Is that a yes?" he whispered.

Augusta grinned. "Perhaps. We'll see what Papa says first. I can't possibly agree to anything without his permission."

Silas chuckled. He leaned forward slowly . . . and pressed his lips to Augusta's. The kissing-bough was suddenly very heavy, and her arm was aching, so Augusta let it drop the floor, choosing instead to wrap her arms around Silas' neck. They broke apart, breathless and grinning, giggling together, just like they had when they were children.

She was quite sure it was a very different kiss to the one he'd stolen all those years ago. Although, come to think of it, it was nearly impossible to steal what had been so freely, happily given.

Epilogue

One Month Later

It really was a perfect day. Augusta's nerves had been jangling all the previous day, in anticipation of her wedding.

She was getting married! She was getting married, and not to someone she barely knew. It was to Silas, her childhood friend. Augusta glanced at her reflection in her dressing table mirror, and her heart skipped.

If someone had told me a few weeks ago that I would be here today, getting married to Silas, I would have laughed.

Augusta fingered the glossy ruby necklace at her neck and fought back a grin. It felt like a dream. A wonderful dream.

"Well, well, are you awake and ready to go?" the Duchess asked, bustling into Augusta's room. "You look beautiful, Darling. I'm glad you're wearing your grandmother's necklace."

Augusta smiled. "It feels right for the occasion. What time is it?"

"Time for us to leave. Everyone is at the church, and I hear it's packed to the rafters. Where are your bridesmaids?"

"Caroline insisted I have flowers, so she and Eliza went out to gather some. I doubt they'll find much at this time of year."

"Perhaps not," the Duchess acknowledged. "But it's a kind thought."

Augusta was wearing an ivory brocade dress, with a thick shawl to protect her against the January cold. The sky was an idyllic blue and the sun shone, but the air was cold and there was still plenty of snow on the ground. Augusta made last-minute checks to her hair—Betsey had done a tremendous job, as usual—and got up from her seat.

"I suppose it's time to go," Augusta said, nerves jangling again.

They heard footsteps hurrying along the hallway, then the door burst open, and Caroline and Eliza scurried in. They were both breathless and pink-cheeked from the cold, and Caroline's belly was just beginning to swell a little. Eliza clutched a posy of greenery, complete with trailing ivy, holly studded with bright red berries and mistletoe.

"I thought greenery and berries would suit a winter wedding," she gasped, grinning. "Caroline has put some ribbon around the stems so you don't prick yourself when you carry them."

"That's so considerate of you both. Thank you," Augusta said, touched, taking the beautiful bouquet and smiling down at it. "Are you ready to go?"

"Ready to watch you marry my brother? Always," Eliza said, grinning.

She had changed so much over the past month. The new Eliza was more confident, more forward, and entirely better suited to handling the rigours and pitfalls of a London Season. Augusta wondered if she and Silas could accompany Eliza to London. Now the Duke was investing in the Mitchell orchards—he'd been very unhappy that his dear old friend hadn't come first to him to ask for a loan or financial help—things were looking better for everyone. With Silas back, new life was breathed into the business.

She hadn't heard much about Ambrose, except that he'd returned to London and was not doing well. He'd taken to the gambling hells apparently, and was now more openly looking for an heiress. Of course, there had been no takers so far. Reportedly, Lady Firnsdale was talking long and loud about Augusta in the salons and at parties, complaining how the wicked girl had "hurt" her precious son. Nobody cared to listen, not when the truth eventually came out. Augusta was frowned at by some of the older, more staid matrons, but she really didn't care much about it. She was far too busy being happy to care.

It all felt surreal, like a fabulous dream. The sort of dream you didn't ever want to wake up from.

Well, now Augusta didn't have to wake up. She could live the rest of her life with the man she loved and with her family around her. It was so obvious to her now that true love shouldn't have to hurt so much, it shouldn't have to involve so much sacrifice, doubt and misery. Augusta only felt like a fool for not seeing it sooner.

She took one last look around her childhood bedroom—she

and Silas would have a modest house on the border of the Mitchell and Radford estates—and turned to leave for the church. Her new future lay just ahead.

* * *

Snow crunched under Augusta's feet, and nerves twisted in her stomach.

"I feel so nervous, Mama," she murmured. Eliza and Caroline were walking ahead, arm in arm and deep in conversation. "Is that normal?"

"Perfectly," the Duchess assured her. "You're sure about this, aren't you, Darling? No second thoughts? No doubts? Because your Papa and I have thoroughly learned our lessons. We wouldn't want to push you into doing anything you don't want to do."

"It's all right, Mama. I love Silas. This is the right thing for me to do. I'm . . ." she paused, gathering her thoughts. "I'm happy."

The Duchess' eyes misted up. "Well, that's what every mother wants to hear. Now, where is your papa?"

"Here, here, my dearest!" the Duke cried cheerfully, stepping forward from around the side of the church. "I'm ready to escort my favourite daughter down the aisle."

Augusta chuckled. "I am your only daughter, Papa."

"Ah, that is just a formality. Now, shall we?" The Duke smiled down at his daughter and offered her his arm. Augusta slipped her arm through his, and they were ready. She held her breath as the church doors opened, and the whole congregation turned to look at her.

She recognised her friends and family, with the Mitchells sitting in the front pews, beaming. She and the Duke began to walk down the aisle, with Eliza and Caroline walking in front of them. For once, the Duke had abandoned his long, elastic stride, slowing down to allow for a more dignified procession towards the altar.

And there, of course, stood the man Augusta had been dreaming about since she was a child. Her fiancé, the man she was to marry. Silas Mitchell. He was dressed in his finest suit, a deep burgundy to contrast with Augusta's gown and highlight her ruby necklace. He was watching Augusta walk towards him, a smile on his face and tears in his eyes.

The Duke stopped at the altar, and bent down to give Augusta a kiss.

"There you are, darling," he said gruffly. "I love you very much. Be happy, won't you?"

Augusta smiled tearfully up at him. "I will, Papa."

He glanced at Silas. "Look after her."

Silas bowed. "I will, sir."

Then, there was nothing for it but for Silas and Augusta to smile up at each other and face the Vicar.

"I love you," Silas whispered to her as the man began to speak.

Augusta smiled. "I love you, too."

Extended Epilogue

Some Years Later, Christmas Day

It was chaos, of course. Christmas Day at the Radfords home had always been chaos, and today was no exception. Now the Mitchells celebrated with them every year, there was an extra layer of excitement.

Colin had carved out the time from his busy schedule of study in Paris to come back and visit his family. Eliza and her new husband, Frederick Evergreen, were also in attendance. Poor Frederick, an only child, was exceptionally nervous amid the chaotic atmosphere, especially with the children running around. They'd only been married a year, and poor, shy, scholarly Frederick was still adjusting. He clearly adored his wife, however, and would have put up with a hundred more Mitchells and Radfords if it made her happy.

Timothy and Caroline's oldest daughter, Molly, was nearly four years old and very loud and rambunctious. Their son, Edmund, born only a year later, was noticeably milder and more placid. Like his Mama, everyone said.

Augusta and Silas had one son, Robert. He was three years old and the apple of his parents' eye. At the moment, he was racing around the drawing room, all but screaming with excitement. The three toddlers were chasing each other around and around the Christmas tree, which they had all helped decorate earlier that day.

The Duke, the Duchess and Helen and Charles were all seated on a large sofa, smiling fondly at their wild grandchildren. Augusta and Silas stood in the doorway, watching with a smile.

"One of them is going to get hurt," Augusta murmured. Silas had his arm around her, and she rested her head on his shoulder.

After their first year of marriage, there'd been no more talk of financial worries. The Mitchell orchards were thrived under Silas's management, and the Duke's investment had been quickly repaid. Silas was determined not to use too much of Augusta's money, except to build their own home on the border of the Mitchell and Radford lands. They lived comfortably if not lavishly, and Augusta could not have been happier.

Ambrose had died only two years after the incident, having plummeted, drunk, into the Thames one night and drowned. His mother had been devasted, and now she reputedly lived a pauper's life somewhere in the city. Augusta had recovered enough from his betrayal and nearly missing out on the love of her life to be able to feel quite sorry for them both. The man had haunted Augusta's dreams—or rather, nightmares—for quite some time.

She didn't know what would have happened if her father hadn't saved her from Ambrose that evening in the hallway. Ambrose had clearly intended to compel Augusta to marry him, but she didn't know exactly how he'd meant to achieve it. Would he have tried to compromise her, somehow, so that she would be forced to marry him? Would he have intimidated her, hurt her, or just tried to blackmail her?

Augusta shuddered. She didn't know how she could have been so thoroughly hoodwinked by Ambrose. It was said that he'd tried to woo a few other ladies in the years before his death. He hadn't been successful. He'd pursued a few naïve young debutantes, but those girls were fortunate enough to have watchful mamas around to send Ambrose packing. He'd courted an older widow for a time, and they had been on the brink of getting engaged when the widow broke off the relationship. If the scandal pages were to be believed—and they were usually right more often than they were wrong—the widow had clashed with Lady Firnsdale and was altogether too clever and independent a woman to give up her money and freedom to a man like Ambrose Finch.

Augusta wondered if the widow thought about her good luck too and congratulated herself on a narrow escape, just as she did.

"Penny for your thoughts," Silas murmured. "You look very preoccupied, my love."

"Do I? I suppose I'm just reminiscing on past times."

"If you're talking about last year, when I put a snowball down your neck, then—"

"No, not that. Also, I think you'll recall that I fully wreaked

202

my revenge this year."

"Hmm. If you say so. What is it, then?"

Augusta sighed. "I'm feeling nostalgic, I suppose. Our lives have changed so much."

"That's a good thing, isn't it? We should always be changing, always moving forward. A motionless pond becomes stagnant and poisonous. I think our life together is perfect."

"Oh, I know. I'm very happy, Darling. I was just thinking about our courtship. . . if you can call it that. We were so close to losing each other."

Silas's arm tightened around her shoulders. "I know. It gives me the shudders sometimes to think about it. Still, what does it matter now? We made it. We're married. We're safe, both of us. I have you, and you have me, and we both have our naughty little Robert."

Augusta smiled up at him. "There might a fourth member of the family coming soon."

Silas sucked in a breath. "What?! Are you saying—"

"Yes, that's right. I think I'm expecting again, Silas."

Silas broke into a wide smile. "Oh, my love, that's wonderful news! How are you feeling? How far along are you?"

"A few months, I think. Already it feels like I'm carrying this one differently, so I hope it'll be a girl."

"A girl would be lovely. We could call her Margaret."

"I was thinking of Felicity. That's a nice name, isn't it?"

Silas considered. "Yes, Felicity is nice. I suppose we can argue about it once our little girl is born."

Augusta snorted. "If I am giving birth to the baby, the only opinion that matters about the baby's name is mine."

"Fair enough," Silas conceded. He glanced upwards. "Hm. Why, would you look at where we are standing?"

Augusta followed his gaze and suppressed a smile. A kissing-bough was hanging in the doorway. These days, Augusta didn't have as much time to help her mother with the decorations. This looked like Eliza's handiwork.

"A kissing-bough? How interesting," Augusta said mildly. "Should we move?"

Silas chuckled. "Are you teasing me again?"

Augusta smiled softly up at him, snuggling in closer. "Of

course, I am. I love teasing you."

"I have noticed that. I must be the most teased husband in England."

Silas bent down to kiss her, and Augusta tilted up her chin to be kissed. It was a soft, sweet kiss, lasting no more than a second. Then, they pulled away, smiling at each other.

"I love you, Silas Mitchell," Augusta whispered.

Silas grinned. "And I love you, Lady Augusta."

The End

Printed in Great Britain
by Amazon